"A terrific first novel full of page-turning action, delightful characters, and a wry twist. . . . Grimspace may be in the air. Bullets, ugly beasts, and really bad guys definitely are." —Mike Shepherd,
national bestselling author of the Kris Longknife series

"An irresistible blend of action and attitude. Sirantha Jax doesn't just leap off the page—she storms out, kicking, cursing, and mouthing off. No wonder her pilot falls in love with her; readers will, too." —Sharon Shinn,
national bestselling author of *Reader and Raelynx*

"A tightly written, edge-of-your-seat read with intense characterization—plus one pounding, hot SF plot."
—Linnea Sinclair, RITA Award–winning author
of *Gabriel's Ghost* and *Games of Command*

"An unflinching tale of survival, redemption, and serious ass kicking. Jax's brutal eloquence will twist your heart when you least expect it." —Jeri Smith-Ready,
award-winning author of *Voice of Crow*

"*Grimspace* is an exciting, evocative, and suspenseful science fiction romance, reminding me of *Firefly* and *Serenity*. Characters and a world you'll think about long after the book is done. Fascinating!" —Robin D. Owens,
RITA Award–winning author of *Heart Dance*

Ace books by Ann Aguirre

GRIMSPACE
WANDERLUST

GRIMSPACE

ANN AGUIRRE

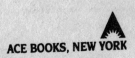
ACE BOOKS, NEW YORK

THE BERKLEY PUBLISHING GROUP
Published by the Penguin Group
Penguin Group (USA) Inc.
375 Hudson Street, New York, New York 10014, USA
Penguin Group (Canada), 90 Eglinton Avenue East, Suite 700, Toronto, Ontario M4P 2Y3, Canada
(a division of Pearson Penguin Canada Inc.)
Penguin Books Ltd., 80 Strand, London WC2R 0RL, England
Penguin Books Ireland, 25 St. Stephen's Green, Dublin 2, Ireland (a division of Penguin Books Ltd.)
Penguin Group (Australia), 250 Camberwell Road, Camberwell, Victoria 3124, Australia
(a division of Pearson Australia Group Pty. Ltd.)
Penguin Books India Pvt. Ltd., 11 Community Centre, Panchsheel Park, New Delhi—110 017, India
Penguin Group (NZ), 67 Apollo Drive, Rosedale, North Shore 0632, New Zealand
(a division of Pearson New Zealand Ltd.)
Penguin Books (South Africa) (Pty.) Ltd., 24 Sturdee Avenue, Rosebank, Johannesburg 2196,
South Africa

Penguin Books Ltd., Registered Offices: 80 Strand, London WC2R 0RL, England

GRIMSPACE

An Ace Book / published by arrangement with the author

PRINTING HISTORY
Ace mass-market edition / March 2008

Copyright © 2008 by Ann Aguirre.
Cover art by Scott M. Fischer.
Cover design by Lesley Worrell.
Interior text design by Kristin del Rosario.

ISBN: 978-0-441-01599-3

ACE
Ace Books are published by The Berkley Publishing Group,
a division of Penguin Group (USA) Inc.,
375 Hudson Street, New York, New York 10014.
ACE and the "A" design are trademarks belonging to Penguin Group (USA) Inc.

PRINTED IN THE UNITED STATES OF AMERICA

10   9   8   7   6   5

For Andres.
You're the reason I get up in the morning.
And sometimes you're the reason I wind up lost
in chicken country.
Which is better than bat country.
This one's for you, like everything I do.

ACKNOWLEDGMENTS

Linnea Sinclair and Elaine Corvidae have been reading my work for more years than I care to count. If not for them, *Grimspace* wouldn't exist. My wonderful agent, Laura Bradford, jumped on this story. Without her, I never would've connected with the talented staff at Ace.

At this point, I need to thank all of the above for their time and expertise. I'm humbled by the chance to work with people who know so much about . . . well, everything.

Much love also to Dionne Galace and Carrie Lofty, who always listen, no matter how crazy I sound or how late it is.

However, this section wouldn't be complete without a mention of some amazing writers who inspired me over the years: Robin McKinley, Patricia Briggs, Sharon Shinn, Patricia A. McKillip, Robin D. Owens, Connie Willis, Jeri Smith-Ready. The list goes on. I spent a great deal of time delightedly lost in worlds they created. I hope readers enjoy their stay in mine.

CHAPTER I

Are you afraid of falling, baby?
    No, I'm afraid of landing.

    [He's laughing, and I'm smiling.]
    Stupid idiot smile, don't you know what comes next?

Wake. Wake now.
    I don't want to see this, not again. It's not helping me deal. This thing is broken—
    Oh no. *No.*
    I sit up, shuddering, shoving the dark mop of hair out of my face, and my fingers come away wet with sweat. With trembling hands, I yank the patch away from my skull. It hurts. But then, what doesn't? What the Unit Psych calls dream therapy, I call torture. Seems too cruel to do this to someone on purpose, and I know they're going to find a way to blame me for the tech malfunction. They always do.

But it's not my fault they're using gear that should've been decommed after the Axis Wars.

That's what I want to believe. But it's getting harder. There comes a point when you want to accept culpability simply because you're the only common denominator. So yeah, maybe it's my fault. I push to my feet, off the sleep-mat, restless, haunted, although they proved a long time ago that it's all just electromagnetic energy, nothing spiritual. Nothing left of the soul, nothing left of *him*.

My AI asks, "Lights on, Sirantha Jax?"

Such a polite Unit spy. The fragging thing reports everything I do, every time I roll over, probably every time I take a piss.

"Yeah," I tell it, and the soft yellow glow, simulated sunrise on the most hospitable of the tier worlds, fills my cell.

Oh, they wouldn't call it a cell. These are my quarters, provided gratis, while my Unit assesses the damage to my psyche, decides whether I'm whole enough to run. But I'm incarcerated, even if I'm being watched by an AI instead of a hulking brute. There are prisons without bars and worlds without sunlight. I didn't know about either one until I joined the Corp.

I pace ten by ten, and when I reach the door, the AI inquires, "Shall I summon an escort for you, Sirantha Jax?"

"No." Wheeling away, I head back to the sleep-mat and sit down, legs furled.

To the AI, I'm sure it looks as though I'm meditating. In fact, I'm envisioning ways to execute something that is not, technically, alive. Perhaps the introduction of a virus into its system . . . I'll have to think about it some more.

An escort.

Clearly, I can't be trusted. If I were allowed to roam the station, I'd jump the first freighter I found bound for the Outskirts. Desert. Frag my contract. And they can't let that happen, not until they determine whether the accident was, in fact, my fault. And they *won't* let me go until they know whether my mind is fried and I can't run anymore.

The first thing carries a prison sentence. I'll be shipped off to Whitefish before I hardly know the judgment's been handed down. It'll be some smug bastard who's never been off New Terra, hearing my case via uplink. I don't know if they've gotten to that point yet, don't know if barristers are involved. I should be consulted for my defense if they make me stand civ trial, but since I *am* Corp, if it comes to that, they'll probably handle it internally, and in which case I'll end up spaced.

Yeah, I've got the J-gene. And it's rare. But if it seems like it's my fault, that god-awful mess on Matins IV, they're going to make sure not a whisper of it gets out. Kai . . . he's dead already. So he isn't talking. This leaves me marching out an air lock to keep shit nice and quiet, keep the Corp squeaky clean.

Funny, the shiny adverts that get us to sign on the dotted line never show what bastards the COs are.

Thinking like that makes me sweat. Feel it running down the divots in my spine to pool in the small of my back, clammy beneath the air refreshers blowing down on me. Maybe it *was* my fault, but I don't want to die, even if I deserve to.

And I could answer the second question right now. Not that anybody's asked me. I can jack in. I can jump.

I just don't want to anymore.

I'm scared.

It's been a week since I heard another human voice. Not counting my AI—I swear programmers code them to be annoying, pedantic little fucks. Oh sure, I could summon an escort to walk me around the promenade, but everyone on station knows what that means. I'm not going to entertain the Corp bureaucrats for even a millisecond. Instead I'm pacing and not sleeping except when I'm forced to dream therapy by the Unit Psych, via sedation and veiled threats. Crying and eating choclaste, a synth-food with no sugar, no caffeine, and only burns your tongue slightly after you've eaten it.

I don't need a mirror to know I'm a wreck. Coarse black hair standing up in long scruffy ringlets, skin pallid from lack of sunlight, and let's not forget the circles beneath my eyes. I've lost four kilos since I came on station, extracted from the wreckage on Matins IV. They didn't need to tell me Kai was dead; I was *there*.

And yet they did, with excruciating, patronizing precision. Fragging bastards.

Four different Psychs came to talk with me, that first day while I was lying helpless in the med bay. One of them wanted to know if I could describe the smell of burning human flesh. The Corp is full of those types, who in another time would've been chopping up their neighbors and burying them beneath the porch. Now they receive specialized certifications and go to work inside our heads.

For a while, I pretend to meditate, giving the room-bot nothing to report. And as I'm sitting there, mimicking serenity I don't feel, my door chime sounds. The AI informs me, "You have a visitor, Sirantha Jax. Allow entry?"

It's either a Psych or a CO; nobody else has clearance. Mentally I shrug, and say aloud, "Why not?"

The AI objects: "I am not programmed to evaluate the prudence of an action, Sirantha Jax. Allow entry?"

I sigh. "Yeah. Allow entry."

At this point, anything is better than waiting. I don't get up as the door glides open, then I wish I had. Because it's nobody I expected, nobody I know. He's tall, seems taller because I'm sitting down, and he has a rough-hewn, authoritative face, the look you see on men who are accustomed to getting their own way, always. Doesn't look as if he's ever cracked a smile, grave as well, the grave. But he's not a Psych, and he appears to be in civ clothing, so not a

CO, either. Shit, he's probably a barrister, which means I'm soon to be a whitefish, no daylight and no parole.

He looks me over, assessing my thin, foxy face and sharp chin. My nose is too long, and a fresh scar bisects my left cheek. I know he's registering the dark hair, light eyes combo that marks my distinctive heterozygous genotype, tied to the J-gene. Mine are icy gray, ringed in silver. Wolf eyes, Kai used to call them. Remembering that fills me with almost unbearable anguish, and the only reason I'm not sniveling again, while stuffing another square of choclaste in my mouth is because this guy is watching me.

"Have a seat," I say, and I'm glad I sound calmer than I feel.

He's got the choice of dropping down onto my sleep-mat with me or sitting in the only chair, over by the desk. They didn't go overboard with furnishings and took away anything I could conceivably use to injure myself. I'm surprised when he hitches up his meticulously tailored trousers and plops down next to me. I'd have figured him for a chair man, all the way, which just goes to show you can't judge by appearances. Or rather, you shouldn't because you'll be wrong a lot.

Assuming the lotus position, he still doesn't say a word, and just as I'm thinking this is getting weird, he cants his head toward his open palm. I lean over so I can read something that's inked onto his hand:

Say nothing for 60 seconds.

I raise my head, about to say, *Are you shitting me?* when his dark eyes catch mine, irresistible intensity. His look bores into me, and damned if I can say a word for that entire minute. It's like he's willing me to silence, a feat that others have attempted numerous times, and failed.

"If everything has gone well," he says at last, "then our people have sent your AI into its maintenance cycle. Still, our time is limited."

"And if everything hasn't gone well?" That isn't what I want to ask. I want to know who the hell he is. Despite myself, I glance over the terminal, flashing blue, the color code of routine maintenance.

"Then someone would already be here to arrest us." He flashes me a decidedly saturnine smile. Yeah, that word suits him.

Huh, wonder why I'm not reassured.

CHAPTER 2

I'm just staring at him, mouth half-open. As soon as I realize it, I find something to say, anything. "Who the hell are you?"

"March," he tells me.

"That a name or an order?" The smart-ass answer comes naturally, even as I'm trying to figure out his angle. What matters is why he's here, and I'm not sure why I haven't queried him.

Maybe it's because I know it can mean nothing good, this illicit entry to my cell, and this is a way of postponing my all-but-inevitable hop from the frying pan to the fire. Such a quaint descriptive when we've been cooking with molecular agitation for so long, but in my circumstance it's just too apropos.

Besides, he'll tell me anyway. His type always does. He has an agenda, and it doesn't matter a damn whether I'm on board with it. Doubt anyone's ever told him no and made it stick.

"Take your pick," he says, shrugging. "We need to get you out. You have three minutes to decide, Ms. Jax, and the clock is ticking. How tight is procedure here?"

When the AI comes out of its maintenance subroutine to find (a) an unapproved visitor or (b) Sirantha Jax missing, Klaxons are going to make this place sound like a bunker in wartime. But I shrug. Honestly, I have no idea. Perlas Station isn't anywhere I've set foot before, and it wasn't a conscious choice this time. This was simply the closest port from Matins IV, where the salvage crew found me, quite inconveniently, alive. I've often wondered why they didn't just finish the job and let the accident go unexplained, a tragedy that the Corp could sweep beneath the metaphorical rug. Dead men tell no tales, and dead women tie up loose ends.

"What makes you think I'm going to leave with you?" Even as I say it, I'm thinking about it, and I'm aware of the seconds winding down. I have to decide fast. If I don't leave, Newel, the Psych who asked me to describe burning human flesh, yes, *that* one . . . he's coming again today. He'll be overseeing my "treatment," now and forever.

Deep down I know it's move or die. Haven't I been imagining desertion the whole time I've been locked up in here? Trying to figure out a way to escape? And now it's been handed to me, I'm like a caged bird, afraid to venture beyond the bars, terrified of what lies beyond. That's new. I didn't used to feel like that, used to be the first to dive into free fall.

Maybe this is a trap. Maybe they *want* me to do this, and I'll be killed during my escape attempt. But at least this way, I have a chance. Here in this cell, I'm a trapped rat, and given the choice, I'll always opt to go down fighting.

"Because you have to. They're not investigating anything, Ms. Jax. This isolation and the so-called dream therapy they're forcing you to undergo, it's not standard. They're trying to break you. They don't want to know what happened; they just want to make sure you're in no condition to talk about it. Ever. And when you crack beneath the stress, they'll write you off and bury you beneath piles of policy. Ninety seconds, Ms. Jax."

With an inward jolt, I realize he's right. Nothing they've done to me is conducive to healing. That's not the goal at all. Most likely, I was supposed to fall apart by now. What jumper could live without her pilot and not go mad? Especially when forced to relive the event, over and over and—

When I cracked, I wasn't going to be sent to Whitefish. Instead, I'd wind up in the Corp asylum where they hide the broken ones. All of us snap, sooner or later—you can't spend so much time jacked into grimspace without losing part of yourself. Jumpers know the risks and yet the drive toward exploration, the need to be the first to see a new rim world, make first planetfall with our pilots, these things fire us along an ultimately self-destructive course. We're a little crazy, the J-gene carriers, or we wouldn't be able to handle grimspace in the first place.

With that, I make my decision and push to my feet. "Let's go."

There's nothing here I want. All my personal effects burned up on Matins IV, and so I'm ready to follow this guy into the unknown, trusting wherever he's taking me is better than where I am. That's a hell of a hope to pin on a stranger.

I half expect him to want to talk some more or outline a plan, but he's on his feet as well, expedience ruling the day. That's a welcome change from the bureaucratic bullshit I've dealt with for the last ten days. I doubt the COs wipe their asses without forms in triplicate.

"Need you out of the uniform," he tells me, so brisk that I don't think even for a moment he's angling to get a look at the body beneath. "They'll probably guess you're making for the docking bays, but it'll help if they can't get a vis-ID at a glance."

He intends me to strip, but I know it's not prurient interest. Even before, I wasn't anything special to look at: lean, strong, and energetic, a good partner in bed, but not because I was beautiful. I think that might be tied to the J-gene as well, the hunger for sensation. People don't understand my loss; the Psychs poke at it with morbid curiosity. Intellectually they know it's bad for a jumper when her pilot dies, but they don't understand the relationship.

Imagine for a moment—lover and brother and guardian and partner and—

There are no words. Even if a jumper never sleeps with her pilot, there are still bonds that can't be articulated to the layman. He's the one who watches while you're lost in grimspace, the hands on the ship controls that interpret your signals as you cue the jumps. Every time you jack in, he's the reason you come out safe again. Perfect trust, perfect symbiosis; there comes a time when words aren't necessary anymore.

Well, I can't waste any more time on hesitation. March hands me a plain brown coverall, and I change quickly under his watchful eyes. My whole body's webbed with faint purple burn scars, souvenirs of the crash, so if he has any sense, he'll look away. But he doesn't. He just stares, eyes on mine. I don't trust him, and he doesn't seem to like me, so we make a perfect match. Dressed, I look like a san service worker.

He finishes the makeshift disguise with a bottle of Spray-bond, aerosol colorant used by part-timer punkers who want to be able to wash out their weekend revels and return to the office looking respectable. In my case, dark hair goes grungy gray, and suddenly I've aged twenty-five years. It's not hard to alter how I move because I feel physically stiff from my incarceration. At a nod from him, I stuff the Corp gear down the recycler, and then he manually keys the door open.

"Unauthorized exit from crew quarters!" my AI sings

out maybe thirty seconds later as alarms begin to sound. I feel faint satisfaction at having thwarted it, even as we move off. "Unauthorized access to artificial intelligence Q-15. Recommend initiation of lockdown. Unauthorized personnel detected in detention level C."

In the distance I hear booted feet coming to investigate. Shit. We hasten down into the corridor, and I can't tell what time of day it is because the artificial lights never alter. Station life would drive me crazy. I need a natural cycle, which is why I often linger planetside after Kai and I— flinch away from that thought, as I follow March at a dead run. God, I hope that's not a prophetic thought.

The Psychs don't realize the reason I'm not completely nuts, since I've been running a lot longer than most, is that my early life granted me the ability to compartmentalize. Just shut stuff off, lock it away. In a room inside my head part of me may, in fact, already be gibbering mad, but I don't let that one out to howl. Just like part of me mourns Kai, curled up in a corner, sobbing like a child. And the rest of me functions.

Just like now. Can't help wondering what I've gotten myself into, but then I've never been one to wait around. And just what in the hell does he *want* with me—if this isn't a Corp trap? I have a bad feeling and a stitch in my side, but March isn't breaking stride, and damned if I'll let him outrun me.

Right before the first checkpoint, a pair of Corp security drones stumbles on us, and he never slows, diving between their blue laser fire like this is all part of the job, coming up beneath in their blind spot. Brute force—he crushes them together, smashing their sensors, so their feed to the security station goes black, then he slams them again in a spray of sparks. I hear the low whir of their tiny thrusters slowing, then they drop, heavy, inert. Maybe two corridors over I hear more booted feet. They're coming to investigate the outage of the two drones.

"Move," he tells me fiercely as the second set of alarms kick in.

Orange alert? Holy *shit*.

That means they don't care if they take us alive.

Up till now, I had always thought of the Corp as a friendly Big Brother, hand out to help, interested in exploration, in science and discovery. And sure, they had a military arm, but that was for defense and protection, not for assault. Now I'm wondering just what I don't know about the Corp, what else they do, quiet and smiling, while yokels lap up their adorable ad campaigns about little boys pointing at the heavens in awe as a shooting star carries the Corp logo overhead.

"If they've gone into lockdown, we won't be able to use the doors," I pant, as he makes for the security station at a brisk walk, not unlike the pace one would use if a bit pressed for time for a moderately important business meeting. "Are you *crazy*? We're going to have to fight our way through half the Corp—"

He ignores me and lays out the first guard with a hard hook before the poor bastard hardly registers we're there. Even with alarms sounding, you just don't expect a man in a suit to fight like a gladiator; you expect him to stride up, and say politely, "I'm sorry, I'm quite turned about. Do you know where the lift is to the hydroponics gardens?" The second man, March takes by the throat and stares into his eyes. I don't know what the frag that was about, but the man just crumples, lying up against the wall as if he's about to piss himself. And once more, March keys the door open, and he's hauling for the next point without looking back.

We pass two more security doors exactly like that while Klaxons blare and more teams deploy. One hand on my cramping side, I can't help but think this is the crappiest rescue I've ever seen and I want *answers*, not that I'm a hundred percent sure I needed rescuing. Maybe that was lack of sleep and paranoia and the general creepiness of Psych Officer Newel. I may have just fragged up and made things way worse for myself, ruined my career and put my fate in the hands of a maniac.

As we hit the freighter bays, a gray squad opens fire. They aren't telling us to halt or to surrender. Mother Mary of Anabolic Grace, they really want to fry us. I dive in behind a ship and growl at March, "You owe me some serious answers if we get out of this alive."

He shoves me toward the boarding ramp of a cutter that's seen better days. From his manner and the way he's dressed, I expected a big hauler or a sporty little cruiser, something with a high price tag and a lot of amenities. Not this junk bucket that looks like it should've been decommed *before* the Axis Wars. The gray squad closes on us with military precision, using cover and working the perimeter in a metric circle. Soon they'll be on us, boarding the ship. A laser blast sears the metal at my feet, and I fall back, farther up the ramp.

Talk about ass choices. I've got this shit bucket and a nutcase or a bunch of gray men coming for me.

He reads my look and shrugs. "However she looks, this ship is sound. Can you jump, Ms. Jax? Our lives depend on it."

Jump? But I don't have a pilot.

My look or my mind? Because he adds, "Yes, you do."

My throat tightens, and I feel a fist curling around my intestines. It's a cramp, rising nausea. It's being told you have to remarry before your husband's cold in the grave. Before I can say a word, he boards. No more conversation. It's up to me now. Stay or go. Reluctantly, I admire the fact that he doesn't bullshit, doesn't explain, doesn't persuade. Maybe he knows I can't resist a mystery or a challenge or both. Or maybe he just knows I'm not looking to die today, because the gray men are almost on me.

I follow.

CHAPTER 3

The inside of the ship restores my faith in benevolent deities.

Controls are new, shiny, and everything's well maintained, clean, from the corridors to the cockpit. It's almost like they're using the exterior as camo, nothing to see here, just another struggling ship. And that's probably not too far from the truth.

It's an eight-seater, at least I see that many places where crew can strap in for a jump. Possibly she could carry more, but there'd be no guarantee what would become of them while passing through grimspace. Generally, only refugees are desperate enough to take the risk. But there aren't six other people on board. In fact, I just see three, now gazing at me, although there may be more in medical or the holds.

"I got her," March says, as the boarding ramp seals behind us. "Use the override launch codes Mair gave us, and let's go."

I can hear the impact of gray-squad lasers striking the hull. Luckily, the Corp's response time isn't good here on Perlas; they've grown complacent, unable to imagine anyone could challenge their authority or breach their security. Something tells me—times they are a-changing.

The others busy themselves right away, as if there's no question he's in charge. While they're not talking to me, I study them one by one: an older man with the heavy musculature that signals an upbringing on a high-G world and another man of indeterminate years, slim and androgynous. The older man, silver hair, neat goatee, runs a device across my temple and smiles. "Positive ID," he tells someone over a comm unit, and I'm left staring at him in bewilderment. Last, there's a woman around my age, blond, butch. She regards me with open animosity, and for a moment, I can't breathe, just scorched by the look in her gray eyes, but then the look's broken like someone cutting a live wire. There's even a resultant explosion.

"Shit," she says, leaning down to punch some things into a terminal, pulling up maps and grids. Even I know that the blinking red square is not a good sign.

The older man takes off at a dead run in response, and March disappears through a sliding door. Not much for talking, that one. Yeah, okay, I understand—action's imperative. But still, I've been in solitary for over a week; I want to know something about the people taking me away. Is that too much to ask?

Shit, it *is*. Someone's finally thought to get the freighter bay turrets online, and the hull's now being hammered. We've got to get out of here. Like, ten minutes ago.

Of them all, I have no idea who my pilot is supposed to be. That's not a good sign. A jumper is supposed to feel instant rapport—how else can I trust him? The Corp offers hundreds of candidates up for evaluation. In its way, the relationship is more important than marriage, more lasting and more vital to my welfare. I had a husband once, but he couldn't handle coming second to Kai, and he left me, several spins before I actually noticed he was gone.

I'm not *ready* for a new pilot, not even one hundred percent sure I can do this. I mean, I'm not fried. It's not that. There comes a point in every jumper's life where she knows she's at the limit—next time she jacks into grimspace, she's not coming back. Navigating those beacons will be the last thing she does, but it's like being an addict to almost any chem. You know it's killing you slowly, but you can't quit, don't even want to, because the pleasure outweighs your fear of consequences.

And I guess most of us would rather go out in a blaze of glory, burned-out, than to be one of the saddest folks alive, someone who used to own grimspace and knows she can't anymore. *Knows.* I haven't hit that boundary yet myself, but I don't think I want to retire. I didn't become a jumper to die old and gray.

But there's a knot in my stomach, and I feel like I'm waiting in a seedy hostel for a stranger, unfaithful, like all the years with Kai, first friends, then lovers—so much more—meant nothing. My palms feel damp, cold, and I wipe them on my thighs while the ship shakes. Before, it was all exhilaration, pitting myself against phenomenal odds and coming out with my mind intact, guiding my ship and crew safely to our destination. I'm the reason we rule the star lanes, me. Sirantha Jax. Well, me, and folks like me, J-gene carriers. There's so few of us; we're treated like Corp royalty.

Until we burn out.

Until we kill our pilots and crew and have to run—

Enough.

"Where the frag is Jemus?" March emerges in fatigues, a black shirt, and a combat jacket, which make him look bigger, meaner but compelling, a fact I resent because I hate how he superimposes himself over Kai's memory, just standing there. This gear suits him better than formality, strips away all pretense of civility and civilization. Kai was slim and boyish, no matter his age. He was, in fact, three years my senior when he died, but nobody would've ever guessed. "And why aren't you in the nav chair yet?" To me.

"Bad news," The woman says, looking grim. "The turrets did some damage in the holds and the power coupling—"

March grits his teeth. "If something needs repair, get your ass down there and fix it. What the hell does that have to do with—"

"If you shut your gob, you dickless wonder, I'll tell you what it has to do with Jemus." The ship rocks, and I grab on to the safety harnesses that hang like webbing from the cabin ceiling. "We're screwed, stranded, and no repairs are going to help." She brings up an image on-screen, clearly from medical, and even I can tell that the guy on the table isn't getting up. His head's, well, open.

Please don't tell me that was my pilot.

"Why me?" I say aloud.

"What the frag was he doing in the holds?" March growls, pacing like a caged animal. We're losing precious time; the ship's going to open up like an Old Terra tin can if we keep sitting here.

"He won't—wouldn't—fly without his lucky hat. One of the san bots took it to storage because he left it in the lounge the last time we played mah-jongg," the doc puts in quietly. I hadn't realized we were on a two-way feed, but it makes sense. He steps away from the body with a heavy sadness that makes me like him instinctively.

"Isn't there *anything* we can do?" They all look at me as if surprised to learn I have a voice. "Get weapons online, something."

The young man with the disquieting eyes tells me, "All that would accomplish is a wanton waste of life. I'm Loras."

Seems like an odd time to be thinking of introductions, but what the hell. "Sirantha Jax."

To my surprise, the blond woman answers, although she

doesn't say it's nice to meet me. "Dina, ship's mechanic, part-time gunner, engineer, whatever needs fixing." She indicates the vid display with a tilt of her head. "The doc is Saul. And now you know the names of all the people you've killed. Maybe."

"Frag you," I tell her, without even asking what she means. Frag her for thinking she knows what happened on Matins IV. She wasn't there. I'm the sole survivor, and even I'm not altogether sure. My dreams tell different stories, day to day. I'm not certain I can trust any of them.

Dina adds to him, though she's still looking at me, "After the *Sargasso*, I can't believe we have her on board. When you heard Svet died in the crash, you said—"

Shit. I've run away with people with a grudge, and hell, maybe they have cause. I brace because this woman seems ready to gouge my eyes out.

"*Dammit.*" The word sounds wrenched from March. Dina and I both turn, on the verge of going after each other, even with the ship about to come down around our ears. "I can do it," he adds, in the tone of a man who has volunteered to be fed to the giant thing that lives in the volcano. "Let's go."

"You're a pilot?" Dina regards him with puzzlement and dawning hope.

He doesn't answer her, glaring at me like this is my fault. March—whatever reason he took it up, whatever reason he stopped, he wasn't a pilot for the thrills, like Kai, no he's an older archetype, dating all the way back to the conqueror Cortez. It's not enough to discover new lands, but he has to see the natives bend at the knee, too.

The fact that I have to place my life in his hands makes me sick to my stomach. I'd never have chosen him, not in a thousand years. There's too much dominance in him, too much that doesn't care what's damaged as long as he gets his way. And I think he knows my reaction by virtue of my expression or some alchemy that I haven't pinned down. He doesn't seem like a typical Psi, but he reads my thoughts too close for comfort.

"Get your ass in the cockpit," he says. "We came a long fragging way, and we're not stopping here just because you aren't sure you like me."

"Where's the jumper who got you here?"

Finally, it comes to me, the question that's been bugging me. Outside the ship he said, *Can you jump? Our lives depend on it.* Perlas is too deep for any ship to hit without jumping; there isn't a far cruiser outfitted that can haul the straight space between those two points. People have died trying. So why then does everything hang on me?

Another explosion; shit, we don't have time for this. The ship won't hold much longer. Dina hisses, and I wheel on her, instinctively bracing. She *really* wants to rush me now, I can tell, but instead she just exchanges a laden look with March, who nods. Giving permission?

"It was her last run," the other woman tells me in a voice sharp and hard as the surface of Ielos, a winter world on the rim.

Last run.

March knows the moment I parse that. Their jumper understood that it was suicide—that she'd never make it out of grimspace intact, not this time. Thus gambling their fate on getting me on board, getting me in the nav chair. When did I become someone worth dying for?

This changes everything. They sacrificed their jumper to get me out of here, so we're going. I'll jump. She died for me. Intellectually, I know someone on this crew put her down, like an Old Terra horse whose wind's been broken. Too great a heart, body can't contain it. It's a kindness most don't have the guts to perform.

"What was her name?" I need to know.

"Edaine." It's the woman who answers me, once again.

I can see in her eyes that she's grieving. That's why she hates me. It isn't personal so much as the fact that Edaine died for me, and Dina wasn't ready to let her go. Whether they were lovers or the mechanic simply loved her, it's not my business. But I can respect loss. Understand it. This ship isn't ready for a new jumper any more than I'm ready for a new pilot. Something flickers in my brain pan, part of my classical Old Terra education, long since discarded for the thrill of grimspace.

He must needs go that the devil drives.

Yeah, that. Sod what we want. We've got to play the hand we're dealt. Not so long ago, I could call my soul my own. Clean. Contracted to the Corp, sure, but I didn't owe any karmic debts. But now I've got Kai and the rest of the crew weighing on me. Plus seventy-five souls who relied on me to transport them safely to their destination, among them the beloved Miriam Jocasta, freely elected Conglomerate representative to all the tier worlds. Now add to that body count this unknown jumper, the pilot in Med Bay, and I'm feeling like a brick. I don't say another word, just head for the cockpit.

It's time.

CHAPTER 4

Try to describe grimspace for us.

At parties, when everyone's knocked back a few, there's always someone who asks me to do that. They don't seem to understand, it's like trying to define red for a blind man. If you're not a jumper, then you're blind to the most extraordinary, primordial colors. And nothing I say will help you understand.

The name's misleading. Grimspace means inexorable, implacable. Not to be appeased. You see, grimspace will have its due from all who traverse it. But it's beautiful there, or we wouldn't be drawn back, time and again, driven on by a jones stronger than anything mankind could devise. Jumpers burn out smiling for a reason.

My pretty, poisonous mistress, I'm coming back.

New ship. New pilot. Same old Sirantha Jax.

I settle into the nav chair and run my hands over the interface, checking the port to make sure it's clean. Knowing that my predecessor fried right where I'm sitting, well, talk about cold chills. I focus on procedure, not the fact that the ship's being bombarded. I've never jumped under these circumstances, but I can do this. I can. *Just be cool, Jax.*

It occurs to me as I'm setting up, ready to jack into the nav system, that it's got to be terrifying for a pilot, working with a new jumper for the first time. And who knows how long it's been for March? Meanwhile we've got people shooting, and I'm supposed to be his eyes, and he acts as my hands. For the duration of a jump, we're literally twined together via wetware, and even if I knew how, I couldn't fly the ship while I'm tracking grimspace, finding beacons the old ones left along the star lanes, so long ago that we've given up trying to date it. In trying to figure out FTL travel, someone, a long fragging time ago, discovered a better way.

Grimspace.

And so, just as I have to trust him to make the right adjustments to the controls, safeguard my body while I'm seeing nothing but a world so wide that I don't have words to encompass it, he has to trust that I'm not going to steer him wrong. Oddly, even though I can *do* it, I have only a fundamental grasp of the principles.

Jump ships all carry a phase drive that accesses the secondary space that bends distance beneath, between, whatever, two points in straight space. To get from here to there, you jump into grimspace via the phase drive, then your navigator finds the beacon nearest your destination, and you make the jump back. The beacons are like doors, portals, something, a corridor back and forth, and the phase drive, well, that's the key.

Eons after discovering its existence, we're still exploring the Star Road. That was our specialty, Kai and me. Making long jumps to places no one's ever been. Tagging new beacons. Logging what's there and providing charts for the Corp, sometimes livable worlds, sometimes gas giants, sometimes asteroid belts where a planet might have been.

I loved it. Loved *him*, after a while.

Lost him.

Oh God, Kai, I'm sorry, baby. It's too soon.

March is looking at me. Waiting for me to jack in. But he doesn't say anything, nothing to ease the moment but nothing to make it harder, either. He doesn't bitch at me to hurry, even though I need to, or tell me that there are lives hanging on me. There are *always* lives hanging on me. Maybe that's why jumpers go crazy.

Control yourself, Jax; don't let nerves get you.

He's not Kai, never will be, but I've got to learn to do this with him. In a way, it's more intimate than fucking a stranger because he's going to be part of me for the duration of our flight. I don't *want* March inside of me.

Loras speaks over the comm, calm, measured. "Launch override codes input, bay doors opening in approximately ten seconds. You'll need to hold them, though. Corp security won't permit them to remain that way long."

I feel the swerve as the ship lifts, reluctantly admire the way March handles the controls. The weapons systems come online, and he fires, disabling the bay doors. They're standing wide now, and I can see through the forward screen that the gray men are fighting vacuum; nothing about this has gone according to Corp procedure. Gray men don't boast flexibility as one of their dominant traits. They expected to stop us in the bay; we weren't supposed to get this far. But we have. One thing about gray men . . . they just don't quit. They're going to hunt us to the end of the galaxy.

Cheerful fragging thought.

"Dina, take over guns. Return fire, keep them off us."

And in a graceful spin, we're out, weapons fire coming in hard on aft shields. They're scrambling ships, but it will take time to find a jumper fit to run, and we've got one ready to go. Me. The stars swim around us, and part of me thrills to it, even as I suck in a breath, preparing myself for March. I'm a virgin on her wedding night, arranged marriage, and I've never even given him a closed-mouth kiss.

"What's our destination?" I ask. "Let me see the star charts."

That seems to reassure him because a good jumper always wants to see the locus of two points in straight space before she tries to translate it. And I'm no exception. I study the maps for a minute, noting that we're making for a habitable rim world. Lachion. It's just an outpost, really, a place to refuel, buy supplies and a whore for the night.

Taking a deep breath, I plug in.

And the cockpit disappears.

Right now I'm simply blind. He's giving instructions over the comm, and I hear the crew acknowledging orders. They've strapped in and donned their helmets. Superstitious spacers say if you don't wear your headgear during a jump, there are demons waiting to suck the soul right out of your body. While that sounds a whole lot like Old Terra sailors who believed sea monsters would eat you if you sailed over the edge of the world, I *do* know it's a bad idea to run unprotected.

We haven't made the jump yet, and I can feel the phase drive powering up, the trembling hum of the seat beneath my fingertips. And then March plugs in beside me, and I can *feel* him in ways I never wanted to. There's no give to him, even here, but I sense a self-deprecating humor that I didn't expect, and it gentles him, making him easier to bear.

You ready? He doesn't need to say it any more than I need to vocalize my response. At this moment, we're beyond all that. We're pilot and jumper, and we're going forth together.

Now.

The world opens up to me, an orchid unfurling at accelerated speed. I think of it as the primeval soup from whence all life originally came, a maelstrom of chaos and energy, sights the human mind isn't supposed to be able to parse, let alone convert into coherent images that can be used to navigate.

Because of the J-gene I can sense the beacons, feel them pulsing like sentient life, and perhaps they are, for all I know. Perhaps if we could find their frequency, we could converse with them and discover we've long been diving down the gullets of cosmic dragons and shooting out their cloacae to somewhere else, and guess what, they aren't exactly happy about it. On second thought, some mysteries simply shouldn't be delved into.

He senses my directives in the same oblique manner in which I'm conscious of his hands on the controls. I feel him making adjustments according to what I see, a symbiosis that's never seemed more miraculous than this moment. It's an eternity; it's a heartbeat, and grimspace gazes back at me, scintillant and impossibly alluring.

That's the bait in the trap, you want to stop focusing on yourself and you want to *explore* in ways that aren't corporeally possible. For the first time it occurs to me—perhaps burnout isn't such a dreadful thing. Perhaps it's nothing to fear at all, simply another doorway opening.

No. That's March. Rare for a pilot to risk breaking a jumper's concentration, but I sense frissons of tension rippling through him, soul deep. *That's how a navigator thinks, preparing herself for the last run. You're not there. You're not.*

Instinctively, I reassure him. I don't know why he gives a shit. But it hurts him to think of leaving me here. I feel it, crashing over me in waves he can't quite subdue. Maybe it's transference. He's grieving, too . . . for Edaine, who was his friend, if not his jumper, for someone named Svet, and for another navigator whose name I don't know. I glimpsed his myriad losses before his walls came up, and I don't know when I ever saw someone so alone.

Before this moment, I never thought about what it's like for a pilot when his jumper leaves him behind. End of the flight, and she's still in the nav chair beside him, but she's gone. The spark, radiance, whatever made her unique. Gone.

I know what it's like to be left behind. And that's rare for a jumper; we don't have long life expectancies.

Almost there.

Gravitational pull. My mind's wide-open, full of flares, sheer artistry that even the best pilot cannot comprehend. At its most basic level, the universe is beautiful. We're about to slingshot through our target beacon and back out to straight space.

I've done it.

Distantly I know that the ship's trembling beneath me again, readying itself for the second jump. And then feel it, the instant before I go blind again. Leaving grimspace hurts. But then, what doesn't?

We should be just a short cruise away from Lachion. So many outposts spring up along the Star Road, and the only thing that comes close to the feeling after a solid run is free fall. For this moment, I don't even mind that March is here, sharing my pleasure, that I'm making him feel good because I do. But he's not sampling that on purpose. As soon as he can, he unplugs, and I do the same. Even though I don't know him, not even sure if I like him, I already miss him. You don't know what it's like to be alone until you've had someone inside your head.

And that, you see, is why so many pilots and jumpers wind up sleeping together. It's too much on the senses— that mutual stimulation needs an outlet, and there comes a point when nobody else will do. You want to share your body the way you've shared your mind, so many times, and the sex is better, stronger, and so intense.

Some pairs do it while jacked in, not while jumping, of course, but in the cockpit, joined both ways, writhing together, ecstasy washing back and forth in a closed circuit, constantly driving things higher. It becomes its own addiction after a while, and I've known pilots who simply can't perform unless they're with a jumper.

Anything else is just too vanilla.

CHAPTER 5

Like he knows what I'm thinking, March flicks me a scathing look as he signals the crew it's safe to unstrap from the harnesses and remove helmets. While they report back, I decide that doing me, jacked in or otherwise, is the last thing on his mind. That's good; it's a complication I neither want nor need. I stretch, conscious of no more wear and tear than a residual headache, like a day-old hangover.

I've had worse.

Leaning forward, I take a look at our updated position on the nav charts, and yeah, we came out right on target. Lachion's less than a two-hour cruise, and I settle back to watch. Don't know what I think I'll learn, but he's good at what he does; sure, capable hands manipulating the controls, attentive to various readings. Stuff I don't understand, to be honest. I'm not a pilot, although I've spent almost half my life on board ships.

"Good jump," he says finally.

And it's a surprise to hear his voice, different, more

forceful. Then I could sense his uncertainties and constant grief. Now he's all steel and implacable resolve again.

"I don't think it was my fault," I blurt, before I've formed the words inside my own head. But I need to say it. I need someone to believe me. Don't know whether March is that someone, but I need some of the weight off my soul.

He cuts me a sharp look, a full ten seconds away from the control panel. "Matins IV?" As if there's any doubt what I mean.

"Yeah." I don't look at him. Instead I stare out into straight space, nothing too fascinating there for one accustomed to wildfire. But it's better than measuring his expression, doubting my own credibility.

"We don't think so, either," he answers, neutral.

Something in his tone tells me he's speaking more for others than himself. Having seen inside him, I can say with authority—March is a man, who, if asked to capture the legendary pink orangutan of New Inglaterra, would devise a foolproof plan to catch said beast and equip himself with all necessary accoutrements, and never mind the fact that he doesn't believe in the thing. So, no, he doesn't necessarily believe me. But that doesn't matter to him because he's been asked to deliver me, and I'm starting to wonder why.

"Why me?" I know I don't need to clarify.

One of the advantages to the pilot/jumper bond is that even when you jack out, you carry certain awareness with you, remembrance of how your partner's mind works. He'll know what I'm asking although he could choose to be an ass and feign incomprehension. I respect the fact that he doesn't.

"You're pretty old," he tells me, not unkindly. I'll be thirty-three this year. "And you've logged over five hundred successful jumps and more new charts for the Corp than any navigator ever. There are people who would like to know the secret to your success, Ms. Jax. I represent those interested parties."

"And they can't find out shit from me if the Corp cracks my brain like an egg and locks me up."

Okay, so . . . the Corp used me for fourteen years, knowing I would eventually burn out. And I said yes because I wanted adventure and excitement, wanted off New Terra. I wanted the universe; why should I settle for one boring man and a passel of kids? And now, someone wants to use me to find out why I haven't burned out yet. You know, I'm a bit tired of being used. They're going to learn I'm not the easy mark they anticipate.

March offers that saturnine smile again. "Just so. We were sent to prevent that from occurring if at all possible."

And he's telling me the truth, as far as it goes. There may be more to it, but he isn't actively lying. I'd know if he was.

"I'm sorry about Edaine."

His smile falters. Dies. "Yes," he says, too quietly. "Me, too."

Don't know why I said that. It wasn't my fault—

Then it occurs to me I'm singing that refrain a hell of a lot, lately. At what point do I accept some blame? No, I never asked her to make her last run with saving me as the objective; that was her choice. But if it weren't for me, maybe she would've chosen retirement instead. I feel like I need to make her sacrifice worthwhile.

"Okay if I go talk to the crew?" I really want out of the cockpit. This is more awkward than waking up next to someone whose name you don't remember.

He nods. And that's all. As I go down the corridor, I can't help but think he's almost as glad to see the back of me as I am to go. They're all chatting, still sitting in their safety seats, although not strapped in anymore. When I come into the central hub, though, conversation dies as if I've lobbed a grenade. I drop down in one of the empty places and fold my ankle up on my knee. Wait.

It doesn't take too long. Most people can't stomach silence; it provides too much opportunity to think about things they prefer to avoid. It's the young man who speaks first, something that doesn't surprise me much.

"Is it true you made the leap to Quaren when you were just nineteen?"

Don't know if I should disillusion him. I didn't realize I'd acquired a reputation. We just do what we do, you know? And seldom think about how the rest of the universe perceives us. "In fact, I was twenty-three. Was nineteen when I made my first jump, period."

I know my service record. Almost fourteen years, averaging forty-one jumps a year for a total of five hundred seventy-five successful runs, and of those, I charted eighty-eight new beacons for the Corp. Decorated twice for bravery beyond the call. And the average jumper burns out in less than ten. So I guess I can understand why someone is interested in finding out what makes me tick. Unlock my secrets, and maybe he could improve productivity for other jumpers. That'd be a good thing, overall.

However, the critter that winds up dissected for the greater good . . . well, I'm guessing it probably doesn't feel too pleased about the contribution. So I'd do well to be on my guard and remember that even the good guys probably don't have my best interests at heart. The only person I could've trusted at my back, no exceptions, had his molecules dispersed with all due ceremony about fourteen days ago.

I fucking miss him.

"There are some things waiting for you in quarters," the doc, Saul, is saying. "Clothes. You can change and make use of the san facilities, if you want." He sounds strange, diffident, at odds with his stolid, steady appearance. "Down the hall, second right. The door will recognize you."

His sincerity gets to me. It's easy to be tough when everyone around you is bristling with rancor and suspicion, but let someone show you some genuine kindness, and you find yourself on the verge of breaking down. So I just nod and follow his instructions. Can feel Dina's eyes boring into my back. That one would rather space me than deliver me safely to Lachion.

Walking away, I hear Dina logging her report: "Aft shields at thirty-five percent in sectors 12 and 18, damage to the holds, structural damage in—" But I tune her out. That stuff is her worry. As long as the ship's in one piece and will get us there, I don't much care.

My quarters are small, no more than a closet with a bunk built out from the wall, but as promised, I find a change of clothes and a san shower. Feels good to be clean, and when I dress, I notice that someone's been studying my file. Because this blue bodysuit is an exact replica of one I wore for a photo op with tall s-leather boots and tribal jewelry from one of the inhabited rim worlds, all handmade stuff, very rare. A gift when we made planetfall since a jumper is part navigator, part surveyor, and part diplomat. I've made first contact with indigenous peoples no less than five times.

The outfit is smooth; it stretches at the neck enough to let you shimmy into it, then the fabric snaps back into place. It's some poly-silk blend that looks elegant but doesn't snag or tear and it's damn near fireproof. I wish I had my boots; they weren't just a fashion statement, as the toes were reinforced and a well-placed kick would break someone's kneecap.

As I'm emerging from quarters, March's voice comes over the comm. "Approaching Lachion, planetfall in half an hour. All crew to stations please."

That seems an unnecessary formality, given the size of the crew, but I watch, hoping to learn something about my companions. And I do. From the central hub, Saul heads for medical, but I already knew he's the ship's doc. Dina told me she serves as mechanic, and that just leaves Loras. He takes position at the comm, so he must be the communications officer, and that usually includes systems work and encryption.

"He's a savant," March says at my shoulder. "He hears a language once, intuitively understands its syntax and structures. Vocabulary takes another day or so."

I jump. "Going to put a bell on you," I mutter.

Is he reading my mind? Or following the trajectory of my gaze, deducing my thoughts via logic instead of Psi? I honestly have no idea, and I've never encountered that before. Nothing in his mind gave me any clue. Unlike Kai, who was a chaotic whirl of impulses, half-formed ideas and inclinations, March was orderly, silent, contained. Even while we were jacked in, I received few things from him that he didn't specifically send.

Compartmentalized, I realize. *Like me.*

I glance at him.

And he smiles, cool and humorless. "They'll be waiting for you when we touch down," he says. "Try not to offend anyone."

Smile sweetly back and reply, "Isn't that *your* job, dickless wonder?"

I'm pretty sure I hear Dina chuckle.

CHAPTER 6

The sky looks like a boiled potato.

An ugly gray-white, overcast, beyond the hangar it's sputtering snow, and March didn't see fit to advise me of the season or provide a winter coat. So I'm shivering, arms wrapped around myself. Hard to look imposing while your teeth chatter.

Don't know what I expected, some kind of diplomatic delegation or another sort of welcoming party? What's waiting for us looks more like a dysfunctional family. There's a tan, leathery man chewing on an unlit cigarillo, yeah, I know—those have been outlawed on civilized worlds for a long time. He's wearing an old-fashioned gun belt, retrofitted, wherein he's carrying the tools of his trade. I *hope* those are spanners.

They don't even manufacture live rounds anymore, do they?

And then there's the old woman with a pouf of silver hair, cosmetics caked into the creases of her face. She

looks like a stereotypical holo-representation of a madame;
I half expect her "girls" to pour out of a nearby ship and
cluster around her, giggling. But nope, that leaves the third
member of the quartet waiting for me, a short, slight fellow
with a receding hairline and a rabbity face, very little chin.
The last person appears to be a surprisingly young woman,
although I've learned not to accept things at face value. But
she's slim—smooth skin, dark hair . . . and she has pale
green eyes.

My gaze sharpens. There's a J-gene carrier, unregistered, out here in the back of beyond? The Corp should
have signed her up, begun her training, and had her making
jumps by now. Well, if not currently, then within a year or
two. I put her age around eighteen, but I might be wrong.

Well, if I'm holding out for a polite introduction from
my new crewmates, I'll wait forever. They've arrayed
themselves at my back, silent. I sense amusement from
March; he enjoys seeing me at a disadvantage, I think. I
don't know why, as he's certainly seen me that way a lot.
From the first moment he entered my cell and caught me
on the verge of tears, he's seen more of that than probably
any other living soul. It occurs to me that, for the sake of
symmetry, I should probably kill him.

March cuts me a sharp look. *Okay, what the hell*—

"I'm Sirantha Jax," I say aloud.

"Yes, we know." Really don't like the way the old
woman smiles; there's a spidery quality to her from her
wrinkle-web face to the strands of hair slithering from her
bouffant bun. "Your reputation precedes you."

By dumb luck, I retain my polite smile because there's
definite nastiness to her tone. I'm trying to decide how to
respond to that, remembering that March told me not to offend anyone, when I feel something drop around my shoulders. Glancing back, I see that it's Saul, the ship's doc. At
least he's on my side. He's given me his overcoat; the
length is about right, but it would wrap around me twice

with fabric to spare. Still, I appreciate the gesture, and I shrug into it fully, nice heavy s-wool.

"Thanks," I murmur, and he steps back, leaving me to deal with these strangers. Oddly, just by virtue of the coat, I feel more armored, more equipped to do so. "March didn't have time to brief me."

And the bastard elbows me in the back because he knows I'm bullshitting. Guess it entertained him to throw me in headfirst and watch whether I'd sink or swim. I'm starting to wonder how bad it would've been, lounging around a Corp asylum for the rest of my days under heavy sedation.

The leathery man chuckles. "That's March for ya. I'm Jor Dahlgren. Good to finally meet you." *As if we've been planning this rendezvous for a while.* I must admit, it's more than a little unnerving to have people making those kinds of pronouncements. His handshake grinds my knuckles together, but I don't wince when I pull my hand back. "This is my mother, Mair Dahlgren, and my daughter, Keri." The girl inclines her head to me like royalty, and the crone's smile widens, revealing yellow teeth.

"The pleasure's mine."

Holy shit, they really are a dysfunctional family. A *family* had the power to dispatch someone to Perlas Station, send my AI into maintenance, and manually unlock my cell door? If so, what're they doing on a backward rock like Lachion? Damn, it's cold here. The wind's slicing right through the overcoat down to the slinky s-silk bodysuit. I may look good, but I'm going to poke No-chin's eye out if he gets any closer.

Jor doesn't introduce the little guy, so I turn to him, and he's bright enough to take the cue. "I'm Carl Zelaco, their financial advisor."

Of course you are. With that face, you couldn't have been anything else.

"A pleasure," I repeat. And March snort-snickers. "I'm

sure we have much to say to one another," I continue, though I'm actually not. "Perhaps we should adjourn inside and talk matters over?"

I don't actually see anything here but this godforsaken hangar. The sky is wide-open, no sign of civilization, but surely there's *something*. Or maybe there isn't, which is the whole point. As I ponder that, the scar beneath my rib cage chooses that moment to itch, and I can't scratch it. Loras seems to be staring at something nobody else sees, but then, March did say he was a savant. So who knows what that's about?

"An eminently agreeable suggestion," No-chin Carl says. "Step this way, we have a rover waiting to convey us to the compound."

Compound? Hate the way my gaze goes to March, for reassurance or clarification, regardless, nothing that I want to ask of him. But I've already done it because he's nodding at me, just as he nodded at Dina on board the ship. There's a five-year-old inside me who wants to kick his shins.

Insufferably, he smiles.

With an inward sigh, I turn to follow the leather-tan man. This rover's new, shiny, with plating that makes me worry about the wildlife. "Are we likely to be attacked?" Even the tire rims are spiked, as if to slam another land vehicle. I'm trying to remember what I've heard about Lachion, but this is the last place any jumper would linger. There's nothing to discover or report, just some mudsiders playing—

Wild West, Old Terra style. Ah, shit.

"Oh, I do hope so," says Mair.

"Probably not," the accountant answers. "We're pretty far from—" He grunts as Jor slugs him in the gut, but I guess he's used to that because he doesn't double up or fall over, although he cradles his stomach as he walks. Huh, he's tougher than he looks.

"You'll be entirely safe with us," Keri tells me, smiling prettily, and I have to wonder why her sweetness scares me most of all.

Dahlgren's got his entourage, and I've got mine, I think with some amusement, although Dina would happily shove a shiv between my shoulder blades and twist. I'm less sure of Loras, and Saul, well, he seems to admire me. Or perhaps he just possesses that old world courtesy bred into some men as a relic from a patronymic culture. Whatever the reason, I'm wearing his coat, and he's shivering, so I count that a win.

That just leaves March. *Obnoxious, odious—*

"Obstreperous," he suggests, sotto voce.

I nod, then jerk my head in his direction. His smile becomes a smirk. Oh shit, he's Psi. He *is*. There's no getting away from him, even when we're not jacked in. But what the hell, I've never heard of a Psi pilot. They're rarer than jumpers and almost always scooped up in early childhood, whisked away to Psi-Corp to learn how to filter out thought-noise. Historically, Psi-sensitives bounced in and out of mental asylums until they killed themselves. Until people figured out they were not, in fact, insane, and they really *were* hearing voices. Thoughts. Whatever.

So add one unregistered jumper, one freelance Psi, and me, and you get—

"—your ass in the rover," March says.

The dysfunctional family sits, regarding me expectantly. Behind me, I sense Dina stirring. I don't need to be Psi to know she's looking at March, asking with a look, *Can I kill her now, boss?* And the bitch of it, I can't even entertain myself plotting long, intricate revenges because he might hear me. And laugh, knowing I can't carry out any of my threats. Oh, but his day is coming. I swear.

For now, I get my ass in the rover.

CHAPTER 7

We're making good time to the middle of nowhere, and I still don't have a clue where we're going or why.

Let me just say, that's getting old. I'm starting to think I was better off in my cell. March offers me a tight smile, as if he isn't sure he disagrees. But before I can go all prima donna and start demanding answers, shit gets interesting.

"We've got Gunnars coming up fast," Keri says, as if she's offering us tea and biscuits, and Jor swears as he swerves hard left, narrowly avoiding a collision with something that looks even sturdier than the rover.

"Those bastards," Mair growls. "They must have us tapped. No other way they could've known we'd be traveling this route. *Nobody* comes this way anymore."

"Unless there's a spy giving reports." No-chin Carl makes this observation, seeming unaware that as the only non–family member in the vehicle, he's most likely casting aspersions on himself unless one of March's crew did it—

This is making my head hurt. I feel like I'm one big

crackling box of crazy, and suddenly, I wonder if this is Unit Psych stuff, if I'm delusional and already locked up in the Corp asylum, medicated within an inch of my life. Certainly I feel paranoid—the world I used to live in doesn't make sense anymore. But lunatics don't wonder if they're mad, do they? Isn't it always the rest of the world that's off its nut?

Jor shakes his head. "Doesn't matter. I'll kill her myself before letting the Gunnars get their hands on her."

Kill . . . who? *Me?* Frag that. What the hell have I gotten myself into?

"Nobody said anything about that." It's Saul, speaking quietly but firmly, from all the way in the back. "That's not part of the plan."

But before anyone can respond, the rover rocks, and I close my eyes, not wanting to see how the countryside slings back and forth as the back tires fight for traction with the Gunnar vehicle slamming us repeatedly in the side. The reinforced doors seem to be holding, but March is really being battered around. I spare a glare for the careful way he's shielding Keri with his upper body, and then I'm smashed face-first into the front seat. When I right myself, hands braced, my nose smarts, eyes are watering, and I feel a trickle of hot blood running over my upper lip.

"She's bleeding," Keri says, and I don't understand the rising note of hysteria in her voice.

Hate driving. *Hate* it. I'm remembering more than I want to about physics: drag and inertia and the momentum of, say, the human body when jettisoned from a moving vehicle.

"Open the roof," Jor barks to his mother, who starts manipulating levers, then the panels part overhead, which seems highly ill-advised, given that there are people trying to kill us, for reasons incomprehensible to me.

"Get those bastards, Ma."

The old woman looks insane as she pushes to her knees.

Her white hair streaming in the wind, she activates another series of controls, and I hear the sound of weapons being readied. She's laughing as she fires, and I have the answer to my question; they do still manufacture live rounds, at least on Lachion. I hear metal hit metal, like a mudsider cannon from some old war holo, and a chunk of their side armor panel blows wide, striking the plain in a cloud of dust.

So fragging cold, the wind's drilling through me. I hear Loras chanting something low and eerie, like an alien prayer, and the Gunnars retaliate, launch a small round device from side turrets. I don't know what to expect here on Lachion, but it strikes the windscreen and detonates in a low hum that appears to play hell with the rover's engines.

"Oh, that's not good," No-chin Carl says, ever helpful.

The rover sputters, turbines dying. Our velocity decreases, then we're hit hard. I feel their grapplers lock down, and they pull back, towing us to a halt.

"Anything I fire's going to hit us, too. The rover can't take any more damage and still carry us out of here." Mair snarls a word that I didn't think old ladies knew. "We'll have to defend," she continues. "If they want us, make them work for it."

Jor simply nods and metal shutters come down over all the windows and I see reinforced steel plating shoot up, covering the doors. The only opening's the roof, and I don't completely understand why they're not sealing that, too.

"Air," March tells me quietly. "The rover doesn't have life support. There are too many of us in here. If we did that, all the Gunnars need to do is wait. We pass out; they cut their way in. Take you, kill the rest of us."

I'm not sure that's a bad solution, actually. March narrows his eyes, and I offer him a very sweet smile. Okay, not Saul. I like Saul. I can't see anything, but I hear the sound of feet tramping over the rocky ground. There's at least six of them, presumably combat trained. I hear the thunk of climbing feet.

March pushes Keri toward the back, and Saul makes room between himself and Loras. Somehow, that pisses me off as much as anything that's happened. "She's *bleeding*," the girl repeats, looking between Saul and Loras as if expecting them to do something. "For Mary's sake, keep her out of the wind."

"I hope you can fight," Dina calls from the back. "Seeing as they're going to hit you first."

She's right. I'm in the second row of seats, right below the gap.

"You better," I tell her. "Because I'm between you and what's coming. When I die, guess who's next, bitch?"

Mair laughs; it's an ugly, grating sound, and I'm not glad I caused it. When she regards me with an approving eye, that's somehow worse. Wordlessly, she hands me a weapon, seeming to assume I'll know how to use it. I turn it over in my hands. I was expecting something more Wild West out of these crazy mudsiders, but this is a standard shockstick—basic principle, hit the bad guy as hard as you can while simultaneously administering a powerful charge that will short his brain pan.

Only one person climbing—why would that be? I heard others approaching . . . that doesn't make sense. Send one at a time to a small opening that's easy to defend? My internal alarms are all going off even before—

There's a low whine as the Gunnar lobs something down between the open panel, and just an instant before it detonates, I hear Keri screaming. Instinctively I put my face beneath Saul's heavy overcoat, as I identify . . . gas grenade. Shit, I didn't even know they made these anymore. Frag this, my eyes stream with tears as I pull myself out of the rover. They don't want me dead; I know that.

That's the one thing I'm sure of, these Gunnars, they're not going to kill me, whatever they do to the rest of this motley bunch. I land hard on the hood of the rover, roll off onto the dirt, and the thud takes the wind right out of me. I can still hear Keri moaning, and Mair curses with a fluency that I've only heard in starports on the rim.

Jor is ominously silent, and the rest of the crew scrambles out after me. Except for March. He's shepherding the girl with an excessive tenderness that makes me want to bury my foot in his balls. Was I ever like her? I don't think so. Life . . . never gave me a chance to be soft. And maybe, if I'm honest, I'm a little jealous—not of March, he's an asshole, but because nobody ever tried to take care of me like that. Not even Kai.

Outside the vehicle, Carl talks quietly with the Gunnars, smiling. I realize he wasn't being stupid earlier; he was boasting. He's wearing a rebreather and a mildly apologetic expression.

"I'm sorry for the inconvenience," he tells me, as if my luggage has been misplaced on an interstellar voyage. "The Gunnars pay substantially better, and I think, given all the statistical data, you'll agree with my assessment. It's the best possible outcome for you to sign on with them."

Doing *what*?

It seems as if there isn't going to be fight. The gas has thoroughly demoralized the Dahlgrens—but I don't know; I feel like busting some heads on principle. I'm bloody tired of being dragged around, here to there, without a word of explanation. And it's been like that a long damn time, nothing's been right since Kai died, and I am *sick* of it.

Mair chooses that moment to stagger from the vehicle; she stumbles, falls, eyes livid with grief. But as she pushes herself upright, more will than strength, she growls to Carl, "Better to die on your feet than live on your knees. You spineless sack of shit."

I somehow know that Jor's not coming out of the rover under his own power. Maybe the gas affected him different than the rest of us. But whatever, why ever, he's gone, and Keri weeps against March's shoulder. Mair, with her wild eyes, looks like the living embodiment of the old Furies, come to reap a man's soul. I'm a little afraid of her, and everyone falls back, as she surges toward the Gunnars. For a moment, I think she'll rend them limb from limb single-handedly.

Carl glances to me in appeal, as if I have some power in this insane tableau. Then I realize I do.

"Frag you." I answer his look in Keri's time-for-tea tone.

And it takes him a moment to process the disparity of the words from the sweetness in my voice. The Gunnars look like killers, all of them. Big men, hard-eyed, well geared, and ready to throw down. That's fine.

So am I.

I'm Sirantha Jax, and I have had *enough*.

CHAPTER 8

"Jax," March hisses. "Loras can't fight, Saul won't. Are you crazy?"

That leaves me, Mair, Dina, and March, if he'll weigh in. Keri is a nonfactor, as she's still sniveling.

So yeah, I guess I am. After all this time, you would think I'd have earned a better death, but at least I'm going out swinging. I test the weight of the shockstick in my hand, and the Gunnars share a look among themselves, like some hive-mind critter, before they burst out laughing. I'm pretty sure these assholes are related, too. What is it with this fragging backwater planet?

"Oh, Ms. Jax, do be reasonable—" Carl says, as I sprint for him, duck a half-assed grab from one of his goons, open-hand-smash the bridge of No-chin's nose, then come down hard on the backswing upside meatwad's head. *Yeah, asshole,* that's *how it's done.* I smell the faint scent of sizzling skin as he crumples, the shockstick throwing blue sparks. Its live hum in my hands proves to the other five that I'm dead serious, and suddenly they realize they've got a fight on their hands.

It's a mistake people have made before. Because I'm small, they assume I'm also spineless, that I won't have the guts to back up the shit I talk. Carl shrieks like a woman, his nose spurting like I've cut his jugular or something.

"He's bleeding." Keri moans. "Mother Mary of Anabolic Grace, what have you *done*?"

Everyone sort of freezes and shares a look of unilateral horror. And I don't understand. It's just a damned bloody nose. I've got one, too. What's the big deal? But I use the time to make myself scarce, as his men rally, swinging slow because they're so big. They connect, and I'm going down, not in a good way. I don't have the strength to go one-on-one with any of these guys, but I'm betting my brain against theirs. These nulls don't know *how* to fight women; it's a different game, believe me.

As I dive between the legs of a big Gunnar, I see Mair wind up and slam her shockstick hard as she can between the V of another guy's thighs. Falling, he makes a noise that I can't say I've heard a human utter before, sort of like I imagine a puppy would sound being put through a juicer. He curls up on his side, covering those extra-crispy genitals with his palm, then she's after No-chin Carl. Guess a broken nose isn't satisfactory recompense for her loss. I wouldn't want to be in his shoes—that's for damn sure. And huh . . . for some reason the remaining Gunnars don't want to mess with Mair—they leave Carl to take his thrashing—and that has them hounding me. I evade a clumsy grab with a feint left, then I sprint for the rover.

Just like that, we've got a fair fight on our hands.

I'm not sure they want me alive anymore, but that's all right because they've got to catch me first. I use the rover, rounding it, then doubling back. If they think I'm going to stand still and take my beating, they're the crazy ones. It's a childish tactic, but it buys me some time as March shakes his head, glares at me, and throws a sloppy roundhouse. He gets stomach-slugged twice in rapid succession and doesn't even stumble. Making a second lap, I decide he's one tough son of a bitch and make a mental note never to gut-punch him. I'll go for the eyes instead.

Midfight, March glares at me, and for that sin, takes a solid uppercut to the jaw. I laugh out loud, starting to enjoy this. Shit, the two behemoths have figured out my little game, and this time, they anticipated my turn. My timing's off, but I dive between them, roll, and come up behind Saul, who regards me pleadingly. Don't know what he's asking, no breath to inquire because I've still got them on me and no way to shake them.

March can hold his own, but I have to deal with this somehow—

But not alone. Leaping from atop the rover, Dina drops down on one of the flagella tailing me. She isn't a huge woman but she's muscular, and seventy kilos, landing hard, will flatten even a big guy if he's not braced. Her shockstick hums as she clubs him efficiently, although one hit really would've done it. Still, I can't help admire her artistry; he's going to have quite a nice pattern in minor burns, assuming he's not brain damaged by the time she's done.

I turn just in time to see March land the telling blow. The other guy's head snaps round, flecks of blood and spit spewing from his open, rubber-lipped mouth. They did it the old-fashioned way: no shocksticks, no finesse, just slug it out until someone falls over. In a one-on-one fight, I'm guessing that's rarely March. And probably because he's bleeding from a split lip and has what looks to be a nice shiner swelling on his left eye, March sinks his boot into the guy's ribs, hard enough that even *I* wince.

That leaves just one standing, against all of us, so I figure it's safe for me to stop running. He seems to realize that around the same time, nearly collides with me, then raises his hands, palms up, in a symbol of peaceable intentions.

"Truce?" he asks, and I realize it's the first time I've heard one of them speak. "The Gunnar clan would like to step back from this particular investment. It seemed like a good opportunity but the start-up costs"—he gestures at the fallen—"are prohibitive."

"They killed my boy." Mair finally rises, stiff and weary, from the broken body of her former financial advisor. Although I'm not a medical officer, I'm pretty sure Carl's not getting up. Ever. "I want them *all* executed, March. Here. Now. Every last one."

"The gas is nontoxic!" The Gunnar defends himself, sounding desperate. "He must've experienced an allergic reaction. Swear it's nonlethal, the rest of you are fine."

The doc hovers nearby, not quite wringing his hands in dismay, but it's close. I wonder if March surrounds himself with pacifists and untried boys for a reason. Make himself look better by comparison, maybe? I smirk as he narrows his eyes on me. God help me, but I love the fact that I can taunt him silently, even with this shit going on.

"Thank you," I say softly to Dina, while the rest wait to hear what March is going to say. I know he's thinking things over, weighing factors of which I, in my almighty ignorance, am unaware.

She shrugs. "You got balls, bitch, even if you're dumber than a bag of hammers. We'll be lucky if we don't die today."

Have to laugh at that, and damn me if I'm not starting to like her, even if she hates my guts. I'm glad she's on my side. Sort of.

"No." Saul speaks into the silence. He's been circling among the bodies or soon-to-be-bodies, administering treatment. "Carl Zelaco betrayed an honorable contract with clan Dahlgren for the hope of financial gain. While clan Gunnar pursued this investment"—he glances at me as if I'm a walking, talking stock certificate—"with regrettable vehemence, they intended no harm to clan Dahlgren, save financial embarrassment. A life for a life; it is fair frontier justice."

March surprises me by nodding—I guess Saul functions as his conscience. God knows I didn't sense anything like one while we were jacked in together. Mair hisses, and I half expect her to fly at Saul. I even step in front of him, although honestly I don't want to take this old woman on. She is fragging *scary*. But then Keri surprises me with a firmness I hadn't expected of her:

"He's right," she states. "Let's go. We still have business to discuss." Right now, there's a resemblance to Jor in the set of her mouth, and her red-rimmed eyes shine with a hard light, although that may be the way the setting sun reflects in her pupils.

"I will *not* forget you," the Gunnar clansman says. And yeah, he's looking at me.

I give him my best grin. "Nobody ever does."

All this time, Loras has been staring up at the sky, as if he lives in a world the rest of us simply cannot perceive. He's dreamy-vague, golden curls and sapphire eyes, a fey, graven look that gives his features an inexplicable purity. Now that I study him closer, I realize he's not young so much as ageless, his face untouched by time or worry. There's a certain kind of madness in his face, as if he cannot care for anything enough to be moved by it, and I have to look away. But he draws my eyes back as he speaks.

"We should go," he says quietly, expressionlessly. Studying the angle of the sun. "If we hope to reach the compound by nightfall. They're coming."

"Shit." For once, March seems to speak for all of us.

CHAPTER 9

"They who?"

It's like the tenth time I've asked, but no one's answering me. Instead they're rushing to and fro trying to get all the wounded loaded into the Gunnar Landcruiser. The dead have already been dumped unceremoniously into the cargo space in back, and it shakes me down to my bones, the way Keri accepts that.

If she knows she can't afford to indulge in grief, moan and whimper and sob on March's shoulder, it can only be because she knows something really bad is coming, something that will require all of us, functioning at our peak, to survive it. My breath puffs out smoky like a devil's sigh, and I'm shivering all over. Their silence is frightening me more than anything I've ever known.

"We've done everything we can here," March says finally. "All aboard, we've got to make tracks."

"We'll never stay ahead of them," Keri answers in a

monotone. "There isn't a land vehicle fast enough, and they can pry off armored plating—"

I realize it's not resolve buoying her up. She's numb with despair, and I know this is my fault even if I don't understand what's happening entirely. But the others are too accustomed to listening to March to heed the girl's objections. One by one, they climb inside, and the Gunnar takes his place at the wheel. It's close, not meant to carry this many, and so I wind up on someone's lap. Not surprisingly, March holds Keri, carefully although not possessively. I'm figuring out she's like a little sister to him. Maybe if I had a brother, he'd treat me like that, too.

I glance down at Dina, who rolls her eyes. "You're so not my type," she tells me, although she does wind her arms about my waist, probably to keep me from hitting my head. "Scrawny little bitch."

"Dahlgren compound is closest," the Gunnar murmurs, presumably laying in the course as his fingers fly across the consoles. "We'll make for it and pray."

Loras pauses in his low chanting. "Already on it."

"Would someone please tell me what's coming?"

"You called them," Keri tells me, pale green eyes eerie in the half-light. "With the blood. They live in the caves and only come above to feed, they'll descend in hordes . . ."

Before I can erupt and start pulling her hair out in sheer frustration, Saul elaborates. "They're a native Lachion life-form, one of the few things that seems to have thrived here—" He gestures, and glancing between the miniscule gap in the plated panels at the barren plain, I can see why survival might be difficult. "Largely because the creatures eat anything that moves . . ."

"Or doesn't move," Mair adds, cheerful as a death's-head.

Saul continues as if he hasn't been interrupted, as if he's giving a lecture, and we ought to have holo-recorders fixed on him, lest we forget something important later. "In some regards they are akin to *Nyctosaurus gracilis*, from the

Upper Cretaceous of western Kansas. That was part of Old Terra," he adds, seeming to notice that some of his audience look blank.

"There used to be great herds on Lachion," the old woman tells me. "Bison. We cloned and raised 'em here. We didn't know about the Teras then. Didn't know why nobody had developed this world. It seemed like hard work but doable."

"But you can't see them coming," Keri says in a reedthin voice. I see March rubbing her back, his expression as soft as I've seen it. "Just hear their wings."

Now I've got this image of these flying things, mouths full of jagged teeth to rend, talons to pry the metal off the Landcruiser, and leathery wings that carry them faster than anything can move on the ground. Plus, you can't see them coming. And *this* is better than my cell, better than Psych Officer Newel? Maybe. Despite myself I shudder, but Dina doesn't stroke my back comfortingly.

Instead she says, "And you called them down on us, dumb-ass."

"Er, yes." The doc looks discomfited. "The Teras are natural hunters, and they've evolved a very complex camouflage mechanism that approximates invisibility. True invisibility is impossible, naturally, but—"

"Quiet." March holds up a hand, and everyone in the vehicle stops breathing. Or damn near. Over the rumble of the Landcruiser, I'm pretty sure I can make out the faint sound of wings. To make that kind of noise, there must be—"Hundreds," he says, after a moment. "And closing fast. Will this heap go any faster?"

The Gunnar shakes his head. "Got her wide-open right now. I've got their heat signatures on-screen, and I figure our paths are going to intersect a good ten minutes before we reach the compound."

"They'll be on us in less than four minutes," Loras informs us. Nobody asks him how he knows that or how he was able to sense the Teras stirring in the first place. I'm sick of asking questions everyone else already knows the answers to.

"Powering up the shock fields." March flips a few switches, and I can hear a new hum in addition to the engines and the ominous rush of wings growing ever closer. Through the seams between panels I can see that the light is going, and I wish that didn't fill me with such inexorable dread.

"That'll deter them a little while." The Gunnar's knuckles gleam white where he's gripping the steering console a little too tightly.

His brothers are starting to come around, some of them. The one Mair whacked in the jimmy asks, "What the hell are we doing with Dahlgrens, bro?" Then pauses, registering the sound: "Mother Mary of Anabolic Grace, we got Teras incoming?" He levels angry blue eyes on me. "You're a hex, lady, dark luck, powerful bad juju, ken?"

"Only to people who try to kidnap me," I tell him sweetly, and March snorts, so I feel obliged to add, "Or rescue me . . ." And then Dina makes a *pfft* sound. "Or who travel with me . . ." My gaze sweeps around the darkened interior, trying to find an ally, but nobody will hold my eyes more than two seconds, it seems. "Fine, frag you all, I'm dark juju, bad luck, and you're all doomed."

"I don't think you're bad luck," Saul says, touching my shoulder lightly. "I think you're the best hope we've had since the Corp bought out and shut down Clericon Stellar twenty turns ago."

Before I can ask what the hell he means, something thumps hard against the roof, slinging the Landcruiser sideways. I almost hear something, just above the range of human hearing, but Loras flinches, trembling visibly, and I can see a thin trickle of blood seeping from his nostrils. Something . . . sonic about these Teras, and poor Loras with his hypersenses, their screams hurt him? Well frag me, that's . . . really . . . not good.

The shock fields hiss as bodies hit them, and I smell the

obscene odor of frying meat. But each time the power surges, the engines splutter, and the Gunnar finally says, "Turn 'em off, March. We're going to stall out. There's just too many of them, and they're overloading the systems."

Mair says softly, in praise, "You bought us some time."

"It'll be enough." Keri lifts her head from his shoulder long enough to deliver this vote of confidence. "March never lets us down."

There's always the first time, I think sourly, and am rewarded with a glare.

"Hard part's going to be getting from the Landcruiser into the compound," the Gunnar says, fighting with the steering column now. I can tell that only his raw physical strength is keeping the 'cruiser from being towed off course. But he's tiring; I can tell that, too. "Unless you've remodeled according to my recommendations since the last time I was there."

Mair's expression seems to indicate she didn't want to take advice from a Gunnar, a fact that we're all going to regret before much longer. But I'm distracted by the way Loras covers his ears, shaking uncontrollably. Once I'd have thought he was weak, terrified, maybe having a seizure, but now I know it's agony, pure and simple. He isn't human. I'm suddenly positive of it. He's more than a savant, and people are treating him like he's furniture, subhuman, not worthy of their regard. Even the doc, who by certain sworn oaths, *should* give a shit, doesn't seem to.

Kneeing Dina in the chest, I crawl over the seat, pushing my way back between Gunnar brothers until I reach Loras. He regards me, eyes wide and blank, tuned to the frequency that seems to be liquefying his brain. It's not just their screams of pain; he can hear everything, their calls to one another, their rage. Hunger. What it must be like, experiencing that, I cannot begin to imagine, but it makes him like me, alien in his way.

And for that I want to help him.

CHAPTER 10

"What can I do?"

Loras doesn't seem to see me, let alone hear the question, so I take his hand in mine, and it's cold, frighteningly so. If someone doesn't do something, he's going to die. Too many fragging people have bought it because of me. I'll be damned if it's going to happen again.

Think, Jax.

For a minute, nothing comes, then—okay, maybe it's a stupid idea, but it's the only one I've got. If one sound is killing him, maybe another pitch can cancel it out; I just have to find the right one. Watching his face, I start singing, running the scale in "ahs," and everyone else turns to look at me as if I'm insane. Maybe I am.

But when I hit an F toward the lower end of my range, Loras responds. His fingers wrap around mine, and he nods. He still can't speak, no more than he could articulate his distress when the Teras came, but that's helping, so I sing it louder. Though I have decent pitch, I'm not trained, so my lungs are starting to burn from holding the note.

March raises a brow at me. "What the frag are you doing?"

I don't pause to answer, but Dina figures it out. "Saving a life, you brainless hump." With that, she adds her voice to mine, finding the note after a few false starts.

And then one by one, the rest of the vehicle joins in. The Gunnars are all tone-deaf and just succeed in making racket, but Mair and Keri hit the right one on the first try. March is the last, and I think it's more aggravation that it was my idea than lack of desire to help Loras. I honestly think they just didn't notice. I don't know why that should be, why they pay so little attention to him, but I'm going to find out.

"Lights of the compound ahead," the Gunnar says. "We can't stay in the vehicle; they'll pull it apart. Do you at least have shock fields installed?'

"The entire perimeter can be electrified, plus all building exteriors," Mair answers. "We have that capability remotely, and the fields extend twenty meters."

"So you can turn it on after we make it inside the fences?"

The old woman nods.

"Well, it'd be better if you had an outbuilding big enough to drive the Landcruiser inside, like I *advised* you, so we wouldn't need to run . . . but that'll do."

"We were getting around to it," Mair says tightly.

"That wouldn't help with so many of them on us." March sounds grim. "They'd just hold on, then we'd have them chewing us up inside when we tried to disembark."

"Once we're safely parked, we could fire up the shock fields on the Landcruiser without worrying about stalling," the Gunnar points out, and I'm surprised to see March concede with a nod.

"If they damage the 'cruiser, with too many panels gone,

the fields won't work. Necessary connections ripped out."
And the Gunnar nods at March's words.

Holding the note almost distracts me from what's going
on outside the vehicle. I can feel it rocking, and the metal
plates scream as the Teras pry at them. I don't think I've
ever been this scared in my life, and I'm starting to feel
faint from the tiny, rare gulps of air I'm permitting myself
to keep Loras among the living. Keri hasn't faltered; neither has Dina, and I spare a smile for both of them.

"Yes," he whispers. "I owe you my life." His fingers
squeeze mine. "It's all right," he adds, louder. Stronger.
"I've constructed the sound barrier myself now, using your
voices, and I'm holding it inside my head."

"So here's the plan," the Gunnar says. "We drive inside
the first set of fences. When I park, I fire up the shock
fields. Mair activates the compound defense grid. Some of
them are going to avoid the shock fields, that's a given.
We're just going to have to run like hell toward the nearest
outbuilding and pray."

"No." Mair shakes her head. "You know they won't return to the caves until they've fed."

"Then what do you suggest?" March sounds as if he's at
the end of his patience.

Mair closes her eyes for a moment, and when she opens
them, it's like she's another woman entirely. "A sacrifice."

And no matter who asks her, that's all she'll say.

One of the back panels finally rips away and I have the
sense of things swarming, although I can't *see* them, and
my flesh crawls. I hear the sound of something swiping,
reaching, and No-Chin's corpse seems to fly back as if
animated, and then I can hear the grotesque sound of
bones snapping, the wet sound of the Teras devouring
their prize. The wind howls through the open Landcruiser, so cold, so dark now, and an endless night full of
slavering fiends.

I don't realize I'm trembling until Loras cups his other

hand over mine. "Don't worry," he whispers. "I am your *shinai* now. I will not let anything happen to you."

My what?

Before I can ask, the side panel gives, and the Gunnar who told me I'm bad luck, well, he goes screaming, arms flailing, face contorted. I'll never forget the way he looked as the Teras pulled him out. Perhaps I am dark luck after all.

"Coming into the compound," the Gunnar says, toneless. Hell of a way to watch your brother die. "Cruiser's too damaged for shock fields to fire. Whatever you have in mind, clan Dahlgren, do it now, or none of us are going to make it out of this alive."

"Clan Dahlgren sacrifices to ensure its own perpetuity." I'm not altogether sure what she means until she bounds out of the Landcruiser, no longer old in her deportment, and somehow, she's sprinting with preternatural speed. I can smell the copper where she's cut herself, and it's an irresistible lure. Clan leader, warrior, whatever else she is, Mair isn't merely an old woman. I've never known *anyone* who could move like that. I want to ask, but now isn't the time.

I sense the Teras wheeling away from the vehicle and giving chase to living, bleeding prey. Keri screams, "Grandmother!" and March has to carry her away, as the rest of us make use of the time she's bought us so dearly. It's the bravest and most terrible thing I've ever seen.

We run, heads down, conscious that the Teras could return at any time. Loras still has me by the hand, and he yanks the door wide, pushing me inside before entering himself. I don't understand his new care for my safety, then I'm awed, humbled, to hear the live hum of the compound defense grid activating. She's out there with them, being torn to pieces, and dying, she saved us all.

Tears stand in my eyes, and Keri's still screaming, fighting March with fists and feet, but he just holds her, gentle but implacable, refusing to let her go back out. She's lost everyone today—her father, her grandmother. And a lot of it is *my* fault. I'll be lucky if she doesn't try to kill me at some point. I no longer find Keri's histrionics ridiculous. Whatever her eccentricities, Mair was a woman worth mourning.

Dropping to my knees, I take stock with a glance. Of his clan, only the Gunnar chief made the run. They were all big men. Slow. Our crew seems to be present, although the doc's blood-spattered and collapses against the wall as if he may never move again. We're in a storage building. I see crates stacked up against the wall, tools. Dina looks angry, which is pretty much on par. Even though I don't know shit about Lachion, I know it's not safe to go back out there. There's no guarantee all the Teras were outside the perimeter when the defense grid came up. We need to hole up and let them fry, trying to return to the caves.

I hope there's some food in here. Fragging starving. It seems like forever since I stuffed that square of choclaste into my face, and before that, I hadn't eaten all day.

Maybe that's an irreverent thought, I don't know. But it's how I function. The part of me that feels unworthy, wounded, totally shaken by everything that's happened, I shuffle her to the back because she's not helping me deal. And the Sirantha who steps up, well, she's a pragmatist.

And she's hungry.

CHAPTER 11

Also, I need to pee.

But I can't see anything like san facilities in this corrugated steel box. Dina has already started to rummage through the crates, looking for anything useful. The main house, with all associated amenities, is probably deeper inside the compound, but I don't think any of us want to go back out there until the drones have a chance to scout around and see what might be lurking in the dark.

Loras has settled down beside me, almost as if he's awaiting my orders, and March still holds Keri, who appears to have collapsed entirely. Rest is probably the best thing for her right now, but her breath still hitches as children's do when they've cried themselves to sleep. Leaning against the wall, I watch Dina rooting around, tossing out items that may be useful. So far, she's found blankets, torch-tubes, and what looks like emergency rations.

I snag one, tear the foil open, and yep, it's the olive green paste that tastes like nothing you'd ever voluntarily eat, and yet simultaneously contains a whole day's worth of necessary nutrients. *Why the hell can't they manufacture these in choclaste?* Making a face, I hand one to Loras, who accepts it and downs his without shuddering. March is watching me, so I pass a pack to him as well. Even if I don't like him, I'm not going to starve him while he can't get his own. He's still got Keri as deadweight.

Dina grabs a couple more and hands them out to the Gunnar and Doc, who opens his eyes reluctantly. Everyone eats in silence. It's hard to know what the hell to say after a day like we've had. The Gunnar just sits like a small mountain, probably thinking about his brothers.

But then I remember I had a couple questions that just won't keep and glance at March again. Seems like he'd know. "How did Mair—"

He pitches his voice low. "She was a first-rank chi-master, one of the last."

I blink at that. "No shit?"

March gives me a withering look. But I didn't even know they existed. All I've ever heard is stories—Old Terra monks, who could adjust their breathing, stop their hearts. The greatest of them could completely control their chi, resulting in superhuman feats. Like the burst of speed Mair summoned when we needed it most.

"Did she have a student?" I ask. And his gaze goes to the girl sleeping in his arms. Well, of course. Everything comes back to Keri.

I sigh. What can I possibly offer to counterbalance her loss? Why did she think I'm worth it? Hell, *I* don't even think so, and I'm generally the biggest proponent for the survival of Sirantha Jax.

Nothing I can do about it, though, and so I turn to Loras. He's been watching me almost in the same manner that he scanned the sky for things the rest of us couldn't see. It's a little unnerving, to tell the truth.

"So tell me about this *shinai* thing."

And March laughs quietly. "That's right. He's yours now. You don't know how long I've waited for this day."

Call me cynical, but anything that makes March so happy cannot be good for me.

"I am now your *shinai*," Loras tells me, but there's sharpness to his tone. "This means I will put your welfare ahead of my own and follow all your directives, except ones wherein you ask me to do harm. That, I cannot do, even for you."

What the frag . . . ?

"Sounds an awful lot like slavery," I say.

Loras studies me for a moment as if he isn't sure if I'm messing with him or not. "That is what *shinai* means in La'hengrin," he answers at last. And yeah, there's a definite edge in his voice.

"How can she be so traveled and yet so ignorant?" Dina asks of nobody in particular, but I'm too busy glaring at March to respond to the insult.

"You have to be out of your mind if you think I'm going to put up with keeping someone *enslaved*." Mary, I want to break his neck. I can't believe I've jumped, even once, with someone so monstrous. I need to scrub my mind clean with a wire brush, everywhere he touched it. Bastard. "No," I tell Loras, shaking my head. "If there's a ceremony or something, let's do it because—"

His blue eyes burn as he claps his palm over my mouth. "Don't," he begs, although his gaze says something else entirely. "You cannot deny me, or I will die. The La'heng cannot exist outside the protection of another species. It is part of the legacy your people left us."

Godammit, before I can help myself, I glance to March for confirmation. I fragging *hate* that I keep doing that. But he's nodding. "Did you really think I run a slave ship, Jax?" Even though he doesn't say another word, I sense his disappointment. And maybe I have let him down. Because even though there's no liking between us, maybe there was a nascent respect.

"You're serious." Dumb-ass thing to say—of course he's serious, and suddenly I do feel ignorant. I have no idea who the La'heng are or why they need to be . . . *shinai*. Even mentally I shy away from the real word—slave.

"Yes," he answers quietly. "When humanity first visited La'heng, we did not greet them warmly. We killed all of their delegations, rebuffed all attempts to establish contact. They correctly adjudged us a hostile alien race and took steps to civilize us."

I don't know how long ago this was, don't know anything about this—I have lived in an oddly insular world, made up of Kai and my CO, who directed me where to jump and to whom I reported when I felt like taking a holiday. "What happened?"

Hate that I'm making him talk about it when it clearly bothers him. Deep down, I know I'm going to hear a tale of conquest and subjugation, and that it's another thing I can feel guilty for, although it's racial, not personal.

"They seeded our atmosphere with a chemical that dampened our ability to fight."

"RC-12," the doc puts in. "It's generally only used to sedate violent criminals. It had never been used on a global scale before."

"They took La'heng bloodlessly," Loras goes on, monotone. "And fed us more drugs to keep us compliant. They didn't take into account our physiology. We adapt quickly, integrate changes. The RC-12 produced a new generation of La'heng young incapable of fighting, even to defend their own lives. We're helpless."

I'm starting to understand, and my stomach rolls over, full of that disgusting paste and burning shame. "So it was decided you each needed a . . . protector?" I can't make myself say "master," but that's what it means. What we've done.

Loras nods. "At birth, we're bonded to someone, who ostensibly will safeguard us and treat us well. Since many of us have a flair for languages, we are sought after on board ships."

"You don't stay with your protectors for life?"

"Generally," he says. "But we can be inherited, like property. And if someone saves our lives, outside the family line to which we're bound, then *shinai* transfers to that new person, a sort of life link, I suppose."

"I got him from my great-uncle," March says then. "But he's yours now."

Mother Mary of Anabolic Grace.

"And if I refuse—"

"I'll die. It was decided that a quick death is preferable for any La'heng unfortunate enough to find himself without protection due to what might befall him thereafter." Loras regards me, mouth compressed.

Which explains why they were all studiously ignoring his distress. It doesn't make it more acceptable, but they all knew what might happen if they intervened. And March, who should've been looking out for him, probably couldn't tell what was going on, all the way in front.

I exhale in a tired rush. "Don't worry about that. I'll try to be a good . . . whatever. I'll watch your back and let you do as you please, okay? Can we think of it as friendship more than obligation?"

Loras stares at me for a long moment. "Could you think of one to whom you are wholly subservient as a friend?"

Guess not. I'm suddenly exhausted and still need to pee.

CHAPTER 12

"Do it outside," March dares me. Mocking. I'd almost forgotten he could do that. "Go see if it's safe for the rest of us."

And for Mary's sake, that's the last straw. I just nod and make for the door. If that's what he thinks I'm good for, live bait, the doll you dangle into the cage to see if the monster's sleeping, then fragging *fine*. I don't see what happens thereafter, but he catches me just before I go out, spinning me back to face him. Keri's curled up on her side, where he presumably dumped her as he came scrambling after me.

"Are you crazy?" he demands.

"Yeah." I hold his look, and I'm just too tired to try to hide anything from him, not that I could entirely. He gets it all, one way or another, then with a muffled oath, he pulls me into his arms, gentle as he was with Keri.

My whole world's upside down as he runs his hands over my back. March is just never, ever nice to me. I don't have any idea how long it's been since he found me on Perlas Station, but it seems like eternity. I can't remember not hating March at this point; it's the one truth to which I cling.

"Let me go before I cut your nuts off," I tell him, then wonder why I sound like that. Soft. Broken. A not-Jax voice.

"Will you just shag her already?" Dina throws a torch-tube at March, hitting him in the side of the head with a satisfying thunk. The light comes on as it lands at his feet.

I think I love that woman. Because he breaks away to glare at her, and I step back. "I was just trying to keep her from killing herself."

"Sure you were." Now the doc's giving him hell. "And that's why you were finger-checking her scapula and vertebrae so carefully for possible injuries, too."

Can't help but snicker.

"I hate you all," March growls. His expression adds, *What'd I do to deserve this?*

It seems like Dina registers that because she answers the implicit question. "Duh. You hired us out of Gehenna. That's where all the assholes hang out. *You* were there, weren't you?"

"She makes a strong case," I admit.

Oddly enough, I feel better, less alone. I still need to pee, but I'm not willing to feed myself to the Teras to do so. We're all surprised to hear the Gunnar finally speak up; he's been quiet so long.

"We need to recall the drones, get a look at their security cams," he says. "If it seems clear, we can make a run for the house. Alternative is to play it safe, stay here until daybreak. It might be a long night, but at least we'll get where we're going."

At that, March nods and snags Keri's bag, rummages until he finds a remote. "Think this is it, let's have a look at what's out there."

He inputs a few commands, and about five minutes later, there's a metallic clang as the drones try to proceed through the closed door. Bright, they aren't. We open it just enough for them to pass through, then close it. Bolt it again.

Everyone watches as the Gunnar reviews the footage, grainy, low-tech stuff. But nothing seems to be moving out there.

"You think they're all dead?" Loras asks.

I can see why that'd be a particular concern for him, seeing as he can't fight, at all. Not even monsters. He's reliant on *me* now for his protection. And if that's not the shittiest twist of fate ever, I don't know what is.

"Hard telling. If they've all fed . . ." The Gunnar pauses, and I know he's thinking about his brothers, taken within the compound proper. "Then they might be nesting."

March folds his arms. "It's choosing time. I'll have to take Keri. I don't think she's going to wake up for a while, and even if she does, she won't be fit to run."

Saul clears his throat. "Especially given the fact that I sedated her."

"We should wait," I say quietly. "It's stupid to go when we're safe enough here. We have blood all over us, so if there are any in the compound, they'll catch the scent."

"Daylight won't help us survive them," Loras observes. "It'll just give us longer to feel afraid."

"They'll be wanting to return to the caves by then." For once, March seems to be agreeing with me. "We have a better shot of everyone making it if we do wait."

The solution's simple, and I have to wonder why I didn't think of it before. "Got an idea. Saul, can I have your shirt?"

I'm not being a perv; he's just got the most blood on his clothing. After a few seconds' hesitation, he pulls it over his head, and I toss him back his coat. They watch as I tie the sleeves around the first drone and push it outside. And the Gunnar nods like it's a sound notion—

But holy shit, I hear wings, and Loras trembles, hands over his ears, since they must be screaming right outside the door. One of them slams hard against the reinforced metal, and I swallow, hoping they can't smell us through the building, that their claws aren't strong enough to get through these walls. I hear the sound of the drone being smashed to bits.

Oh, Mother Mary, no, please don't let me have fucked this up.

I don't notice I'm rocking back and forth on my heels until March puts a hand on my shoulder to steady me. "It was a good idea," he tells me softly. "We'd have died trying to get to the main house. We're safe in here. And this way, nobody secretly feels we're being too cautious." A little louder, he adds, "Going to call the Dahlgren First and have him spread word that there are Teras inside the perimeter." Shortly thereafter, he gets on the radio and does so.

Throat thick, I nod. I've just realized that if I'd gone outside to pee, well, what happened to the drone, that'd be me right now. He really did save my life. *Oh shit.* I have a smart-ass comment about being his *shinai* on the tip of my tongue when, for probably the first time in my life, I hold it. Not because March deserves something more sincere, although he does, but because what's been done to the La'heng just isn't something I should joke about. And at least I've caught myself before I can be an insensitive asshole.

"Thanks," I answer. I'm not just saying that because he complimented me. And by the shine of his dark eyes, he knows that.

He just shrugs, but it feels like an apology, as if he knows he pushed too far. It'll do. Dina's watching us, and she just rolls her eyes, smirking. "Let's get some bio in place if we're staying the night," is all she says.

All she really wants is two empty buckets, and we argue a little bit. I finally say, "Okay, you must get off on guys watching you piss, then. I'm sorry, I didn't realize."

"Bitch." But she's smiling as she helps me rig a primitive setup of blankets on wire fastened to the shelving on either side.

I'm the first to test out the ladies' bucket and man, I think I have a peegasm when I finally let go, groaning. The guys are all smirking when I come out. I know they heard me, but whatever, dammit. *Can we try to be a little bit grown-up? Please?*

March seems to think about that, then shakes his head. But he grins at me. He's removed his jacket, tucked it underneath Keri's head. I dislike seeing the gentle side of him; makes him harder to hate, and I've been doing that so well. Doing my best to ignore both him and Loras, who I swear is trying to piss me off with his attentive-slave impression, I walk past and drop down beside the Gunnar, who looks as sad as a human can without actually weeping.

"So what's your name?" I mean obviously it's something Gunnar, but surely they don't just number the big lugs.

"Lex," he answers tiredly. "Alexander." His gaze goes to Keri, and I wonder what's on his mind. "I'm going to have to marry her," he adds, when he sees me looking. He sounds about as pleased about that as I'd be to hook up with March.

Really starting to like that glare, by the way.

"How come?" I think he needs to talk more than I want to know. And that's fine.

"Clan competition is fierce here," he tells me. "As I'm sure you've figured out. We have to race for new technology, resources. Everything. There's a very definite hierarchy, and we two have been at each other for the top spot for years now. That's why we went after you so hard. Couldn't let Dahlgren get the edge."

"How the hell do I qualify as either?"

"Commerce," he tells me. "Right now, the only source of trained jumpers is via the Corp. They control all trade, more or less, although they would deny that's their intent with their refusal to permit unaffiliated academies. Imagine the money that could be made if someone successfully created an alternative."

"You not only want to try and figure out what makes me tick, you also want me to train jumpers for you."

I've put the pieces together now. My disgrace on Matins IV probably seemed like a hell of an opportunity. How often does a jumper wind up like that? Ordinarily they'd have no hope of turning one of us; part of our indoctrination is a "Corp for life" mentality. That's what No-chin meant when he said the Gunnars would pay more, and it'd be better for all concerned if I signed with them. Teaching . . . never even thought of that. Obviously, the Corp has instructors, former jumpers, who choose retirement over burnout, and they impart what we need to know about grimspace. We make our first practice jumps with them, all jacked into a test ship that simulates what we'll one day do all by ourselves.

He nods. "We could create new trade routes. Establish a free market, and it would help a lot of outposts, not having to pay Corp tariffs for their supplies. But Mother Mary, in one day, such losses . . ." Lex closes his eyes. "The only hope either clan has now is consolidation. We become Gunnar-Dahlgren, marry up, and combine our ranks, or we get wiped by the other clans."

"When shell freezesh over," Keri says, slurred, sedated.

"Well, put on your overcoat, sweetheart."

Hard to say who looks more shocked to hear that coming from March.

CHAPTER 13

The inevitable argument's postponed when Keri passes out again.

March pulls her up against him, a wise idea—sharing body heat since this shed lacks climate control. But everyone's regarding him speculatively, wondering what he has in mind. Being March, in the face of such avid curiosity, he leans his head back against the wall, closes his eyes, and goes to sleep. Just like that.

Hits me then—that's a soldier's skill, being able to turn off and on. It's an invaluable talent, one that allows them to stand watch easier . . . but it takes years in the field to develop it, usually on rough assignments. I frown as I study him, trying to put the pieces together. He's clearly a merc, and I'm willing to bet if I got a glimpse of his bare chest, he'd have some battle scars to show. Not that I want to see March without a shirt, Mary forefend. But how does a Psi-sensitive stay hidden for so long? And he's clearly got some ability to control it, or he would be nuts by now.

There's something about that bugging me, some thought I had that would help me figure him out, but right now I'm just too tired to get a fix on it. As I'm sitting there, rubbing my hands over my arms absently, Loras brings me one of the spare blankets. I wish it was a genuine kindness, but I can tell by his expression it's part of the whole *shinai* thing. No wonder March was so glad to have it end—being served by someone who resents it with every fiber of his being, well, it kind of sucks. I mean, not the help. I'm glad of the blanket, and I wrap up in it with a murmured, "Thanks."

But just the fact Loras feels like he *has* to wait on me. I hate that.

It's cold enough in here that I can see my own breath. With all the other stuff going on, I hadn't noticed . . . but I gave Doc back his coat when I fed his shirt to the Teras, and I'm freezing. Loras stands for a moment, staring down at me. He's wearing a simple pair of trousers and pullover, so I don't know how his teeth aren't chattering.

Glance across the room and find Dina looking extremely pissed off, since she's sandwiched between Doc and Gunnar. "Say 'cream filling,' and I kill you. Seriously."

I muffle a laugh, but I manage not to say it. Somehow.

"You want me to . . . ?" Loras gestures at the others, huddled up.

And I hate even more that he feels like he needs to ask permission. Mother Mary, it's common sense. I scowl up at him. I am not personally to blame for what my race did to his, however long ago.

"Okay, you have to follow my directives, right?" At his nod, I continue, "Then you're forbidden to do anything but what you want. And if you'd like to come down here so we can both get warm, do that. If *not*, do what the hell ever. Because I'm tired, and I am sick of this shit."

At this, March's eyes snap open, and now *he* looks extremely pissed. "I can't believe I never thought of that."

Bastard was faking, so he wouldn't have to answer

questions. He gives me a grin and closes his eyes again, while Loras stands there, looking dumbfounded. "It would be very foolish for both of us to be cold," he says finally, and drops down beside me.

I get the feeling this is the first time anyone's said that to him. Hope it's easier on him, and me, too, for that matter. I'm not cut out to go around giving orders about every little thing. Too much of that, and I'd be killing him instead of watching his back.

"Good call."

He settles in beside me, shoulder to shoulder, and we wrap up in a second blanket. Takes a little while, but I can feel myself warming up, and as my body temperature rises, I get sleepy. *Gonna close my eyes for a minute . . .*

Next thing I know, I'm feeling *so* good, not exactly sure where I am, and it doesn't matter because I'm toasty warm, lying in someone's arms. I nuzzle my nose against his throat, stretching luxuriously. I want to make love, soft and slow. My half-awake brain tells me it must be Kai, because he's the only one I ever slept with like this, and then the other half rouses and points out that's impossible.

My eyes snap open.

A torch-tube glows in the middle of the room, providing a little light. Enough to see that March's face is right above mine, and he *knows*. The floor can open up to admit me now, thanks. At some point, he must've given Keri to Loras and come to huddle with me himself, though damned if I know why.

"You were whimpering in your sleep," he whispers. "And jabbing with your elbow. Almost broke his nose."

"And you thought you could fix it?" I pitch my voice low because the others are all still sleeping, but I'm angry over his presumption, angry that I slept better in his arms than I have since Kai died.

He shrugs. "If nothing else, I'm too big for you to hurt

me." At my look, he adds, "Okay, too big for you to hurt *accidentally*."

And he doesn't need to say that I settled down as soon as he pulled me close. I *know* I did; I can almost remember the dreams that made me restless, and I can almost see his resigned expression as he pulled me against his chest, wrapped his arms about me, can almost hear my own small sound as I relaxed like it's somewhere I'm supposed to be. I really *am* insane. I remember Dina mentioning that he lost someone in the crash, and I want to know more. Does he blame me? Should he?

I don't even know the answer to that.

"Why do you hate me so much?" For a moment, I can't believe I asked. It's got to be the false intimacy, sound of other people breathing, lying in his arms in the dark.

"I don't . . . hate you." His voice sounds gruff.

I gaze up at his face, trying to read his expression, defeated by shadows' fall. "Dislike me profoundly and intensely, before we ever met."

"Look, I'm not having this conversation right now. Go to sleep, Jax."

"Go to hell, March." But I'm smiling as I say it.

As I doze off again, I'm pretty sure he says, "Been there, done that, and I'm keeping a spot warm for you, babe."

The next time I wake up, it's to hear:

"No. How can you ask me to *do* this, March? It's monstrous and barbaric."

Great. I guess they're making wedding plans. My eyelids feel like they've got paste under them, and I am, mercifully, by myself. Maybe I dreamed that whole weird interlude during the night. *Please let me have dreamed it.*

Because I don't want to carry the awareness that I fit nicely against March's chest and that his heartbeat is a comforting way to fall asleep. I especially don't want to remember rubbing my face against his throat and liking it. I think I need to kill him. For a moment, I try to imagine a giant rock landing on him, but I can't—

Mother Mary, I *am* deranged. Because I can't bring myself to picture any real harm coming to him. In fact, it alarms me to think of losing him. When nothing else makes sense, he's rock solid. Inexplicably, I feel like I can count on him.

I'm defanged where he's concerned. Or something. It hurts when I press, a wound I didn't even know I had. I don't want to rely on him in any capacity. Mary knows, I've learned the hard way that nothing lasts forever.

"If you would stop thinking like a stupid kid for a minute," the Gunnar says, "you'd realize this is the only way to save both our clans."

Oh smooth, Lex. That's the way to get the girl.

"I'm not a stupid kid . . . I just hate you! Which seems to be the best proof of my intellect that I could offer."

Wonder if that's how March and I sound. If so, that'd be why people think we want to shag each other. And maybe they're not entirely wrong, since I can't deny he has a certain raw charisma. Regardless, I'm now convinced that Keri's going to wind up a Gunnar. It's a foregone conclusion.

I climb out of my warm nest and start folding up the blankets. Someone's already been outside to empty the buckets, so I guess that means it's safe. Everyone seems to be here. Dina, Doc, and Loras are sucking on packets of paste, looking no more pleased than I'd be if I were eating one. All three are riveted on the funny little love triangle, funny because I don't think March realized until now that all his protectiveness had created one gi-enormous crush.

Which makes me wonder how he missed it, being Psi and all. He can't seem to help rummaging around my head like it's a jumble sale, but he has no clue what's going on with Keri? *Interesting.*

Case in point, he turns to glare at me.

CHAPTER 14

It's sputtering snow when we finally emerge from the storage shed, from what felt like an endless night, into a white-gray morning. There's a lesson in that, I think. No matter how interminable something feels, there is always, always an ending. Sometimes that's good, and sometimes it's bad; sometimes it's a matter of indifference, and sometimes it's heartbreaking, and your life is never the same thereafter.

March surprises me by holding up a hand as the others set off. I wait without protest, but not because of what happened last night. That's not it. *Is* it? He goes back into the building and brings me a blanket, wraps me up in it poncho style. I give him a half smile, not understanding the shift.

But I murmur, "Thank you," and we go along behind the others, him matching his strides to my shorter ones. The silence is oddly companionable.

Fried and fallen Teras bodies lie strewn all along the perimeter. They died in the night, trying to return to the caves, and in death they lose their camouflage. Dark and ugly, like something from a child's stories—it is difficult to believe something like this evolved naturally. The stench is dreadful, and more than once I swallow down bile that wants to become vomit, but I don't have anything to up-chuck. The paste metabolizes quickly so your body receives the nutrients right away. And I chose not to eat it this morning; I'm hoping there will be something better at the main house.

"I haven't been fair to you," he says, so quietly I almost don't catch it.

But he said it. I know he did. I actually stop walking. Pause and gape up at him. "You—"

"You heard me." March scowls down at me, and I know he doesn't like saying it any more than I would. "I'm going to do better."

Our eyes meet, and I notice for the first time that his eyes aren't simply dark; they possess gold flecks as well, an amber ring around the iris. He also has the most ridiculous lashes I've ever seen on a man, a sharp contrast to his hard-hewn face. He's almost too rough-featured in fact, unless you focus on those long lashes. After that look, mustering a smart-ass response takes some doing.

"Well, it'd be hard for you to do worse. Come on."

We start walking, and I increase my pace to catch up with the others. I don't want Dina thinking I want private time with March. Mary forefend.

I don't know what I expected, not like I had a chance to look around last night. But the compound seems to be a series of outbuildings along a path that leads up to the main house, a structure of old-fashioned stonework. The whole enclave is surrounded by intricate wire-and-steel fencing, crackling an electrical warning as we pass by.

As we near the main house, clansmen whose names I don't know come to meet us. They live in what I take to be apartments or longhouses nearby. Keri greets them and invites them inside. The rest of us trail in her wake, and I gaze around, surprised at the elegance of her home.

Floors are marble, walls are paneled, and if it's not real marble, real wood, then they still paid a fortune for such high-quality synth. It even rings true when I rap my knuckles on it in passing. They have Giovanni paintings and sculptures from the Sheng Dynasty, just before Taiwan was reclaimed by China, or so my spotty recollection of Old Terra history suggests. It's a gorgeous place, and I feel bad just walking on this rug. My shoes sink six centimeters, and who knows what's on them?

We proceed to a meeting hall that looks almost like a senate chamber. Keri proceeds to the podium, where a Speaker would ordinarily stand, and she does so with a dignity I wouldn't have expected. Once there, she advises her clansmen of the bad tidings with solemn poise, and in turn, they report some losses in the night. One day, she will be a woman of great strength, I think. Depressing to contemplate, when she reaches her prime, I will be quite old if I even survive that long.

"Leadership is what separates a principal clan from a weak one," she tells her people, once the initial shuffling has ceased. "And they will not yet listen to my voice on the Clan Council. Alone, I cannot hope to hold the position of strength we have enjoyed. So it is with a heavy heart that I propose consolidation. In making a marital merger with clan Gunnar, we double our holdings, double our population, and double our resources. Hereafter, the clan lines will be joined and known as Gunnar-Dahlgren. I put the proposition to a vote, as it affects the way you live, as much as me."

The rumble of voices greets her pronouncement, and I watch from my vantage near the back. I don't know how this impacts me, but I feel a peculiar tension, studying her face. Glancing at the Gunnar, I see his investment in the proceedings. Both clans have lost so much. From what I can gather,

they are taking a vote. A black bead means no, a white one
means yes, and they pass around a silver dish. It is a remarkably elegant system for its simplicity. Finally, a dark-haired
man stands, having counted the tokens, spokesman by some
tacit understanding or perhaps tradition.

"Rydal." Keri recognizes him with a nod.

"The vote is tallied in favor of consolidation," he says
with sad gravity. "We judge it preferable to a hostile
takeover."

Although I am not sure, I guess that would involve
wholesale slaughter of the clan and seizing all assets and
territories. March catches my eye and nods. I feel like I've
just seen the world change in some fashion this morning,
and I don't understand the sensation. Lachion has never in-
fluenced the larger universe so far as I'm aware; these are
mudsider politics, nothing that will make a difference.

Keri inclines her head, then fixes a pale green gaze on
the Gunnar. "Have your First speak to mine; we have con-
tracts to negotiate."

"My First died out on the Nejanna Plain," he tells her
flatly. "It will take time to decide who should fill the breach."

You can almost see the sparks crackling between them,
and I decide they're going to be bitching at each other
longer than I really want to listen. Seems like I'm not the
only one who feels that way because the Dahlgren clansmen trickle out in twos and threes, and even Doc shifts his
weight on the balls of his feet.

I clear my throat. "Breakfast?"

Even though I direct the question to nobody in particular, Loras pushes away from the wall and beckons me. I
fall in step beside him as he says, "I'll show you to the din-
ing hall. There's usually something laid out for another
hour or so."

"Communal meals?" I can't imagine the workload that
must mean for the cooks. Unless . . . "Do they have food
processors?"

"The lesser clans, no. Some are astonishingly low-tech, but this one has done well. There are even bots in charge of cleaning and maintenance here."

That remark reminds me of my cell AI, and my mouth tightens. "Fantastic. Can we expect . . . Oh, that smells good."

Something sweet and smooth is brewing. I know the scent, I've had it once before—it's a hot drink that goes into your veins like pure chem, leaves you bouncing until you crash. I seem to remember it's highly addictive. There's also the aroma of honeyed pastries, fried s-meat, and some kind of fruit, a sharp, succulent tang. We come into a large open room with a couple of bots circulating, ostensibly keeping track of the food laid out on a long table. It's a well-lit space with windows on three walls, arrayed with round tables.

I make myself a sandwich out of the meat and the sweetbread while Loras looks on in horrified astonishment. "I don't think you're supposed to . . ."

Shrugging, I say, "It gets the job done," and take an enormous bite.

Actually it's better than I expected, this blend of sweet and savory. He sighs and fastidiously selects some fruit. We've almost finished by the time the crew catches up with us. I'm drinking a cup of the dark, pungent stuff that will probably make me jittery; the taste is a little difficult to pin down, but it seems to have a trace of choclaste.

I don't know what happens next.

But as March drops down in the chair opposite me with a smile, I'm pretty sure I'm not going to like it.

CHAPTER 15

"You're serious," I say, after hearing what they have in mind.

March nods. "That's the plan."

Doc looks faintly apologetic, as if he suspected what my reaction would be. And if he supposed I'd be horrified at the thought of a ten-planet tour, all in different quadrants, without scheduled R&R, well, he'd be right. That doesn't even factor in the expectation of recruiting unregistered J-gene carriers for our as-yet-fictitious academy. And what about the gray men hunting me? The minute I'm ret-scanned in any Corp way station, they're going to dispatch the nearest unit.

With some effort, I manage to make myself sound reasonable and not just start ranting, my first impulse. "Look, first, you're talking about a really long haul. I've always had plenty of rest between jumps, and we don't know what our timetable will be. I have no idea what this could do to me."

Dina leans forward, elbows on the table. "It kills you."

Something in her gray eyes tells me she's talking about Edaine. And I won't go there with her right now, though I know I'm not the reason the other jumper pushed herself so hard. She might've made her last flight as a sacrifice for me, but I didn't cause her total burnout. That decision was hers, and I'm just a convenient source of expiation.

"Everybody dies," I answer. "It's just a matter of when and whether you do anything worthwhile beforehand." But I don't take it any further, and as far as I'm concerned, that's a concession. Instead, I ask, "What am I supposed to say anyway? 'Come join our renegade training facility. No, we don't have anything built yet, but they're working on that while I find the founding class.' "

"I expect you'll refine the verbiage," Loras puts in. "That's part of your skill set, isn't it? It's why you were so good at making first contact."

And damn him, he's right. I *do* have a knack for swinging luck my way. Always have had—it's one reason I live through things that destroy everyone around me.

"The gray men—" I start to object, but March shakes his head.

"You won't be traveling first-class anymore, Jax. No more clean Corp stations."

Takes me a minute, but I get it. We'll be avoiding regulated routes, slinging out through the beacon nearest our objective, then scrambling signal so they can't tell where we've gone. There are a pretty low number of potential destinations at each point, so they may locate us via legwork, but that will slow them down some.

By keeping on the move, we stay one jump ahead of them. Literally. That means I won't have long to convince the unregistered resources to join up. It sounds crazy; the Corp is just so big. How can we imagine, even for a moment, that we might muster the resources to challenge its monopoly? Grimspace belongs to the Corp; it's an undisputed reality and has been, longer than I've been alive.

I realize I don't even know the details of how Clericon Stellar went down. They were a start-up like we hope to be, and they failed. If we're going to do this, I need to find out why. Information may be our only hope. There might even be other renegade jumpers, although I've heard nothing. Stands to reason the Corp wouldn't want that getting out. In fact, I bet I've been listed as officially flatline by now, so maybe they've called off the gray squads and are pursuing me through unofficial means.

As my training informed me, Corp intelligence tracks our jumps into grimspace and there are pinch-faced men that go over flickering screens, trying to make the numbers match up. Of course, in revealing this, they were reassuring us that we wouldn't get lost. But now it makes me wonder how many unsanctioned jumpers their data miners tallied and what happened to those people if they got caught.

Deep down I don't need to be told; I know. And unless I want it to happen to me, I've got to make this work. It's a different life. No more am I Sirantha Jax, Corp superstar. Now I'm just Jax, and I need to prove myself all over again. Well, that's fine. I've survived worse.

I don't let myself think about Kai.

Glancing up from my silver mug, I find them all staring at me. "Okay." I glance at Doc. "What's the first planet on the list? And how did you find these sources? The Corp has tons of people constantly looking for the same thing. There aren't enough J-gene carriers to replenish the pool, based on burnout rate. In about ten turns, there aren't going to be enough trained jumpers left to meet demand."

Saul pulls a silk screen datapad from his pants pocket and slides it across the table toward me. I hit the lower left corner to increase resolution so I can read, and first it's just a list of names: Marakeq, Gestalt, Freeley, Darengo, Collins, Sureport, Venetia, Lark, Belsev, Quietus. But after a moment, it sinks in.

"These are all either nonhuman or class-P worlds."

The Corp doesn't interfere on class-P worlds, where native technology falls somewhere between Bronze Age and pre-Industrial. Once we make first contact, we log our findings, then categorize the planet as primitive. In most cases, we could determine that much from orbit, but the Corp likes to know the exact level of development: what sort of tools, customs, whatever we can learn in a single visit. After that, interstellar trade and travel remains restricted until such time as the citizens develop sufficient technology to come looking for us on their own.

Furthermore, those five class-P worlds? They're the ones where I made first contact, but I can't imagine myself going back to claim sons and daughters, taking them away to the sky. How in the hell can I rationalize that? Culture shock might kill them, let alone grimspace.

"I don't think you grasp the scope of what Mair wanted to do," March says then.

"So tell me."

"We aren't interested in spiriting away a couple adventurous souls here and there," Saul explains. "We're looking to relocate whole villages—we'll cull them from remote areas where their disappearance simply goes unsolved. Certain anomalies in Old Terra history make me believe this may have occurred before. Ever heard of Roanoke?" I shake my head and he adds, "No matter. You needn't examine all the evidence as I have. But this is why Gunnar-Dahlgren needs to be fixed to support a surge in population. We're not simply starting an academy, although that's part of it."

"A colony of jumpers."

It's a mammoth undertaking. I don't ask if they have transport ships. Surely they must have passenger freighters somewhere on this rock, if they're serious. I don't know how I feel about that. Part of me thinks any breeding experiment is doomed to failure, and Mary knows we've seen bad results from this kind of thing, time and again. Purpose becomes twisted, and even a scientist with the best intentions, like Doc, gets swept up in the trappings of godhood. People shouldn't be pushed to mate to produce a certain type of child; I feel strongly about that.

"Nobody will be forced to do anything," March says with a disgusted sigh. "Doc's isolated something that the Corp never saw. He's been going through medical records for years." Which doesn't quite explain how he found it, but maybe he's simply smarter than the average Corp scientist. Given that they're mostly bureaucrats these days, that hypothesis doesn't stretch my imagination much. "So there's another factor that determines how *long* someone can handle grimspace, and it's tied to the genotype."

He pauses, and we stare at each other. I feel as if he's willing me to make a mental leap, like he'll be disappointed in me if I can't put it together on my own. Then it dawns on me, a feeling of astonishment and awe—sunrise on Ielos. I sat in the thermal rooms with Kai once, watching slow red-orange break of light refracted over the glaciers. That's how I feel now.

"Not a bloodline," I say slowly. "You're looking to engineer a new species. You want human recruits from class-P worlds with strong J-gene strains. Alien DNA provides for longevity—compensates for burnout."

March watches me, probably tracking my mental processes. He knows when I work it out. I dub that unknown factor the L-gene, whatever allows inhuman navigators to withstand grimspace better than we do. A number of alien races can sense the beacons, but many despise us for our conquistador attitude, and the rest consider us food.

I say it aloud for the benefit of the others. "You're going to make something new from mingling alien and human DNA. I'm right, aren't I?"

Dina crams the last of a sweetbread into her mouth and says through the crumbs, "Hey, you're not as dumb as you look after all."

Maybe I really was better off in my cell.

CHAPTER 16

So we're going to Marakeq.

I wish I could say I enjoyed my time on Lachion, but with Lex and Keri growling like a pair of Anduvian ice otters in mating season, the rest of us just lay low. Barely, I manage to restrain a wince when I see that they're hauling crates of the nutri-paste, presumably to replenish our stores.

Great. We'll survive any emergency. We'll just wish we hadn't.

The morning of our departure, I run into Keri outside the training facility. I've spent a lot of time in there because it gets the blood pumping, and pure physical exertion means I don't have to think. Something in her face tells me I'm not going to like what's coming, and I brace myself instinctively. It's a wonder she hasn't confronted me before now; I feel responsible for a lot of her problems.

She doesn't say hello, merely looking me up and down with an air of indefinable scorn. I know what she sees, a woman past her prime with burn scars raying out from the edges of my workout gear, but I don't shift beneath the weight of her eyes. I just wait.

"I don't like you," she says at last. "But you're necessary to bring my grandmother's vision to fruition. Make no mistake, that's the only reason you're alive."

A bitchy reply springs to my tongue, but I swallow it down. I started trouble on this planet without knowing the rules. If I'd made a habit of being that careless on other worlds, I'd have died long before now, and this time, her family paid the price for my unsteady impulses. So I owe her, and she's entitled to hate me as much as she wants. Right now, I'm none too fond of myself, either. I have to look at myself in the mirror, knowing I lived where eighty-two died, one of whom was the man I loved. Not to mention the loss of Miriam Jocasta, a diplomat of incredible eloquence and grace; she had been instrumental in achieving peace during the Axis Wars. The woman was an icon, and I killed her. Maybe. From the line of their questioning, the Psychs had certainly been inclined to think so, at any rate.

Frag, I wish I could remember.

"You want to go a few rounds with me?" I blot away the sweat and head back to the training mat without waiting for an answer.

Since she was Mair's pupil, she'll probably kick my ass ten ways from sunrise, given she's younger and faster and probably stronger, too. I'll take whatever she dishes out, but I won't hand it to her on a plate. She'll enjoy my beating more if she works for it.

Her smile seems tight somehow, wicked with anticipation. "Gladly. And should there ever come a day when I need you no longer, I'll see you dead."

There's no more talk after that. She positions herself in a half crouch that I've never seen before. No big surprise— my combat training was purely perfunctory, augmented by a propensity for starting trouble in spaceport bars. Mary, she's fast. She's clocked me between the eyes with the heel of her hand before I hardly register the movement, and while I'm reeling, she sweeps my legs out from under me.

I land hard on my back, exhaling with a huff, but I roll before she can smash her foot into my stomach. With a mental shrug, I grab her ankle and yank, thinking we'll take this fight to the ground, but she executes a neat maneuver that breaks my hold. The girl is good. After that, I submit to my beating; my fighting is clumsy as hell compared to hers. Sweat pours off me in rivers by the time she seems satisfied, maybe an hour later. I'm aching in places where I didn't even know I had muscles, and there's a deep bruise forming where she kicked me in the hip.

"If you'd wanted to, you could have taken those Gunnars by yourself."

She shakes her head. How I hate the fact that her perfect cheeks are simply flushed with a rosy glow. "I'd have needed Grandmother's help, but it was the height of stupidity to fight in the open. There's a reason we use ammunition that disables vehicles instead of causing bodily harm. There's a reason we fight our battles inside, safely in the confines of the clan arena."

"I didn't know," I say, humbled. "I'm sorry about your father. And your grandmother. As for seeing me dead, well. Give it time. This ten-jump journey might do the trick."

She seems torn between pleasure in that prospect and chagrin. Finally, she responds, "I hope not, for we'll still need you to head up our training academy when the program progresses to that point."

"Essentially then, you came to tell me that you are resigned to working with me to honor your grandmother's wishes."

For a moment, there is something regal in her young face, the set of her shoulders. I can imagine condemned princesses facing down their executioners with the same blend of fatality and poise. Maybe I don't entirely like Keri, but I respect her now.

And I think she knows that because a smile flickers at the edges of her mouth like a corrupt holo-file. "Kicking your ass was a nice bonus, though. I have too much business here to accompany you, but I wish you luck. Not that I think you'll need it with March heading the expedition."

Maybe she doesn't intend it so, but that feels like a barb, so I answer, "Yeah. At least you'll have Lex with you to get things done."

Her sharp inhalation sounds like a hiss. Yeah, I know. I'm lucky she doesn't punch me in the face again. I probably deserve another black eye, but I've never been good at the antiquated doctrine of turning the other cheek. Why give them the chance to hit you a second time? I say knock them out the first time they swing, a combative philosophy that probably explains my current situation.

But she surprises me by laughing. "Much as I hate the bastard, he does have a certain personal force."

"He's a mountain."

"Has his own gravity," Keri quips, and I realize we're smiling at each other.

Life goes on whether we want it to or not. And laughter is a constant.

"Good luck rebuilding things," I tell her. "Going to clean up, then go get a good seat in the rover. I want to see what it's like all the way in back."

"I wish . . ." She seems hesitant, and I pause, letting her assemble what she wants to say. "That is, Grandmother had all these ideas, tactics you were supposed to use, approaches for the different worlds. She'd done extensive research on culture, traditions, both primitive and alien . . ."

"That's why she wanted to meet with me," I guess aloud. "To go over this stuff before we set out."

Keri nods. "But most of it was inside her head. Not long ago, she started to get suspicious of standard datapads and sys-terminals. She said the Corp could probably mine what you stored somehow or what you were searching for."

Once I'd have dismissed that as the paranoid delusion of an old woman who'd missed a few too many antiaging treatments. Now I consider the prospect for a moment before allowing, "It's possible. Do you have any of her research, at least? The info she unearthed regarding our target ten would save me retracing her steps."

"I'll give you her PA. Anything she stored would be in there. She wouldn't use standard datapads or sys-terms any longer. Just a moment."

Maybe five minutes later, Keri returns with a smooth silver sphere. I've seen these before, although I've never even held one. They're ridiculously expensive, closed to any other system, and require three levels of encryption confirmation before they will relinquish their data.

"I hope you have her codes. Don't know anybody who can hack one of these."

She leans in and whispers.

"Thanks." Nodding, I commit that to memory and pocket the device.

With a wave, I head off to the san-shower in my lodgings, which are substantially nicer than anywhere else I've stayed. There's a sterile quality to any Corp quarters, regardless of locale, like they don't want you to feel at home. It's practical, choosing furnishings that are easy to clean and maintain with the constant rotation of crewmen in and out. But the end result remains unchanged; people don't *want* to stay.

My in-room wardrober contained only basic patterns, but I still prefer having my own clothes—items in fabric, color, and style that I've chosen myself. It's hard to be confident and in control when you're wearing what someone else selected. Makes you feel like a child, even if nobody ever picked out your clothes when you were a kid.

Casually, I rake my new things into a bag Dina donated. Yeah, I know; I expected the thing to blow up, but so far it hasn't, and there doesn't seem to be anything wrong with it, either. So I sling it over my shoulder and head for the rover. I'm not going to check on anyone else. When I woke up in Med Bay, after Kai died, I promised myself I wouldn't let anyone get that close again.

Guess I'm early because nobody's around yet. So I tap the door once, and the panel slides open, allowing me to grab a seat in back. If anyone shoots at us on this run, always a possibility here, I don't want to be under the gun hatch again. It's fragging cold, and I wrap up in my double-breasted s-wool overcoat to wait.

My patience doesn't last long, though, and I remember the PA in my pocket. I fish it out and thumb it on. It hums as it powers up, and a tiny little keypad ejects from the front, inexplicably reminding me of teeth. I'm nervous as I enter the codes Keri gave me. For all I know these things detonate if keyed wrong, and my fingers feel big and clumsy. But no boom when I'm done, just the sound of security disengaging as the thing clicks open, revealing a touch pad and a small data screen.

The instant I touch the pressure point, though, a smooth, asexual voice speaks. "Welcome, Mair Dahlgren. It has been seventeen days since your last entry."

Is this thing an AI or just part of the data entry software? Can it feel loneliness if neglected? I pause for a moment, then answer, "This isn't Mair. She died almost a week ago, and her granddaughter gave me this unit to assist in carrying out her final wishes."

"I am sorry," says the little machine in a tone that approximates sincerity. "Please provide proof of identity with thumbprint and voice sample. Speak your name clearly, and I will update my records to reflect transference in ownership."

"Sirantha Jax."

There's a pause, then a ray of thin yellow light emits from the data screen, sweeps the upper arc of my face, and I realize I've been ret-scanned. My heart thumps, thinking that the data will be beamed to the Corp along with my last-known location, and all this will have been for nothing.

I'll wind up in the asylum after all, beneath Newel's tender care. *Oh Mary—*

"Congratulations." The unit smoothly interrupts the near panic of my thoughts. "You are confirmed as new owner of PA-245. In the event you should misplace or forget your codes, depress the emergency access button on the bottom of the device, and I will offer you the choice of retinal scan, voice confirmation, or thumbprint to reset your security access."

Right, it's a closed system.

"What if I want to change Mair's old codes?" Keri knows them after all, and I don't trust people instinctively. This gadget is mine now, and I want whatever data I impart to remain confidential.

"Do you?" it asks.

"Yeah. Let's get that done."

Such an advanced interface. This can't be a simple software package. It's capable of reasoned interaction. Most programs would've simply recited the instructions for doing so.

"I'm bringing up input parameters on-screen. Please key the new codes, then confirm with reentry."

Wow. Maybe I'm giving the thing too much credit, but it seems to understand why I wouldn't want to speak the code aloud, although voice recognition is clearly contained within its field of expertise. As I choose my three codes, then tap them in, twice, I wonder about its limits.

"Are you an AI?"

Is that a rude question?

"New codes confirmed," it advises me. And then, almost kindly: "I am Artificial Intelligence 245, personal assistance and data management, fully equipped with the Helpful Administrator personality chip. Do you require further aid?"

"Yeah. Show me what Mair dug up on Marakeq. Please." I feel dumb adding the last word, but I can't help myself. There's something . . . different about this little machine.

And as the others start to arrive, I settle back to read.

CHAPTER 17

Here I am in the cockpit with March again.

I've hardly seen him in the last week. I get the feeling he's been avoiding me, but I'm not sure why. The way I figure, I'm the one who should be embarrassed, but I refuse to let it bother me. I didn't start my life over just to turn into something I'm not. As I've never cared what anyone thought of me, I'm certainly not starting with March.

He watches me settled into the nav chair beside him. We're cruising, already a good distance from Lachion. I took my time making my way up here; in fact I made him summon me, something I can tell pissed him off. I check the port, even though I know it's clean. Stalling, because I have a fist squeezing my intestines, sweat popping out on my upper lip, and a snail of discomfort crawling down my spine. It doesn't get easier; we just don't have people shooting to distract me.

Kai started every flight perfectly. He'd lean over, a lock of ash blond hair flopping into his eyes, and he'd give me the tender, sheepish smile I came to love. Saying, "For luck," he would brush his lips against mine. But I never felt like I needed luck with Kai. He *was* my luck. We were golden; nothing could touch us. I wish I could remember what the frag happened on Matins IV, whether I killed him—

"Steady," March says, resting a hand on my forearm.

I recoil reflexively. The warmth of his touch lingers, but I don't want him to comfort me, if that's his intent. He has no right, and he shouldn't know the things he does. I didn't confide in him.

"I'm fine," I bite out.

"He's *gone*," he growls. "Not coming back, Jax. And I'm all you've got."

His words make me gulp twice in sharp succession, suddenly light-headed. Much as I don't like March, I respect him—or I *did*. For a long moment, I gaze at him, jaw clenched. *You think I don't know that? You think I'm ever able to forget that?* Heat suffuses my cheeks, and I feel myself trembling on the verge of something extreme, like I might cry. Or kill him.

I know which I prefer.

"Tell the crew to strap in," I say, my eyes on his. "You speak to me like that again, I jump us all the way past the Polaris system. And if you don't think I'll flatline everyone on board, take another look at the wreckage of the *Sargasso* from Matins IV."

"You talk tough, but—"

"But what?" I'm out of the nav chair and in his face. "Take a closer 'look,' asshole. Am. I. Bluffing?"

He doesn't want to. But I know the moment he does because his face goes queer and ashen. "You're saying you did that on purpose . . . ?"

I shake my head savagely and drop back into my seat. "But this time, I've got nothing left to lose *except* my life. You keep pushing me, and I'm not going to give a shit about that, either. I don't care if you think it's pathetic that I"—my voice breaks, but I'm not going to let these tears fall in front of March—"miss him. Keep your opinions to yourself, understood?"

I don't add: *You're not even worthy to say his name.* But it's there between us. He knows. To my surprise, he's the first to break eye contact.

"Just do your job," he mutters. "Sometime today would be good."

Without another word, I take a look at the star charts. Marakeq would take months to reach if we didn't have a jumper on board, so it's not as far as it could be. The information I salvaged from Mair's research advises me that it's primarily a swamp world with isolated pockets of civilization, and the dominant life-form appears to be amphibian intelligence. We're further handicapped by the fact that the planet is both class P and nonhuman. Nothing like setting the bar high, right?

As I plug in, I hear March telling the crew to prepare for jump. I'm blind again, waiting for him. Hating him. Then I'm crowded full of him as the phase drive starts powering up. Before his walls come up, separating us as efficiently as a room partition, something I never had with Kai, I glimpse something.

Something I'm not supposed to see. And it changes everything.

But I don't have time to reflect; the ship trembles beneath me, and I need to focus on getting us to the beacon intact. So I push the new awareness to the back of my mind and ready myself for grimspace. Oh, it feels good, a rush I almost forget each time I leave it behind. But Mary, the colors—I'm aware of the cadence, the cosmic tides, and the sequence of vibrations that tell me inarguably: *That way.* And March responds to my directives as an extension of me. His hands are mine, sure and confident, guiding us through the primordial soup. Even as I hate him, I wish I could show him what it's like—

You already are.

I'm not sure what that means, and I want to challenge the barriers he's put up to find out, but I can't divert myself from navigation. If I let my concentration slip, there's no telling where we'll end up. So I keep monitoring the wildfire outside the ship; everything seems so small, and our hull looks like it should ignite plowing through the ether, but the colors don't touch us.

Now and then I see shimmers, reflections of others, maybe traveling parallel, maybe time trails. Grimspace ghosts. Sometimes I wonder if I'll ever see shadows of myself, the echo left by my own passage on another vessel. That's a paradox the Corp didn't encourage us to contemplate, and right now, I understand why.

We're here.

I sense his assent, and the ship shudders, making the jump back to straight space. I don't need to see the astrogation charts to know we hit the mark, but before I can savor the pleasure of a solid run, the phase drive whines in powering down. I've heard that sound before, and its feedback screams inside my skull. Hope to Mary we don't need to leave in a hurry. The frog-folk aren't likely to give us any trouble in orbit, but if gray men or others track us down, it could get real messy without a phase drive.

Sighing, I tug the plug out of my wrist, and there's a moment of vertigo as I accustom myself to seeing with my eyes again. Everything flickers before coming into focus, and sometimes I wonder whether I'm real at all, maybe I'm a program someone's coding for an interactive holo. The absurdity of the thought makes me smile—who the hell would want to pretend to be me?

March taps the comm panel. "Dina, I need you to—"

"Already on it," comes her waspish reply. "What am I, stupid? That's a rhetorical question by the way. I'll let you know when I figure out what's wrong."

Unlike last time, I don't head out of the cockpit right

away. Instead, I shift in my seat, watching him fiddle with the controls. I know he doesn't need to be so proactive, adjusting this and that once he's input our cruising course. All he needs to do for the next several hours is monitor our progress. I smile as I realize that means he's nervous.

"I know what you did," I tell him. "And why."

"No idea what you're on about, why don't you be a good girl and get me a drink?"

Oh, he's trying to distract me now by pissing me off *again*, but it won't work. "You can't bullshit me, March. I *saw*."

He turns his head to face me then, and I see a surprisingly vulnerable slant to his mouth. "You were upset," he mutters. "I just didn't want you killing us."

"So you made yourself a target. Better that I'm mad at you, hating you, than hurting, is that it?"

"Exactly," he answers, too quietly.

Perversely I feel like that's just about the sweetest thing anyone's ever done for me, and yeah, I *know* how that sounds. But I'm . . . not right. I wasn't, before Kai, and now, even less so. But regardless, it touches me that he chose to piss me off.

Exhaling, I say, "Don't do that again, March. Please. I appreciate the concern, I do, but . . . I'll never get over it if I don't deal with it. And if I'm going to hate you, I want it to be real, not over mind games. I know you're good at them, better than me, but I really don't want to play."

He narrows his dark eyes on me. "I'll do whatever's necessary to protect this ship and my crew. I'm not making you any promises, Jax. I'm still not convinced you aren't a liability, not convinced we shouldn't have waited for someone more stable, even if that meant it took substantially longer."

That hurts, and it's meant to, but I don't flinch. Because even though he's doing his damnedest to play the hard-ass, make me think he doesn't give a shit about me, I know that's wrong. I saw. I *felt*. Just enough to make me wonder what else was there, before he slammed the door so hard it convinced me he has something to hide.

And I'm going to find out what.

CHAPTER 18

As usual, we're in the middle of an argument.

However, I am just an observer in this particular squabble, sitting in the hub with my ankle propped on my knee. Dina beetles her brows, and she's up in March's face, doing everything but shaking a fist. I don't think she'd bother, though. If she intended to hit him, she wouldn't give warning; she'd let her knuckles do the talking. In the time we've traveled together, I've learned some respect for the woman.

"I'm telling you, we need to take the ship down," Dina says heatedly. "If you four launch in the pod, then I'm fragged if they track us down before you get back. And what if I need to do some work outside the ship? You going to leave me up here doing the walk without backup? Plus, I can't shut down certain systems while in synchronous orbit. They'll find it easier to locate us."

"She has a point." Everyone glances at Doc, who shrugs. "I understand you're worried about the ship being damaged on the planet, but if something happens up here, we're no better off, and we'll have lost Dina."

"And nobody wants that." I don't mean to sound quite so acerbic, but Dina just grins. To her, that probably felt like an endearment, and I can't help grinning back.

Dina backs off, now that she has popular support. "Take us down then. Find a landing spot, ideally a clearing with some cover."

"Anything else, your majesty?" March sketches a bow that would do credit to someone meeting real royalty.

"Frag you," she returns without heat. "My family was deposed fifteen years ago."

My brows arch as March returns to the cockpit, but Dina's already turning away to get back to work on the phase drive. That leaves me glancing at Doc for clarification, and he shakes his head before heading to medical. Finally, I turn to Loras, who sighs.

"I believe Dina comes from the Imperial family on Tarnus, or rather, what used to be the Imperial family. There was a populist movement on her world, perhaps twenty turns ago, and—"

"It ended in a bloody coup?" I guess.

Not that I don't want to hear the two-hour lecture that Loras would have volunteered on Tarnian history, but well, I don't know shit about the universe, and I don't *want* to know. The only thing I'm good at is grimspace, and it'll eventually kill me.

"That is an oversimplification," Loras observes with a sliver of disapproval, "but essentially correct. I believe Dina had been exiled in disfavor for . . . consorting with her handmaidens and taking an unseemly interest in alien technology, so she was not in the capital at the time."

I can't resist the urge to tease him. "Consorting, huh?"

"Trust you to fixate on the prurient and miss the trauma she survived."

"Trauma?" Even as I repeat the word, I know I've been a moron.

"She's the only survivor from the royal family, and they only permitted her off planet for two reasons: her predilection for her own sex and her promise she will never return."

"Her promise?" That doesn't seem like much of a warranty, even relying on some antiquated code of honor, not that I think Dina would abide by such a thing. I'm parroting shit like I'm brainless, but I guess I just never imagined there was anything more to her than met the eye.

"If she sets foot on the surface of Tarnus, the chip in her head will discharge," he tells me dispassionately. "Any attempt to remove it will also result in detonation. They made sure she will keep her word."

And though I've heard some horrific things in my day, I can't help but shudder. Instinctively I know that the implant contains some ritualistic element, probably designed to shame her. I can't quite reconcile this with the tough ship's mechanic, but I know he's telling me the truth, or . . . most of it.

"What aren't you saying?"

Loras shakes his head with a faint half smile. "There's a lesson in that, Jax. Nobody here is what he or she seems."

Before I can ask, the ship bucks, and March's voice sounds over the comm: "Everyone strap in, it's going to get a little rough."

For once I do exactly what he says without finding him to argue about it. A few minutes later I'm glad I did because the ship's shaking, and I can feel us wallowing back and forth as we enter the atmosphere. Loras murmurs that we're hitting thermal pockets, and I can't tell from his expression how bad that is. March is probably struggling to keep the nose up, increase drag, trying not to liquefy our hull.

"He doesn't use autopilot much, does he?"

Loras glances up from the console and seems to decide

it's time he strapped in as well. "I don't know," he answers. "We haven't flown with him any more than you have."

"Right."

I feel like a shit for forgetting the poor bastard who died on Perlas Station. Before we can say anything more, we pitch sharply, and only the harness keeps me from being flung against the far wall. As it is, I'm going to have an impressive web of bruises all over my throat and shoulders. I feel my stomach surge into my throat because this reminds me of—

No. Oh no. This is like dream therapy, all over again.

My fault . . . why did they think it might be my fault? I got us to Matins IV, didn't I? I didn't hurt Kai. I wouldn't have. *But what . . . ?* I can't remember; there's a red haze around everything. It hurts, and I feel like—

We hit hard, and I feel the ship careening. Screaming metal, something tears loose. When there's a hangar or a port, you can expect a certain amount of help—a computer beaming ideal trajectory, cooperative deployment of thrusters. Here, it's just March and his best judgment. I'm holding a scream inside my head, and my throat seems swollen shut. I see nothing but the dark, spreading across my field of vision like a plague.

She's screaming. I hear screaming. I'm pinned. Both *my arms feel like they've been torn off, but I can hear her screaming. I have to help her, Mary give me strength, help me move this. Hurts. I'll crawl. No. No. Too late—I can smell the—*

There's no burning meat, Jax. You're safe. Everyone's *all right.*

This is the first time I've heard him when we weren't jacked in. But suddenly my head's full of him, and I don't know where I am. But I can feel my arms, and I'm whole,

just like he's promising. I become aware of someone
crying—rough wracking sobs.

Oh Mary, it's me.

It's going to be a while before I can speak, and I don't
even want to think of opening my eyes because the crew is
probably watching me with the horrified fascination usually reserved for the interstellar freak show. But I sense the
negative even before I process his response. *They're checking out the* Folly. *We took some damage coming in.*

Considering my meltdown, that seems like quite the
understatement. Now I can feel his hands on my back,
stroking, soothing. Guess he was right; I'm nowhere near
stable and probably a liability to the mission. Shit, I can't
even handle a rough landing.

You're one of the strongest people I've ever met. That
shocks me out of my self-pity. I wonder why he's saying
that, and as if I'd asked the question, he goes on: *I could
hear you screaming all the way up in the cockpit. And the
second I touched you . . . Jax, I saw it all.*

Shit. I did that? Gave him the charnel house from
Matins IV to bear along with everything else? Mother
Mary, is there no limit to the pain I'll inflict?

He gives me a little shake, and I open my eyes. We're
still in the hub, but he's got me on his lap by the console.
There's nobody else around right now, as he said. I'm starting to realize that March's word is gold. He might be a lot
of things, but the man doesn't lie as far as I can tell.

"Was I screaming?"

I don't remember. My throat isn't sore, although the rest
of me is.

"No," Doc says from the doorway. "At least not so the
rest of us could hear." I register March's surprise, but Saul
continues, regarding us with an inscrutable expression.
"He came from the cockpit at a dead run, yanked you up
out of your seat. What happened, Jax?"

"Psychotic break." I feel like I'm signing away my personal liberty by admitting as much, like maybe the Corp had a point in keeping me confined.

But Doc just nods, looking thoughtful. "Let's get you to medical."

It's only then I realize that I'm still sitting on March's lap, and his arms fall away from me with the slow, swimming reluctance of a mudsider learning to move in zero G. And I say quietly in the confines of my own head: *Thank you.* Not expecting to be heard. To my surprise, as I fold to my feet to follow Saul, I receive a very soft response that maybe I am not meant to hear.

I will always come for you, Jax.

CHAPTER 19

Ten minutes pass in silence.

Doc's bedside manner is a little disturbing, but then he's a geneticist more than an actual physician. I need to remember that. Finally, he concludes his battery of tests and regards me with an expression I can only describe as bemused.

"You have some unusual activity in the temporal lobe, both within the amygdala and the auditory cortex. We could work to neutralize those abnormal patterns, but I don't know whether that would be treating the problem or the symptom."

"Pretty sure it'd be the symptom. I have some . . . bad memories."

"Yes, I expect you would," he returns mildly. To my surprise he doesn't display the same kind of morbid curiosity as the Unit Psych. "Seems a hard landing acts as a trigger. Do you know of any other events that might set off a similar reaction?"

I shake my head. "Thought I was anesthetized to it, after they made me revisit it so often on Perlas."

"They did *what*?"

Frowning, I explain what my confinement was like, and by the time I'm finished, well, I don't think I've ever seen Doc look so outraged. He asks me a series of questions regarding the frequency and timing of my treatments. "Barbarians," he mutters. "Wish I'd known this earlier. It explains a few things."

"Like what?"

He pauses. "I can't be sure without further testing, and I'm not certain I want to subject you to it, but . . . Jax, I think they may have used subliminal suggestion in your dream therapy to guarantee your eventual breakdown."

"In case the Psychs and solitary weren't enough?" The bitterness in my own voice surprises me, and what's more astounding, I don't doubt it's possible. But there's a more pressing question on my mind now.

Doc regards me solemnly. "I think it's critical we figure out what happened on Matins IV. They think you know something—and perhaps you do."

"Why didn't they just kill me?" It's the first time I've asked that aloud.

"I don't know, my dear. But I suspect it's vital we discover that as well."

"So you don't think I'm crazy . . . or dangerous?"

"No more than anyone else," he answers kindly, "under the right circumstances."

I don't know why, but that placates my fear better than anything else he could have said. Humans are capable of horrific acts, but the aftermath of Matins IV left me feeling like I deserve a special spot among monsters. And I don't even know why. Examined intellectually, the feeling doesn't make sense. I *know* we made the jump; we arrived intact and something . . . happened as Kai tried to put us down on planet. I just can't remember what. But how could that be my fault?

My gaze wanders around the sterile medical exam room, white and gleaming synth. Saul's instruments align with mathematical precision, revealing a great deal about his character. I hop down from the table and decline his offer of a sedative.

"No thanks. It won't accomplish anything if I sack out in quarters. Once I start *asking* to forget, well . . ." I smile wryly. "I might as well have stayed on Perlas."

"I can't imagine you ever take the easy road," he observes, putting away the scanner he used to check my amygdala, whatever that is. "That's what March can't resist, you know. That grit."

"He acts like he can hardly stand me—"

"There are reasons." Before I can frame the question, Doc shakes his head. "Oh no, I've said too much already. Get out of my med bay, you're fine."

"No, I'm not. But I think maybe . . . I will be."

Saul gives me a knowing half smile as I turn down the hall, heading back to the hub. I can hear Dina swearing from somewhere else within the ship, and Loras seems to be analyzing a status report at the comm terminal. Well, things can't be too bad if we've got systems online, right? He ignores me, a fact I find comforting. It'd be so much worse if he behaved solicitously.

I still feel somewhat shaken, but I've got a little distance from it. Time to compartmentalize, push it back and pretend the woman who broke down belongs to someone else, another Jax. So I square my shoulders and go in search of March.

When I find him, he's in the cockpit, but what bothers me is . . . he's doing nothing. Just slumped in the pilot's chair, gazing at a panel whose numbers mean nothing to me. A cold chill crawls down my spine as I realize I've never seen that look in his eyes: a veritable wasteland, bleak and grim. In anyone else I'd call the expression despair, but I can't reconcile that to what I know of him.

"What's wrong?"

I'd intended to demand to know our plan of action, status of repairs, how long we might be grounded, and when we're heading out to meet the natives. But his eyes knock all that right off my agenda. Now I just need to know why he looks like this.

"Better question is what's right? It'd take less time to answer." He manages a shadow of his usual saturnine smile, but I'm not buying it.

"Seriously, don't bullshit me."

Sighing, he sits forward in the pilot chair, tapping a figure on the display panel with an index finger. "That's population. Something bad happened here, Jax. There's nothing left alive above five kilos."

For a minute I can't even process that. The amphibians we came to visit beneath Corp radar, the genetics we intended to tap . . . gone? Figuring out what happened, that will be work for anthropologists down the line.

"How is that even possible?" I can't begin to guess.

March shakes his head. "I don't fragging know. The Mareq were tribal, barely even aware that there were other settlements within reasonable walking distance: different traditions, different dialects. Don't know how a plague could spread, given they had almost no contact with each other. And they were a peaceful race, as far as our records indicate."

"You think someone did this on purpose." It's not a question, and I know damn well that's what put this look in his eyes.

"Nothing else makes sense," he says, too quietly.

I think about that for a moment, and I'm surprised to see my hand hovering a few millimeters from his shoulder. Is that what I want? To comfort March? Perhaps I give myself too much credit, believing I might have the power.

It's been over a standard month since I touched anyone else of my own volition. The last time, I was with Kai, preparing for our jump to Matins IV. Hovering there, my fingers look thin and spidery, blue veins too prominent across the back, a map of bad choices. Maybe those arteries writhe with some poison that contaminates everything I touch. So I drop my hand, and for once he doesn't notice, still staring at the panel.

There's something I have to ask, and a few months back, the question would never have occurred to me. But now I'm born again in speculation and paranoia. My skin crawls with it, and my mind fosters suspicion like a beloved child.

"Did Zelaco have access to Mair's research?"

March's head jerks up. "Possibly."

"Let's assume he did," I say, carefully neutral. "Would it be within his character to provide some intelligence to the Corp for the right price?"

He sucks in a slow breath, both hands fisting on his knees. "Absolutely. He wouldn't have revealed our base of operations; he wouldn't have risked them striking at Lachion while he was on planet. But if he calculated our risk of failure greater than our chance at success, he certainly would've padded his take by selling you to the Gunnars and added another slice by offering what he knew of our agenda to the Corp."

I feel numb.

"So we're looking at ten dead worlds, potentially. If you can't cull the competition, destroy their resources. March, what if they took samples? What if they know about Doc's cross-germination idea?"

"Doubt Zelaco knew the science of it. Doc's been very tight with that." But he doesn't sound hopeful.

In fact, he looks almost totally defeated, and I realize he's paying me a compliment, letting me see him like this. Maybe it's quid pro quo. He's seen me at my worst, so he can offer it back. Whatever the reason, I won't snipe at him, not now.

"Are we still going to look around on planet?"

"Might as well," he answers. "Dina's going to be a couple of days getting us flightworthy. We took some hull damage coming in, and the phase drive—"

"Broke down conveniently," I finish. "Zelaco, or more to the point, someone he hired had access to the *Folly* while we were en route to the compound?" When he nods, I add, "At this point, I think we can assume there are gray men headed for our location."

March offers a tight smile. "There's a bright spot, at least."

"Or it's possible we're sharing a paranoid delusion."

"Occam's razor," he murmurs, shaking his head.

"Huh?"

"Just someone who lived a long time ago and died in obscurity. We need to move unless we want to become anecdotal footnotes ourselves."

Reality as I know it is no more because I'm in complete agreement with March.

CHAPTER 20

It's hard to imagine this planet holding the key to any-thing.

Through the view screen, I see the soil bubbling with algae as the rain pours down. Everything is green, but it's unwholesome, dripping and dank. The atmosphere is borderline breathable, but we need filters to scrub out chemicals that might burn our lungs. I make no protest when Saul plugs my nostrils; that's not the way I want to die.

Most of the time, I imagine myself passing while I'm jacked in, taking my last look at grimspace. Sometimes, mainly when I'm drunk, I see myself as an old woman, keeling over while eating smooth sweet slices of kavi and ogling handsome waiters. That death wouldn't be hard to arrange, particularly on Venice Minor. In fact, I could probably pay someone to see to it.

"You think about that too much," March tells me, as we're checking our gear.

"Everyone needs a hobby."

With a look he informs me that I'm unspeakably maca-bre, but I just shrug. Ship sensors indicate there's a settle-ment about four kilometers away, so we're going for a hike. The *Folly* doesn't have anything like a land vehicle, just the shuttle, which won't clear the jammed bay doors, courtesy of our crash landing. We could sit around waiting for Dina to get that fixed, but neither March nor I qualify as patient. Besides, we've already ascertained there's nothing big left out there.

What could possibly go wrong?

Loras takes one look outside and declines to set foot on planet; he doesn't bother with an excuse while Doc states gravely that if there are no living Mareq, he will only get in the way. Dina presents the best case for staying behind, as the ship needs repairs.

For a moment, I feel as if they're throwing us together on purpose, as we'll probably spend the night at the settle-ment. Even if there's nothing dangerous left mudside, we could still fall down a hole or get sucked into the swamp. Whatever March says, I'm not walking back in the dark.

But I don't notice any significant glances, no conspira-torial grins, so I don't think it's matchmaking. Seems more like they just don't want to wander around this shit hole, and as I step off the loading ramp, I can't blame them. I sink two centimeters into the mud, and the stink of putrid vegetation almost overwhelms me, even through the filters.

"Our own slice of heaven, huh, Jax?"

As the rain plasters my hair to my head, I sigh and shoulder my pack. "Right."

Guess this might have been paradise for the amphibians. Part of me aches, like this is my fault, like I'm the butterfly whose wings create hurricanes. I try to push it back. But it's hard to escape the feeling that my life has become a curse, a thread that ought to have been snipped at Matins

IV, and that I'm only going to keep causing pain until I have the good sense to die. But even if that's the case, I'm just not selfless enough to fix it.

He fiddles with a handheld nav device, getting a fix on our location as opposed to the settlement. I'm almost surprised not to be chided for my thoughts, but then he can't live inside my head, can he? I suppose I've gotten used to the idea that he might, that he's privy to everything about me.

Realizing he doesn't and he isn't, now . . . I feel lonely.

"Let's go. Sooner we get moving, sooner we get there. See if we can make sense of what happened here."

Nodding, I fall in behind March, not because I acknowledge his authority in any fashion but because if by some chance we were wrong, and there's something big and ugly left in these wetlands, I really prefer it eats him first. Give me a chance to run.

"Nice," he says, sparing a glance over his shoulder. "Really nice."

Oh sure, *that* he hears.

For the first time it occurs to me, as we're walking, maybe it's not entirely March. Maybe it's something I'm doing, something I didn't even know I *could* do. I think back over the times where he's tuned to my frequency, and it's often when I was thinking something I *knew* would needle him. This last time, I heard him back, without effort, without equipment. What that means, exactly, I have no idea.

"It means our theta waves are compatible," he answers, surprising me. "It's almost always a one-way feed. I get impressions from other people, what kind and how deep depends on how disciplined their minds are and how much I want to know. Used to be uncontrollable, couldn't shut it off."

"How did you—"

"Mair. She wouldn't teach me the higher forms, but she saw what a mess I was and taught me how to quiet my mind. Shut out the noise through meditation."

Well, that explains a hell of a lot. "I'm sorry. I didn't know."

His next words come out strained. "Before she took me in hand, I wasn't even human, Jax. You have no idea how many people I've ended. Broke minds to set an example, for the hell of it, or just because I needed a quiet kill. I spent years on Nicuan, feeding their endless wars. By the time I stole a ship because they shorted my pay, there was nothing left. Mair rebuilt me, brick by brick."

A chill shivers through me, more than the icy rain coursing down my neck. I've seen echoes of that darkness in his eyes sometimes, a soulless echo he keeps in check. Am I safe out here with him?

"Who else have I taken from you?" I probably wouldn't have the nerve to ask if I could see his face. But looking at his broad back in the battered flight jacket, I can just manage it. "I know about Edaine. And Mair. I didn't realize she was your mentor . . . that only makes it worse. But there's someone else, isn't there?"

And it's part of what he's been trying to hide from me, each time we jack in. Part of the reason he wants to hate me. I know her name. *Svet.* Dina said it weeks ago. But who was she to him?

I hold my breath as we walk, ducking beneath low-hanging vines and ferny fronds that clutch at my clothes as we pass by. The sounds seem louder around us, insects buzzing and chirping, a small symphony fusing with the slurp of ooze around our shoes.

"I'm not having this conversation with you, Jax. Not now."

"Why not?" Second time he's given me that answer, almost verbatim.

At that, he turns to face me. "Because we're in the middle of nowhere," he tells me deliberately. "There's nobody to see, nothing to stop me but my conscience. And I've only recently decided you don't deserve killing."

My breath rushes out of me in a sound that can't rightly be called a sigh. It's more of a whimper, and I'm embarrassed because I sound like a wounded animal. I don't know what I thought . . . that his animosity had become at least partially feigned? That I'd proven myself somehow. I guess I thought because he spirited me away from the brain butchers on Perlas that I could, to some degree, count on him for protection.

But as it turns out, March is the chief advocate of wanting me dead.

And what better way to accomplish that than to lead me, trusting as a sacrificial goat, out into the wilderness? No wonder nobody volunteered to come with us. Was there *ever* anything on this planet? And why wouldn't he have detected the anomaly in life signs from orbit? I remember Keri giving me the PA; she knew the codes. Maybe she planted all the data about Marakeq. Maybe they realize I don't know anything, nothing but grimspace, and I've been played.

Maybe March doesn't give a shit about the grand scheme. I give him points for the thespian performance in the cockpit. I bought into it with all my credits. Believed he was suffering over the fate of these poor bog-runners. I'm so stupid. I should have known there was a reason for his sudden shift, why he came running to help me.

His assurance, *I'll always come for you, Jax*, takes on sinister tones.

There probably isn't a grand scheme any longer, and all their hope of an academy died with Mair. Maybe this is their way of righting the wrong on Matins IV. I thought it myself; I shouldn't have survived where so many other, worthier people died.

Wonder how far we are from the ship and whether they'd act against me if I came back alone. Do they know? I can't believe Doc and Loras do. Saul has been the essence of kindness from the beginning, and Loras, oh shit,

Loras will *die* without me. Those two can't possibly be involved.

Does he plan to return without me? Report a tragic accident and move out? The Corp would probably stop hunting them with confirmation of my death. *Neat and tidy, isn't it, March? And then you can wait for someone stable, just like you said.*

Clean slate.

My face feels like it's blazing with heat, and I see clearly for the first time, every detail down to the rain trickling down his brown face. I back up a pace, then two, fumbling in my pack for anything like a weapon. Come up empty-handed. I'm not scared so much as angry, mostly at myself for being so fragging gullible, and if he takes a single step toward me, I'm going to kill him with my bare hands or die trying.

I know which I prefer.

CHAPTER 21

"You can't be serious."

But he doesn't make a move, so I think he knows perfectly well that the time for bullshit is done. He fooled me once, shame on him, but I'm not falling for it again. Instead, I'm gauging the distance, trying to calculate an approach where I can prevail against his sheer physical strength.

I have to be honest with myself, though. The odds don't look good. I probably have a better shot running away from him, and I possess too much self-preservation to cavil. Survival is survival, and he's just said he wants me dead. So I feint left and dive right, but before I can tumble past him and hit the ground running, he catches me around the waist, easily, as if I were a recalcitrant child trying to avoid chores.

"Jax." He pitches his voice soft, soothing. "You're losing it again. Maybe not a full break, but you're not rational. If I intended to hurt you, why announce it?"

I don't respond except to struggle with fists and feet, my heart pounding in my chest fit to explode. It's something else now, and I'm trapped. He's a wall as I pummel him, managing to do nothing but bounce off him like he's the ultimate immovable object. And he doesn't react except to leave his arm around my waist, keeping me from falling, even when I collapse.

Because he's right—I'm fragging insane. I hate feeling like this. For the first time since I left Perlas, the tears come, and I can't stop them, sobbing as the rains wash over us, heavier now. As if from beneath a blanket, I hear the rumble of thunder in the distance.

Afterward, the only reason I can look him in the eyes is because he doesn't comfort me. He doesn't murmur soft words or stroke my back; he just keeps me upright, out of the mud, and the moment it seems like I can stand on my own, he lets me go.

"I'm so sorry," I say, low. "Don't know if it was the crash or something the Corp did to me afterward, but—"

"Shut up and let's go," he says brusquely.

For some reason, that makes me smile, but he doesn't wait around for my reaction. I'm left staring at his back as he heads down what passes for a trail, a clearish patch between the trunks of bloated trees. Oddly, I feel lighter. I have no idea what my Unit Psychs did to me, but I think my head's a minefield strewn with triggers, and maybe if I survive each explosion, what emerges from the wreckage will be me, really, truly me.

At that he spins, spearing me with a look. There's such heat in his eyes, never seen this expression, not from anyone. It's not desire, but something deeper, darker. Instinctively I fall back a step.

"Not 'if,'" he growls. "I'm tired of catching glimpses where you're thinking about dying. Yeah, before we met, I wanted you dead, not because I felt sure you were to blame for Matins IV. Because you walked away. But get it through your head, Jax. I will *never* let anything happen to you, not now. You're one of mine, whether I like it or not."

My legs won't hold me. Or maybe my feet are simply swept out from under me by the wash running between gnarled roots. I wind up on my knees in the mud, face up-turned, not to him, but for the rain, almost praying to be made clean. The fabric of our coveralls is supposed to be waterproof, but nothing can withstand the saturation found on Marakeq in monsoon season. We're both soaked through, and I feel as though I'll never be warm again.

"March, please," I whisper, beneath the sound of the water. I don't know whether he can even hear me. "You have to tell me."

I gaze up at him, touching him only with my eyes. And I recognize when he accepts the inevitability of this exchange. For the first time I grasp that bending doesn't necessarily mean weakness. Defiance doesn't always equate to strength. And before he replies, I know he's not going to deny me a third time before sundown.

Raindrops spatter his hard face like tears, and when he reaches for me, I let him draw me up. We stand joined only by our twined fingers, as he answers in a broken voice, a not-March voice, "All right. All right, Jax. You win."

"I don't want to win. I just need to understand."

"How much do you remember about the flight before the crash?" His hands tighten on mine, hurting me, but I know he's not even aware of it.

I swallow hard around a lump in my throat. "It was uneventful." This part is rote; I've repeated it so often: to the Psychs, to my CO, in the silence of my own head. "We were just coming off R&R, so I was well rested. Kai and I intended"—small inner flinch at speaking of him in past tense, yes, he's really gone—"to pick a mechanic and a medic from the pool and do a routine exploratory. But somebody got sick, a jumper who was supposed to make a passenger run. There were all kinds of diplomats and dignitaries waiting for the jump-flight off station to Matins IV. My CO asked if I'd mind filling in, more R&R to follow, since he knew passenger flights weren't my favorite."

"Asked or ordered?"

I shrug. "Same thing."

"So what went wrong?"

He squeezes so hard that I have to pull away, rubbing my fingers to bring back the circulation. Soon I may have bruises, purple fingerprints where he ground skin against bone. There used to be flesh, muscle, but I've withered like the crone dolls children make from the husks of sere, out-of-season fruit.

"I don't know." Hurts to say that for what seems like the millionth time. "Safety check went fine, the flight itself . . . nothing out of the ordinary when you consider we had seventy-five souls on board and only eight crew, most of whom weren't accustomed to serving on passenger flights."

"It was a big ship then?"

"An X-class professional transport vessel. Kai had only piloted one like that maybe two or three times in his life, apart from academy sims."

"But he was certified, competent to handle it?" When I nod without hesitation, since Kai was the best damn pilot I ever knew, he asks, "What about you?"

I give him a half smile. "Size doesn't matter much to a navigator. Interface is everything."

Not until afterward do I realize how suggestive that sounds. To his credit, March stays focused, although I wonder where he's headed with this. Probably he could've accessed my Psych reports to find all this out.

"So you made the jump, then it was a straight cruise to Matins IV . . . ?"

"Yeah. There was a conference, something to do with . . . I can't remember, actually. But I'm sure it's public record."

"Tell me the rest, Jax." Maybe he doesn't realize how demanding he sounds.

"That's all. In my head it's like there's this big red hole. I remember making our final approach, Kai kissing me for luck and me . . ." I suck in a sharp breath. Oh Mary, can I truly say this out loud? Yes, I can—quid pro quo. "Teasing him. As he started making adjustments to the controls, being extra careful because it was a strange ship, bigger than he was used to, I asked, 'Are you afraid of falling, baby?' " My voice breaks, and I feel tears welling up, salty heat that doesn't matter in the rain. "And he answered, 'No, I'm afraid of landing.' H-he laughed. I smiled. I don't remember anything after that, March. On Mary's Sacred Shroud, I don't. Next thing I know I'm on the ground, pinned. People are . . . are . . ."

"Shh," he whispers without touching me, which is good, because I'd break. "I know all that. Stop now. Stop."

"Your turn."

I'm not an idiot. I already know that someone important to him died in the crash. Question is, who? The body count from Matins IV stands at eighty-two, and that planet should have been my grave. I'll spend the rest of my life carrying scars from wounds that ought to have killed me. Should be dead twice over. The facilities on planet weren't sufficient to handle burns like mine, so they jumped me to Perlas. I'm told I lay there for twelve hours, listening first to screams, then to silence, before the salvage crew arrived. The landing authority figured there was no hurry . . . nobody could've survived.

"I'll tell you, Jax." He offers a smile laced with wry humor. "On Mary's Sacred Shroud, I will. But right now we need to move."

I follow the trajectory of his gaze downward and see that we're sinking into the ultrasoft Mareq soil. Vines stir around us in a way that I can't help but find disturbing, like the planet's alive, tentacles of a beast about to feast.

Shit.

March pulls me out of the mud with a hard tug, then we sprint deeper into the trees. Hope to Mary he knows where he's going.

"Me, too," he mutters.

Huh, wonder why I'm not reassured?

CHAPTER 22

We stumble on the settlement by chance.

My legs ache because we had to run in long, bounding strides to keep from sinking, slip-sliding along in the driving rain. I feel the sting of it on my skin long after the downpour finally abates. And my fingers feel cramped because he never let go of me; I understand why. Getting lost here would be a death sentence.

The community looks about as I expected.

But the mud mounds are the best biotecture I've ever seen; class P or not, this civilization clearly understood the value of a harmonious habitat. We walk through the deserted arcology and see no signs of struggle, no damage to external environs. Though I don't know what's on March's mind, I'm wondering what the hell happened here.

If we go inside one of the structures, we'll need to do it on hands and knees. The openings are more suitable for children, and I recall from my reading that the Mareq seldom reach more than 92cm at full maturity. A chill rushes over me as I realize we may be the only sentient creatures left on planet. I've visited dead worlds before, logged the existence of ancient ruins, but that doesn't possess the same immediacy as knowing you've glimpsed the death of a thriving culture.

As we explore, the sky overhead darkens to slate, and the gauzy star that functions as this world's sun slips below the horizon. Apparently this is the closest thing to true night Marakeq possesses, a dreamtime twilight where the trees take on fantastic shapes.

"I thought this run would tell us something," he says finally. "What type of weapon was used, where they went . . ." Sighing, March taps the communicator to get in touch with the *Folly*.

"Everything all right?" Doc's voice sounds reassuring, even from four klicks out.

"Yes and no," he answers. "We got nothing, but we're safe enough. Going to spend the night and head back to the ship in the morning. March out."

"Let's find a place to pitch camp," I say, tilting my head toward one of the larger structures. "In there might be good."

"You think? If it was a disease that took them—"

"Where are all the bodies?" I shake my head. "Plus a disease that's fatal to the Mareq probably wouldn't even translate to our systems. We're fundamentally different; they're not even warm-blooded."

As we're crawling inside the mound I indicated, something about what I just said resonates. I stop just inside the low arch, and March butts me with his head. "Get moving, Jax. It's fragging cold, and it's starting to rain again."

But I'm waiting for my eyes to acclimate to the dim interior. Hoping I'm right. And yeah, there are small bulges all over the earthen floor.

I laugh softly, delightedly. "They're not gone. You said yourself, it's *cold*, March. They're in the ground. Sleeping until it gets warm again."

"And their heat signatures have equalized to the earth around them. Shit, you're right. We *were* sharing a paranoid delusion."

"Partly at least, and I don't think I've ever been so happy to be wrong." I'm beaming at him over my shoulder.

He smiles back, a real one, not the parody that twists his mouth and never reaches his eyes. "Me, either."

Backing out, we make a quick visual inspection inside all the buildings and find most of them are occupied, their residents asleep for the winter. When we find an empty edifice, probably a meeting place, not a home, that's where we make our last stop, hands and knees muddy beyond belief from all the crawling. Inside the hut, it's surprisingly inviting, cozy, the sloping walls covered in soft moss.

"So what do we do? There's no guarantee we can wake them, and I'm not sure that's a good idea, even if we can."

"First thing we do is warm up," he answers, digging through his pack. "Or we're going to die of exposure. Get your blanket, your lips are blue, Jax."

There's no way he could tell that. Too dim in here, everything is gray. But I do as I'm told, fish out my supposedly weatherproof bedroll and wrap up. Sometimes it's stupid to argue. But why am I not surprised to learn that dinner will be squeezed out of a packet? I sigh and suck it down.

Later, I feel substantially warmer, and I've nourished my body, if not satisfied it. March sits across from me, leaning against the wall. His eyes are closed, but he's not asleep. He might as well hold up a sign that says: *I don't want to talk.*

So I shut my eyes as well, and I'm nearly dozing when he murmurs, "I hate how well you understand me."

"You're not exactly inscrutable."

"The rest of the universe doesn't agree with you, Jax."

At that I grin and open my eyes. "Right, sorry. You're the soul of masculine mystique. Better?"

A pale flicker tells me he's probably smiling. "Not what I meant, but I'll take it. Have you seen the ship's official manifest?"

Talk about non sequiturs.

I shake my head. "Why would I?"

"It's registered as a privately owned vessel out of Gehenna, full designation—*Svetlana's Folly.*"

Now it makes sense; he's just no better at segues than I am. "Who was that?"

"My half sister." He sighs. "Long story, all that matters is . . . she was among your crew on the *Sargasso.*"

I want to show sympathy, but that'll earn me a rebuff quicker than anything I could say. So I just ask, "She joined the Corp?"

I sense more than see his nod. "She was tired of living hand to mouth. Said I'd one day grasp the value of working for the establishment. I didn't want her to go, but she wasn't somebody who listened to advice. When I could finally afford my own ship, I named it to poke at her that I'd made good, right? Without selling my soul to the corporation. We were supposed to meet up after she made the Matins run. Said she had something important to tell me and wouldn't trust open comm channels."

I flinch. *March, I'm so sorry.* But I don't say it aloud, and I don't even know what I'm sorry for, really. Being alive? I don't recall what happened; I truly don't. Clearly, the Corp intended it to become my fault; they shaped my treatments so I wouldn't be mentally competent to deny charges laid against me. Whatever else, that's one reason they didn't kill me. A living cat's-paw serves a number of purposes, PR and otherwise. They probably hoped to get me to the point that I would confess, sobbing and broken. Apologize in tears to the bereaved families; you can't buy press like that.

"I understand," I manage through an aching throat.

And I do. Much as I'd like to, I can't blame him for feeling I'm tainted by what happened on Matins IV. I can't blame him for seeing in me a living reminder of his sister's death. He probably wishes she was sitting here instead, and no, I can't blame him for that, either. I wish she was, too. Instead of family, now all he has is a ship bearing a name that probably hurts each time he hears it.

"No," he says quietly. "You don't. If I hate you for what happened to Svet, then I'm no better than the Corp, practicing prejudice because it's convenient. And I've spent my whole life fighting against what they represent. I *wanted* you to be the cocky, care-for-nothing nav-star we saw on the holo. That woman, I could've despised. But . . . you're not. Maybe you were, I don't know. But that's not the woman I see now."

Through the damp fabric of my coverall, bundled in my blanket, I feel naked. Raw. He sees more than I want, more than I can bear. It's like standing before him on Perlas all over again while he stares at my scars, pitiless and unmoved.

"What now?" My voice sounds husky, and I don't even know what I'm asking.

His shoulders surge in what I take to be a shrug. "We head back to the *Folly* tomorrow. It'd be wrong to disrupt their life cycle for our agenda. There are nine other planets, so we hope for better luck."

See, this is where March differs from the Corp. Both agree the Mareq should be left alone. The Corp, however, take that stance because they believe the Mareq don't possess anything that would benefit them. Thanks to Saul's research, March knows better; he just won't exploit them. I understand why the others look to him—and what I thought before, Doc serving as his conscience, that's wrong. Because that's woven so thoroughly throughout his being, it doesn't register as a separate impulse.

"I liked it better when you sat around thinking about huge rocks falling on me," he mutters. "Don't romanticize me, Jax."

I sputter a laugh. "Are you kidding? Have you *seen* your-self?"

"Says the woman who looks like that."

I can only imagine the mud-encrusted, matted-hair picture I present. Well, that comment silences me since he's right, but I smile as I dig the toe of my boot back and forth, making patterns in the soft earth. Then I freeze as I uncover something shimmering-translucent. I don't think he can see it from across the way, so I lean forward, raking more top soil away to see.

"March," I whisper reverently. "Be careful in here. We're in the nursery."

At that, he knee-walks over to examine my find, and I'm surprised to see his face light with a smile. "You're right."

On my knees in a mud mound with thousands of little Mareq sleeping beneath us, I feel the most astonishing tranquility. We're surrounded by life, by perpetuity. They have language, customs, and these bog-runners will never have to worry about grimspace or the Corp. Who's to say they're not better off?

"Wishing you were Mareq?" he asks, then emits a throaty sound that mimics their speech better than I would've credited. He continues to croak, teasing me.

I don't mind. The air's clear between us, at least. Clean slate. But it's hard to say who looks more astounded when the egg I uncovered trembles and splits to birth a slimy, big-eyed Mareq that latches on to the back of March's hand.

Poetic justice.

Managing not to laugh, I ask, "So I've been meaning to inquire . . . how d'you feel about fatherhood?"

CHAPTER 23

Doc's amusement is contagious.

He's tapping away at a terminal, educating the new father on nurturing his young. I can't help but snicker at the picture March presents. Because he couldn't transport the little guy back to the ship in the cold, he tucked it into his shirt, where it promptly attached to his chest.

Dina has propped herself against the wall just outside medical, so she can mock him conveniently. "Tell me you did this on purpose. This is how we're getting our DNA sample, yes? Because nobody's dumb enough wind up like this accidentally."

"I'm *that* dumb." March glares at her.

She smirks. "I always secretly suspected."

"Leave him alone. You weren't there, were you?" So I'm siding with March? That's got to be a first.

"Tell me you've figured out a fix," he begs Saul. "Come on, it's . . . licking me."

Doc seems fascinated by what he's reading. "Well . . . yes. That's how it survives the first standard month. Apparently the parent that awakened the offspring expels protein-rich mucus through its pores, which the progeny ingests until it is old enough to digest more complex organisms like vegetable matter and insects."

Dina's smirk becomes a grin. "This just gets better and better. You two smell utterly foul by the way. Just saying."

He looks at the small lump beneath his shirt. "You're kidding, right?"

The little Mareq makes a weak sound, and I wince. "We have to find something it can eat, or we might as well have left it to die in the cold."

March sighs, still looking down. "Why the hell did you wake up early, huh?"

Loras sits at the other terminal, skimming the minute data files. At that he glances up and says, "Apparently it's your fault. Well, you and Jax together. According to Canton Farr—he's a Fugitive xenobiologist who studied the Mareq covertly—for a birth, two conditions must be met. First, it is uncovered by the parent that will rear it, and second, that parent declaims what Farr calls the 'Coming-Forth' song."

"This is your fault," March says, glaring at me. "You dug it up."

"Yeah, but who sang the Coming-Forth song? That'll teach you to tease me."

"Pointless bickering!" Doc shakes his head, glancing between us. "I'll do a biomolecular analysis and synthesize something. March, you'll want to depilate your chest before applying the nutri-gel first time, and you'll need to leave it on constantly for the first month, unless you're bathing. Then someone else will take over, but we'll want to avoid switching hosts as much as possible. The little one chose *you*, after all."

"You're shitting me!" March makes two fists, but who's

he going to hit? I've never seen him look like this. "I have to keep this thing on me for a month? Can't you rig something up? A surrogate?"

"You *are* the surrogate," Loras points out.

"As far as I know, no one's ever raised a Mareq outside its own habitat," Doc answers, his tone remarkably gentle. "It's vital we stick as close as we can to what we know of their natural life cycle." With that, Saul gets busy, trying to generate something the baby can digest.

With its protuberant eyes, yellow translucent skin, suction toes, and scrawny useless limbs, it's actually so repulsive it's almost cute. Then again, it's not attached to *my* chest. The creature is no more than an oblong blob beneath March's shirt, barely seeming to breathe. I don't know how the oxygen-rich environment is going to affect its development or what other chemicals it needs to thrive.

"We should analyze the atmosphere here and the contents of the soil. Maybe take some of that mud with us for when it's older?"

Dina smirks at me now. "You're nesting. I mean you finally shagged, right? You two went out into the wild alone and came back with a baby. Should've figured your children would be ugly but daaaaamn . . ."

"Go *fix* something," March bites out.

To my surprise, she does, but not quietly. "I get this ship flightready in less than forty-eight hours, and I'm begrudged a little amusement? When the revolution comes, I will destroy you all."

"The revolution came," Loras calls after her. "You lost."

Her response echoes back: "Kiss Jax's ass."

And I laugh softly.

"Body temperature's a little on the high side since we're warm-blooded, but its life signs are good. Just need a little more of this amino acid . . ." Doc mutters. "Hm, try this? Theoretically, it's a close enough match, and if the little fellow doesn't eat soon . . ."

"My chest hair," he protests, as Saul comes for him with a glove full of goo.

"Good point." Without so much as a "please" or "you look lovely tonight," Saul yanks my coverall open to the waist and slathers the stuff on my sternum. "Pass the baby, let's see how I did. March, go depilate yourself."

He heads for quarters, muttering, "This has to be a bad dream."

"We need to know more." Loras glances up from his research, uninterested in the spectacle. "We might be able to stumble through the first month, but we've no idea where to go from there, nothing about their skill development. The undisputed Mareq expert is Canton Farr, but he published his last article more than two turns ago."

Oh Mary, it's slimy, licking me with its slithery pink tongue. *Probably going to be a wonder at catching bugs, later.* The nutri-gel is sticky, but its heartbeat grows stronger, steadier, thumping against my chest. The toes feel really bizarre against my skin. But there's a certain pride in what I'm doing, even if it's beyond disgusting.

"Last-known location?" Doc asks, still monitoring me and baby-it.

Loras shakes his head. "Doesn't say, but we don't have the range to search the full archives anyway, not to mention it would give away our position if we tried. I'm thinking we need to bounce a message to Keri and see if she can find out for us."

"Do that," March says from the doorway. "Encrypt the relay if you can."

"Consider it done." Loras waves and heads for his station.

"So what're we naming him?" I grin at March, who's staring like he's been hit with a shockstick.

His mouth opens, but all that comes out is, "Huh?"

Belatedly I notice his eyes aren't on mine, and I glance down. Shit, I'm standing around bare-breasted, nursing like some class-P village woman, my scars shiny with slime. Rest of me is covered in dried mud, and my hair looks like it belongs to a New Terran dirt-dauber priestess, so yeah, I've never looked better. But frag him, what do I care? I'm doing a good thing here.

Doc seems oblivious, so I glare at March. He's clean, the bastard. "Hey, I took your turn while you were making yourself silky-smooth. You could say thanks."

He clears his throat. "Thanks, Jax."

But I don't recognize that tone. Shrugging, I say, "I'm dying for a shower. Doc, you wanna grease March up?"

"Yep," March mutters. "That's shooting *right* to the top of the list of questions I never want to hear again."

The baby doesn't want to let go of me, and in the end, I have to gently peel its little toes away one by one. However, once it tastes the gel on March's skin, it seems content to latch on. I think it's the food source; thing isn't old enough to form emotional attachments, if the Mareq even do that as we know it. We really need to find this "expert" Loras was talking about.

What was his name? *Canton Farr.*

I don't stay to listen to March's whimpering, miserable moans, and I'm proud of myself because I don't collapse laughing until I'm safely in quarters. But as I straighten I get a look at myself in the mirror above my bed. Mother Mary of Anabolic Grace, it's worse than I thought. I squeeze my eyes shut and fumble to the san-shower because I don't want to see that filthy hag again.

Maybe an hour later, and yes, I took that long, my door chime sounds. Quickly, I scramble into the loose ki-pants and cami that serve as my pajamas and answer it. I'm surprised to find March standing there. The baby's well fed, it seems, and making odd little whirring sounds that I interpret as contentment. Think this is the first time he's sought me out since Perlas, where he had no choice.

His gaze drops to the sliver of skin where my trousers

and shirt don't quite meet, and I become aware of my hip-bone riding above the fabric. With a tug, I fix that and step back so he can come in, if he wants.

But he shakes his head. "I just wanted to thank you."

"What for?"

"Making me do the right thing." He glances down with some expression I can't begin to interpret.

But I know he didn't mean it, those first frantic moments gazing at the thing stuck to his hand. Didn't mean it when he muttered we should leave it. Through our interference, the little guy was born out of season, and none of the mature Mareq will stir until it warms up. Far too late—and March would never hurt something that couldn't fend for itself, not even with neglect.

"You've never needed me for that," I say softly. "And you never will."

He's smiling as I close the door in his face.

CHAPTER 24

We're two standard days out of Marakeq, cruising straight space, when Keri's reply reaches us.

Stupid to jump until we know where we're going, since by some miracle the gray men haven't descended on us yet. Maybe Zelaco didn't make contact with the Corp after all. Maybe that was just March and me relaxing with a round of worst-case scenario. That'd be a nice fragging change.

Evidently her encryption ware isn't compatible with ours because the message plays in skips and hisses: "... wish I knew what the ... but anyway ... Lex ... exploded. Why do you ... Farr's last-known location ... Hon-Durren's Kingdom."

I think I speak for everyone when I say, "Shit."

Loras plays it twice more, coaxing a few more words from it, but nothing that adds to overall coherence. Everyone's oddly subdued, and for once, I know why. Doc mumbles and heads off to medical, probably to record his will or something.

"So how bad *is* this guy, really?" I ask Dina, who sighs.

"Put it this way," she answers. "He calls that shit hole on the Outskirts his kingdom. Seriously. Do you need to hear more?"

"Long haul in straight space," March says, sounding thoughtful.

I sigh. "No shit. Why don't we just let Doc do his best and get on with our mission? We need more samples, don't we? This training academy isn't going to build itself."

For once Dina agrees with me. "Sounds good. Let's give Hon a wide berth and say a Hail Mary for baby-it."

Wearing his "captain" expression, March says, "Look, it's my fault this thing hatched early. I can't in good conscience proceed without doing everything possible to ensure it thrives. Let's ask Doc what he thinks."

Loras studies March with an impassive mien. If this comes to a vote, I suspect he'll be the tiebreaker. Then he beeps Doc in medical to ask, "If we choose not to seek out the Mareq expert, what are the chances we can successfully raise the hatchling to an age where you can obtain viable amounts of genetic material for your research?"

Even through the screen, Doc seems startled. "I thought this was decided. Very well, let me run the numbers." He taps some figures into his handheld and sighs. "Highly probable we'll kill it within the first month without expert guidance. If it lives that long, I can take some decent samples, but for the sake of my research, I prefer we take the route that benefits the specimen."

"I say we go, too," March puts in. "You and Dina vote against?"

I glance at her. Doc's detachment has made me twitchy. How ironic that Doc is arguing for the benefit of the creature, though not for purely humanitarian reasons. On the whole, this side junket seems like a waste of time.

With an apologetic look at March's chest, I mutter, "Yeah. Let's keep working toward the original goal."

Dina nods. So yep, it's up to Loras now. Everyone turns toward him to see which way he'll swing.

"We should go," he says at last. "Nobody will die if we push back our schedule, but the little one might if we fail to learn how to care for him properly. And I won't be party to devaluing his existence because he's nonhuman."

Ouch. That cuts deep on so many levels. As a humanoid alien, Loras would know all about being made to feel lesser.

Though nobody else would notice, I see the way March relaxes. His shoulders lose a tension I hadn't registered consciously until it dissipates. This meant a lot to him, and I need to find out why.

"You okay?" I ask.

"Yeah." He makes some effort to shake it off, apparently registering my concern.

In two days, he seems to have gotten used to having baby-Z attached to his chest. I'm not sure what Z stands for, but the name stuck. I've caught March whispering a few times, trying to mimic the only recorded example of Mareq speech among Farr's work. And, of course, I've played surrogate twice more while March was in the sanshower. Nobody else will touch the thing, not even Doc. He said he'd done enough, between the food source and the patch on its skin that provides other necessary chemicals not naturally present in our environment.

"If we're going," I say, "let's combine what we know about the place." I wrack my brain for a moment. "It was built as a supply station before certain beacons were discovered. Since then, trade routes changed."

I don't want them thinking I'm ignorant; I know why Hon-Durren rules that corner of space. Nobody else wants it. But still, the man isn't someone you cross lightly. He styles himself a raider, though nobody knows how many ships comprise his "armada," because he tends to kill people who come calling, bad for us and worse for Canton Farr.

"Farr might be all right." March answers me without seeming to realize I haven't spoken. For the first time I wonder if the others know. Obviously Mair did, but what about the crew? "He's a Fugitive, after all, and if he was in deep shit after pirate-publishing his work on a Corp-restricted world, where better to hide out?"

Dina nods. "And Hon-Durren hates few things more than authority."

I'm familiar with the Fugitives as well, scientists who flout Corp regulations regarding restricted worlds. Every now and then, they orchestrate an impassioned protest, shouting that the Corp has no right to limit knowledge. Though I used to see them as a fringe faction, rabble-rousers and dissidents, I don't disagree with their ideas anymore.

And technically, we're worse than Fugitives, who are so careful when they study on class-P worlds. Under no circumstances would one of their scientists reveal himself; in fact, a few have died of some simple illness rather than compromise an alien culture. As for us, we're more like Freak Show Talent Scouts, although I don't know of any that have kidnapped a Mareq hatchling. Maybe we're just in a class by ourselves.

"Come on," March says then. "Time to jump, Jax."

"It's still going to be thirteen days in straight space, even from the nearest beacon," I tell his back, and he waves in acknowledgment over his shoulder.

As we settle in the cockpit, he gets on the comm. "Head to the hub and strap in, people. We're going to pay an old friend a visit."

"Acknowledged," Loras returns.

I pause in checking the port to slide him a glance. Looks like the nav chair escaped damage in the crash, but Dina probably already inspected it. She really is good at her job.

"You know him?"

"Long time ago," he mutters.

"That's all you're going to tell me?" I gaze at him, incredulous.

He nods. "Right now. We have work to do."

Sighing, I realize I can't argue that. The sooner we leave this system, the better. We've probably been here too long already.

The comm crackles, and Dina announces, "We're ready."

March taps a few panels, and I feel the comforting throb of the phase drive powering up. The whine that accompanied its use last time translates to low purr instead, so I know we're good. "Let me see the locus of a long haul between our current position and Hon-Durren's Kingdom," I tell the nav computer.

"No match," it answers, sounding almost smug.

Fragging AIs.

March thinks a moment, then suggests, "Try DuPont Station."

Shit, nobody's used that name in . . . well, forever, but . . . of course, that's where we find the file. According to official record, DuPont Station is derelict, but anyone taking these maps verbatim would receive a rude awakening. I study the coordinates and realize I've made this run before, maybe five turns back, although my final destination differed.

"Hate the Outskirts, but at least there's minimal Corp presence." If there's a place where lawlessness is the rule, rather than the exception, then we're headed right for it.

March grins at me. "Truer words were never spoken, Jax."

Not until after I plug in do I realize I don't feel the same nausea and dread as the first two jumps. Whatever else he is, he's *my* pilot now. And part of me feels like I've made the adjustment too fast, as if I'm betraying Kai in some fashion.

"He's gone," March reminds me gently. "And I'm all you've got."

Hearing those words doesn't hurt as much this time. I know I'm never going to kiss Kai for luck again, never going to wake in his arms, never going to see him smile, never hear his laughter ring out. He's gone, and I'm alive, whether I want to be or not. Only the ache remains.

When March jacks in beside me, he doesn't bring up the mental partition. He's still compartmentalized, just like me, but he's not hiding anymore. Among other things, he lets me see that he needs me to see this thing through. I wonder if he'd let me rummage through his mind, as he seems to do with me or whether he'd slap my metaphysical hands.

Then I register his unmistakable amusement as the seat vibrates beneath me. *Make yourself at home, Jax.*

I'm starting to do just that as the trembling increases, and I decide that the way we're rocking isn't right. That slinging side-to-side motion almost feels like we've been hit—and then I hear Dina shouting via comm: "Make the Mary-sucking leap already! Since when does the Corp hire bounty hunters . . . ?"

With a flick of his palm, March shuts Dina up, and the world explodes in color, scintillating, dazzling patterns that form and fold in on themselves. My whole body aches because this is homecoming, and I'll never belong anywhere more than I do here. Grimspace steals my soul a sliver at a time, and I love it too much to mind. Each time I leave, I forget a little of the majesty, or I wouldn't survive the loss.

I can't worry about the ship that fired on us as we made the leap, can't let myself wonder whether they had a jumper on board and if they're giving chase. It takes every ounce of concentration to make the mental translation from straight space, then feel my mind's eye spinning like an old world compass.

But this is different, different than flying with Kai, different than the first two jumps with March. Because I can feel what it's like inside his skin, each breath he takes and how his heart beats. I feel the steady pulse of baby-Z against his chest, the faint stickiness of the nutri-gel that March no longer notices. And I'm aware of his hands on the controls as I never have been. I could almost fly the ship if I had to, because we're not him and me, we're . . . we, then I sense his astonishment, sharing my mind's eye as we gaze outward to grimspace.

Maybe I gave him some sense of it before, but this time, he sees *completely*, and I know he does: the glory, the colors, and the almost-manifest monsters that writhe along the hull. The *Folly* plows through liquid fire; the world without is a conflagration of possibility, ideas and dreams barely conceived and waiting to be given form.

But March and yes, it's the March-me spinning my mind's eye away from the beacon. *He's* doing it, and I didn't even know this was possible. He's trying to show me—

Shit. There's a ship coming up fast behind us. I don't know whether they stayed with us through the jump or whether we've stumbled into a time trail. Regardless, I don't want it following us into straight space, because it doesn't seem friendly, and I sense accord from March. We've got to get rid of them and fast, before I exhaust my mental energy. We both know some ships make the jump, and for some reason, never come out again, but the March part of me loves a challenge.

Come on, assholes, let's play.

CHAPTER 25

I know what we're going to do before he does it.

The spin feels ugly, graceless, and my stomach hurtles into my throat, bounces back as we whip the way we came. Suddenly we're coming at them hard-forward, and they have to choose, collision or roll. What happens when two ships crash here?

I'm pretty sure I know why we've never heard of it happening; no one lives to tell the tale. I taste March's satisfaction, the pumping adrenaline. Mary, he lives for this, and with his—our?—pleasure pounding through me, I'm not even afraid as the other ship slings sideways out of our path. This is glorious, exhilarating, and I sense his agreement.

Then we make the loop again, going nowhere, over the top, back the way we came, again and again, until I feel dizzy. He's actually doing it, though I've never seen anyone create grimspace ghosts on purpose. Now there are so many copies of *Svetlana's Folly* that even I have a hard time telling which vessel's ours.

This is the longest I've ever been jacked into grimspace, and I feel my body shuddering, although I feel strangely detached from its meat. The vista in my mind's eye expands until I can see farther than I ever have. What would be the horizon beckons, if this place possessed such a thing. It's not a door but something else and—

No. Jax, no. Find the beacon.

But it's not that easy. For the first time during a jump I'm aware of fierce physical pain, and the outward tug grows stronger. I'm not sure I can resist it, and what's more, I don't want to; I want to see. I want to know. I've spent my whole life preparing for this final journey, and maybe through the door-that-isn't-a-door lie the people I've lost. Maybe Kai's waiting for me with a kiss and a smile.

Don't you dare leave me, Jax. Don't you dare.

And then I feel stronger somehow. March wraps himself around me in ways I didn't know were possible. Everything I am is filled with him. Every cold and shadowed place, he kindles with light, warmth, clutching me tighter, until he's all I know, and I can't hear the siren song anymore.

Stay with me. Stay.

The pain returns as I try to focus, seeking the signal that's always helped me orient in the past, but it feels thready and weak, diluted by my weariness and whatever's gone wrong inside my flesh.

I think, here.

March responds with sure hands, knowing we have to get me out of here, or I'm going to be lost. As the ship shudders, making the leap back, I'm not sure where the frag we are, certainly a first. And my sole satisfaction is that the bounty hunters who hounded us here don't seem to know which *Folly* to follow as our ghosts split in different directions like the scattering of a school of fish.

My hands shake as I unplug, and when I try to open my eyes, it feels like the light is made of knives, stabbing straight in my skull. I touch my face. Find it wet. And my fingers smell of copper. Never known a run this bad.

"Jax . . ." His voice sounds rough, raw. "You're close, aren't you?"

I don't ask what he means. But for a moment, I can't speak, can't do anything but try to stop the steady stream of blood trickling out my nose. Then I hear him moving beside me, and soon there's a cloth in my hands. I wish I could see his face, but I can't bear the brightness in my eyes. At this moment I'm beyond empty, remembering the delicious pull and the way he wrapped around me. Now, I have neither; I'm just Jax, alone inside my head in a way I never have been, and it isn't halfway to enough.

"Maybe," I answer finally, and then try to drive some of the despair out of my tone. "You said it yourself, I'm pretty old. Had a good run."

"Bullshit. I just got used to you."

I want him to lift me up out of this seat, hold me in his lap like he did after the crash. But he's already nursing one helpless infant, so I stand up blind, finding the open doorway with my fingertips. Before heading for my quarters, I offer a bittersweet smile.

"Haven't you figured that out yet, March? Sometimes bad things happen for no reason, and there's nothing you can do about it. How close did I come anyway?"

His muttered curse tells me he hasn't even thought to find out where we are. "Not the best jump," he says, after a moment. "But not terrible. We're about three weeks out."

Eight days then. I added eight days to our trip, but that's what it has to be, because I don't have another jump in me, not for a long fragging time, maybe never. I'll have to assess what I've got left after I rest. The way that I feel, it's just impossible to tell.

"Do we have the supplies to cover the longer haul?"

He sighs, and I hear him tapping away. And then: "Yeah, but after day seventeen we're going to be left eating nothing but paste. Hey," he calls after me. "Have Doc check you out!"

I dismiss that idea with a flick of my fingertips, but as I'm coming out of the cockpit, I collide hard with someone. I feel hands on my upper arms to steady me, but the faint floral scent surprises me; I didn't realize Dina ever smelled so feminine. "Asshole," she gripes. "Watch where you're—oh *shit*, Jax. Are you . . . What happened?"

I just shake my head and brush by because I don't want to talk to her about it. March can tell her anything she needs to know, or anything he feels like she does. Right now, I just want to be left alone.

"No visitors, no exceptions," I tell the room-bot.

"Acknowledged," it chirps.

I don't clean up. Though I'm probably a mess with all the dried blood, I just don't care, need to crash out on my bunk and close my eyes. Darkness falls fast—this sleep feels heavy and inevitable as my own death.

Yes, I must be dying because I hear Kai's voice . . .

"Ground control, this is the Sargasso. *I'd like you to double-check the suggested trajectory and coordinates. Our readings don't agree. That's going to put us on the ground about one hundred klicks from the landing site and—"*

A hiss from the comm system, then an irritated male voice says, "The information you received is correct, Sargasso. *Follow procedure. Control out."*

We exchange a look, frowning. Although we're not jacked in anymore, we share the feeling that something's wrong. I've had that sense since we left Soltai Station, and now that we're making our approach to Matins IV, the bad mojo doubles. Waiting for clearance in this giant bolt bucket, so different from the fast, elegant ships we usually take out with a minimal four-man crew, we do our own math and come up with coordinates that differ dramatically from what the Corp landing authority has provided.

When I nod in encouragement, Kai presses the call button again. "Ground control, this trajectory is not going to create sufficient drag for a vessel of this size. What you've given us is a crash waiting to happen."

There's a long, ominous silence, then: "Sargasso, you have seventy-five VIPs on board. Are you refusing to comply?"

Kai looks deeply troubled now, torn between the need to obey the Corp and the fact we're both certain they're on the verge of doing something terrible, either from incompetence or some agenda we can't begin to guess.

"No," he says slowly, "but—"

"This is your third denial of an approved flight plan. We have no choice but to categorize this as a mutiny attempt and respond accordingly."

And then they aren't talking to us anymore. There's only silence, which is worse.

"Going to autopilot," the computer announces with seeming delight. "Override codes accepted. Trajectory and coordinates received."

Oh no. No.

"We can't survive a hit like this—there's no way—" I'm scrambling at the terminal now, trying to restore control on our end.

"Siri, what the fuck're they doing . . . ?"

"Wish I knew, baby."

Dream-Jax hasn't registered the full implication yet, but the rest of me knows what's coming. I want to scream, but this is scripted, so I just watch in puzzlement, part of me still not wanting to believe that the Corp, our benevolent big brother, will let us come to harm, or worse, cause us

harm. Kai, he's terrified, reaching for me as the planet
rushes up to meet us. All around me the world dies.

I wake screaming so my throat is raw, and there's
someone pounding on my door, shouting, "Jax! *Jax!* Captain's override, dammit, let me in!"

It's all coming back to me. Unit Psych Newel whispering through my dream therapy, "You wouldn't accept the Corp flight plan, would you, Jax? You used your own calculations. Just say it. Say it, Jax, and this will all be over. Say it, and I'll make everything all right."

Unlike so many other induced nightmares, this one carries a ring of truth. I know what they did to me, now—I just don't know why. As I'm lying there, bathed in icy sweat, I hear March swearing, muffled murmurs of conversation:

". . . been almost three days," Dina's voice. "I thought she was dead." She doesn't sound heartbroken that I'm not, actually.

"Open up, right now," March growls, "or I get the cutting torch."

"No visitors," the room-bot tells him sweetly. "No exceptions."

If I didn't feel like such a pile of shit, I'd find that funny as hell.

CHAPTER 26

So I'm up on Doc's exam table once again.

I'm starving, but he won't let me eat until he's finished with his tests. Not sure what the deal is, I feel fine. What I really want is a big bowl of pasta and a san-shower, not necessarily in that order. But he insists he needs to check me out because it's not normal for someone to sleep for three days without any sign of dehydration.

I try to tell him it's happened before, anytime I have a bad run—my body shuts down like that—but he's not listening. Instead, he's frowning over images of my brain. "That's impossible," he mutters.

Sighing, I ask, "Can I go? Please?"

"Hm? Yes, go ahead. Get something to eat, and drink plenty of fluids."

I take his advice, after cleaning up a bit. The san-shower makes me feel almost human, and a change of clothing always helps. Today, I feel stronger than I have in months, so I dress accordingly: black bodysuit, black boots, and a touch of perfume. As always, my wild hair is hopeless, so I simply scrape it back.

Then I head to the galley, where I intend to eat a big plate of pasta, New Venice style, which means lots of s-cheese and red pepper. I find Loras there, picking at his fruit. Looks like something's bothering him.

"You okay?" I ask the question as I key my request and the kitchen-mate hums as it gets to work.

"I should not burden you with it," he says, after a long moment.

But that's a roundabout way of saying yes, so I spin to look at him. "What's that supposed to mean?"

He shakes his head. "You've been ill."

"Just exhausted, but I'm all right now, so talk to me." The kitchen-mate beeps, letting me know my food's ready, and the doors slide back to reveal a steaming bowl, which I handle carefully as I join Loras at his table.

He watches me with unmistakable intensity, and just as the silence begins to feel uncomfortable, he sighs, and says, "You haven't thought about me at all, have you?" To be honest, I haven't. I'm not even sure what he's getting at. "March told us, Jax. Everyone knows you're getting close to burnout, and if you keep jumping . . ."

It takes me a minute but I make the connection. "Oh shit."

His mouth twists. "Yes, precisely. Is there any chance March was wrong? That you can make the rest of these jumps?"

I wish I knew. Somehow I thought it'd be clear, that I'd be able to pinpoint how many jumps remain to me. I always thought jumpers chose to go out in style instead of the sad impotence of retirement. Now I'm seeing that simply isn't so.

Because even now that I'm rested, I don't know how much I have left in reserve. My next jump could be my last, or I might make twenty more. I'm just not sure, but I am positive I'm not as strong as I used to be. The cruelly candid Jax forces me to acknowledge that March is the majority of the reason I made it last time.

With a soft sigh, I shake my head. "I don't know."

"Do you have any near relatives?"

"Just my parents, but I haven't spoken to them in years." It's one thing to feel resigned to my own death, quite another to know I'm condemning someone else. "I could look into adopting March, though." As the words leave my mouth, I know I've only made things worse.

He stands, slamming his chair back, and I register the glitter in his eyes as anger. "This is just a big joke to you. I wish you'd let me take my chances on Lachion."

There's nothing I can say to that, and so I watch him go. Now I'm the one picking at my food, though I was starving a few minutes before. Knowing I need the energy, I force myself to eat.

"You just never stop making friends, do you?" Dina saunters to the kitchen-mate and makes herself a hot drink.

Guess she ran into Loras.

"Yeah. If it wasn't for you, I'd be the biggest asshole on this ship."

But she just grins as she joins me without waiting for an invitation. "So you're really dying or what?"

"Not if I can figure out a way around it." Saying it aloud cements my resolve. "It'd be different if it was just me, but it isn't. I'd forgotten that."

Dina takes a sip from the gleaming silver mug. "If you were married or life-bonded, your partner would serve as next of kin."

I raise a brow. "Is that a proposal?"

"Mary forefend. I was just giving you the big picture."

As I shove a bunch of noodles in my mouth, something's nagging at me. I chew slowly, thinking it over. "Technically, I think I *am*."

"What?"

"Married."

She pauses, mug in midair. "You heartless slut. Making illegitimate lizard-babies with March and leading him on. He's going to be devastated."

"I think it's more of a frog-baby actually." But I wave away her bullshit, convinced I'm on to something. "Seriously, listen. I got married about ten turns ago. He was Corp, permanently assigned to Soltai Station, which was my home base also, but the way I traveled with Kai, well, it was more than Simon could stand. We separated, Mary, I don't even remember when. But I don't think we ever dissolved the marriage legally. He said something about wanting to keep the higher bennies, and I didn't mind. Kai wasn't the marrying kind."

"You got higher bennies for being married?" Of all things to focus on . . . but she looks pissed off.

"More R&R, family days, that kind of thing."

"What about life-mates? Do they get equal treatment?"

"I don't know," I say in exasperation. "What the hell do you care how the Corp handles same-sex benefits? Are you looking to sign on?"

She sighs, conceding the point. "Fine. So you think your estranged husband could save Loras? Is that it?"

"I'm not sure, but . . . is there something that states Loras must be in physical proximity of his protector at all times?"

"Not that I know of, but I'm not an expert on *shinai*-disposition by any means. So you're thinking—"

"If something happens to me, Simon nominally becomes Loras's protector but would remain unaware of his existence. Until Loras receives his first order from Simon, which will never come, my last order should be binding."

Dina smiles slowly. "That's remarkably clever. Since you told him he's forbidden to do anything but what he wants, if he doesn't want to go looking for Simon—"

"Then he stays on the *Folly* and does whatever he

pleases. In theory that cycle could continue, as long as Loras lives."

"With us, he doesn't need to worry about actual physical protection," she concludes. "That's a tidy solution. Obviously, the *shinai*-bond isn't supposed to function like that, so you'll need to check with Loras to ensure it will suffice, but otherwise, I think you may have found a loophole."

"Would you do me a favor and talk to Loras about it? He's pretty pissed at me."

"Sure."

I feel a little lighter. Even if something horrible happens to me soon, and it most likely will, maybe I won't drag Loras down with me. It's been years since I spoke with Simon, but I wouldn't send Loras to him, even if we were on friendly terms. To the best of my recollection, he's a serious, dutiful man, who lives for rules, regulations, and order. I don't know what I was thinking when I married him except that he had a nice ass and gorgeous eyes.

"Dina . . ." I pause, wondering at the wisdom of bringing this up. But she probably still thinks that Edaine knew she was going to die. "If it means anything, Edaine didn't make the choice to leave you. She didn't know it was her last flight until she jacked in."

Her face pales, gray eyes livid. "How do you know that? How can you?"

"You can't *tell* with any precision, Dina. It's a myth, put out by the Corp so jumpers won't be afraid. They started telling us that to keep their shuttles running and their shipments on time. So we go on believing we'll know our last flight before we get to it, believing we'll have a choice between burnout and retirement. But that's just not the case. Maybe some jumpers figure it out, after a terrible run like I just had. Then they have the choice of never jacking in again, but I don't. Not unless we want to spend our lives on Hon-Durren's Kingdom."

"All this time," she says, studying her hands, "I thought she just didn't have the balls to say good-bye. I thought she was trying to be brave, keeping it to herself. After everything, all we were to each other—"

"I know that's not the case. She must have felt terrible regret when she realized she'd never see you again."

Her eyes shine too bright, and I make an abortive move to comfort her, at which she jackknifes to her feet. "Touch me, and I kill you." And she bolts from the galley, leaving me to deal with her dirty mug.

Sighing, I finish my pasta.

CHAPTER 27

We're sick of the ship and sick of each other.

A three-week haul is just too long at close quarters. No-body's mood improves when the kitchen-mate runs dry, and we're left sucking supper out of a packet. At first, Doc tries to keep everyone polite and social, but after the millionth game of mah-jongg, I'm done. I've spent the last four days in my quarters, reading Mair's files on the other nine planets. I don't know if I'll live to see them, but it can't hurt to be prepared. And PA-245 is better company than most of my shipmates.

But I don't know whether to be worried or relieved when March broadcasts on the comm, "We have visual on Hon-Durren's Kingdom, docking in less than an hour."

"If they don't shoot us down first," I mutter.

"Are you presently in physical danger?" the little machine inquires.

"I'm not sure. Hard to know what to expect of Hon-Durren, he embellishes his own legend so much." Don't ask me why I'm answering; we've been having conversations like this for the last four days. "Listen, I've got to go, 245."

I close the sphere with this weird feeling of regret. Know that sounds stupid and maybe a bit nuts, but I *like* my PA. And that's not typical for me. I despise most AIs, who seem to be coded to maximize the annoyance they can cause.

Since I'm not sure what the near future holds, I don a gauzy red shirt, yes, the color of blood and mourning— both seem apropos under the circumstances—and a pair of s-leather trousers. You never know what climate control will be like on these old stations, so I add a matching black jacket and stuff the PA into my pocket on impulse.

Then I tug on my boots. The wardrober on Lachion got them just right, so there's room for me to conceal a blade there, if only I had one. That might just get us in trouble, though. Do wish I had some jewelry, since throw-backs like Hon-Durren respect lavish ornamentation. As I don't, I improvise with perfume.

To my surprise, the ship's already empty when I emerge from quarters. At first, I'm more than a little pissed, but that's the nav-star coming out. I'm not a celebrity, not even in an artificial, Corp-crafted world, and since this isn't a jump, they're capable of handling the situation. Now I have some distance from the old Jax, I can admit March was right. Thought I was special because I possessed some pull in the Corp, because I tagged some new beacons, encoun-tered a few new races, and didn't die of stupidity.

But when you come right down to it, that's a shitty rea-son for thinking you're somebody. The J-gene isn't some-thing I accomplished on my own. It was a genetic lottery, which I won, then spent almost fifteen turns acting like it was entitlement.

No wonder most of them hated me when I first came on board. In retrospect, I don't see much I like, either. And it finally occurs to me . . . maybe they didn't disembark so much as were taken, in which case, they may be relying on me for help.

Shit. Subtlety is not my strength, and I can almost hear March chuckling over the understatement. So what am I supposed to do?

Thinking about it yields no ready solution, but I'd rather die than sit another minute on this ship. So that decides it. I press the panel, and the boarding ramp lowers with a whir that sounds louder in the empty bay. As I step off, I realize I don't have a remote keyed to the ship, so I'm stuck here until I find the others.

It's cold, as docks tend to be, just a few meters of metal separating space and me. *Definitely not a high-tech place.* I see no bots performing maintenance, though there are a couple other ships nearby, and all of them look worse than the *Folly*. There's only one door, so I head toward it. Perhaps I should be nervous; the place seems to be deserted—

An antiquated speaker crackles, and a deep male voice asks, "Who're you then, pretty?"

It's been a long damn time since I heard anything like that. Even before Matins IV, I was never apt to win any beauty pageants. And I guess my unseen interrogator's waiting for a response, but I don't see how I'm supposed to reply.

Then I hear March in the background, muffled but distinct: "She's with us."

The leprous metal door clangs open, and I'm permitted to enter Hon-Durren's Kingdom. The view is decidedly industrial, derelict mining trolls and scavenged parts spread like mechanical intestines along the walls. I proceed with caution and come down a long, dim corridor into a larger space.

Wish I'd seen the place before we docked; now I'm wondering about the design of the station itself. Three more corridors adjoin from here, north, east, and west. I think this must've been the docking authority, where spacers paid for

their bay and use of other facilities. Now it's just empty but
for a couple of closed-up windows that seem to bear out my
theory.

"Come west, Jax." That's Doc, being helpful.

If it were anyone else, I'd probably turn east, but I trust
Saul as much as I trust anyone. And then I start to hear
voices, so I follow the hallway until I emerge in what has to
be Hon's "throne room," hung with war trophies and con-
traband weapons. My shipmates stand in a semicircle, as if
awaiting judgment. In the far corner, there are tables and
benches occupied by a scruffy lot of the usual suspects, but
the larger space remains devoted to an elevated pilot's
chair, festooned with coiled wire and chains.

Mother Mary of Anabolic Grace, is that him?

If people are talking to me, I don't hear it, just gazing at
the man sprawled on the makeshift dais. Damn, he's . . .
delicious: at least two meters tall, muscular, skin so dark it
almost gleams blue, and long, wild braids trinketed with
platinum and diamond glints. Just looking at him, I want to
say he deserves every bit of his roguish reputation.

And please, can I be plunder?

Probably accustomed to this reaction, Hon gives me a
slow grin, revealing white teeth, except for the front two,
which appear to be solid gold. His voice is low and rich,
lightly accented with a Darengo drawl unless I miss my
guess. "Seem you keepin' better company, March. Maybe I
don't kill you after all."

At this point I notice the tension in this tableau. "Was
that an option? If I get a vote, I'm going to say you don't."

"Jax . . ." March casts me a dark look. Maybe he thinks
I'm going to frag things up, but it doesn't look like I can
make it worse. He cups a hand protectively over baby-Z,
and I wonder if that topic's been bridged yet.

"You got some stones, bwoy, askin' me for a favor."

Oh, that's interesting. March never did tell me what history he had with Hon. Looks like I'm about to find out, and

as I'm waiting, it occurs to me that the other three are pretty quiet. Especially Dina—if she's locked down her mouth, then we're in serious shit, aren't we?

Beside me, March nods almost imperceptibly. "I know we didn't part on the best terms after the Nicuan conflict," he says, "but this is actually a humanitarian mission."

What a great laugh, deep, ringing, and infectious. I fight an answering chuckle even though I don't know what's going on. "Not on the best terms—you funny, March. First you stole my woman, then my ship, left me to die on that Mary-forsaken rock. But you make me curious, so I'll give you a minute before I kill you. Tell me your story."

March seems stuck, though. His body language tells me he's at a loss, so I step into the breach. If there's one thing I know how to do, it's run my mouth.

"I'm sorry I missed the introductions." I step forward and offer my best smile. "But I'm Sirantha Jax. And we've come looking for Canton Farr. Do you know him?"

He's already nodding. "My library man, yah. What you want him for?"

"During our travels, we found this little guy."

Against March's muted protest, I give Hon a glimpse of the docile amphibian curled against his chest. Z raises his head and peers around with protuberant eyes. Yeah, he's definitely grown a bit, and he's taking an interest in his environment.

"Grrrr-upp," Z says, from deep in his throat.

We've managed to surprise the big man. "What the hell is that?"

"He's a hatchling," Doc volunteers. "And Canton Farr is an expert on the Mareq. So if we have any hope of raising this fellow, it's imperative we confer with him."

Folding his arms, Hon studies the lot of us, as if wondering whether this is the whole story. Of course it isn't, but I know they don't want me blabbing anything else.

"Well, I make no cred killin' babies," he says finally. "But I give you access to Farr, you gift me someting back, yah?"

"What do you have in mind?" March asks, closing his shirt over baby-Z, who doesn't go quietly, and his burgeoning paternal instinct strikes me as pretty damn funny.

Hon glances between Dina and me. I suppose we do make a nice visual contrast—I'm dark where she's fair, and she's thick where I'm thin. "Oh . . . I think we can work something out."

I'm afraid to look at Dina.

CHAPTER 28

Instead of executing the lot of us, Hon throws a party.

I think it's a display of power more than true hospitality. Everything in his demeanor says—*You are subject to my will, and I choose to be merciful, remember this.* Or maybe he'll just seize any excuse to celebrate. He really is a throwback, albeit an utterly delicious one.

No chance to talk to anyone else, as the throne room comes alive with lights and music, a thrumming bass-heavy beat that sounds tribal, and as the rovers get to their feet to form a stomping, spinning circle of dancers, I notice almost no women, and his interest in Dina and me becomes less flattering and more alarming.

But I can't worry about that right now. They're laying the tables with fresh food, and it smells fantastic. My mouth waters at the prospect of eating something that doesn't need to be sucked out of a packet. They offer fresh fruit and vegetables, so there must be a hydroponics garden somewhere on station. Next they serve meat in sauce, which means it's likely synth-protein in disguise. For the perfect finish, add steaming baskets of bread with peppered oil for dipping. And let's not forget the sweet, cold Parnassian red.

Yeah, I'm going to be here awhile.

I lose sight of how many times my cup's refilled, but it doesn't seem to matter. Everything loses its immediacy, gaining a pleasant veil, where the most important thing I need to do is shrug out of my jacket and join the dancers. Someone takes me by the waist, and I stomp along with him, trying to mimic the side-winding circle we seem to be making. I should really be wearing a big bell skirt for this, more dramatic in the spins.

After a while, I lose track of how many men catch me and spin me toward them. But I definitely notice when Hon steps in. Not seeing him would be like missing a solar eclipse. For a few moments, we simply dance, and I hear Dina saying, from somewhere, "If she wants to shag him, *let* her. I don't want to die for saying no, although if I was going to try a man, it'd be him."

Then he leads me from the revelry, past the pilot's chair toward a sunken area filled with padded couches. He indicates I should sit, and I do, feeling the music pulsing through the soles of my boots. As he drops down beside me, the lights flicker over his skin, painting him in silver streaks and giving his strong features an almost demonic cast. But there's fascination in his darkly glittering eyes; he's everything a civilized woman isn't supposed to want. He might treat her like an empress or a whore as the mood strikes him, but she'd never possess the faintest doubt that he owned her, body and soul.

"Where you get such fine scars, lovely?" His voice rumbles like a purr near my ear, and I glance down in confusion, before realizing the diaphanous fabric of my blouse reveals the old burns along my arms and shoulders.

"Crash landing." That seems like an oversimplification, but I retain just enough presence of mind to be wary.

"Musta been a bad one," he comments, touching my shoulder lightly. It takes a moment, but I realize he's tracing the pattern through my shirt with a fingertip.

I nod. "They don't come any worse."

He regards me a moment, seeming thoughtful. "I think I know who you are now."

Shit. Be cool, Jax.

"Oh?"

"Your bad crash was the *Sargasso*, yah?" Hon doesn't wait for an answer. "So you must be March's jumper."

There's no point in lying; that will just piss him off because he's already sure. "I'm not on good terms with the Corp anymore, though." Like that needs to be said.

He laughs. "We're both kill on sight, I think."

I think I just increased my value to him, although I'm not sure if it's because I have a Corp bounty on my head or because I can jump. Maybe it's a combination of the two. So what now? I can't afford to make him mad, and the wine's starting to wear off.

"Yeah, although I'm sure they've listed me as officially flatline. The bounty hunters they're sending after me are strictly on the slide."

"So tell me, Sirantha Jax, are bad things chasin' you here?"

I jerk my eyes back to his face, but he doesn't seem angry. In fact, if anything, he looks amused. "I don't know. Think we lost them in grimspace, but—"

"Don't worry, pretty. I'll fix it."

Well, I don't have the slightest doubt of that, but I'm not sure his solution will benefit us. I'm frankly astonished that we didn't get blasted before docking, and I have to wonder what March said that garnered safe temporary passage. Knowing March, it may have been something like: *Don't you want to see my face when you kill me?*

"Are all the station's external weapons functional?" Hopefully he won't take that as me probing for information that could be used against him.

Hon gives me an indulgent smile, leaning closer. Damn, he smells good, a spicy, smoky scent that renders him narcotic. "Don't fret 'bout that. Nobody gets in I don't want here, true. Now I'm gone ask you, what you know 'bout my business outside?"

"Nothing, really." And that's the truth; most of what I've heard is speculation. Because who the hell ever gets to meet Hon? If they did, this place would be overrun with women wanting to play pirates with him.

"Me, I got a fleet of ships, and we appropriate goods from the Corp shippin' lanes, keep what we need and sell the rest in the Outskirts." He seems to study me as if waiting for me to ask an obvious question.

So I consider for a moment. "That means you have jumpers. From where?"

In fact, this gets me thinking about Edaine. Where did March find her? The Corp led us to believe we were the only source of trained jumpers. Of course they also had me thinking my shit didn't stink, so maybe I should stop believing *anything* I learned from them. It might make adjustment to the real world easier.

Hon grins, his gold front teeth gleaming. "The Corp's very wasteful. Hide jumpers away, don't even try to fix them. I smuggle them out, two or three at a time."

He must be talking about the broken ones, who suffer bad jumps and can't quite rebound. They wind up nervous, twitching, and heavily medicated in station asylums. And there are others, who possess the J-gene and begin training but lack the mental strength to handle grimspace. They're the saddest of all. But I gather he's making use of these lost souls somehow.

"How can you repair them?"

"My biomechanic. Not much personality after he's through, but my jumpers get the job done."

Part of me feels repulsed. Clearly he's talking about a

mechanical integration that robs them of their humanity, but then again, what sort of life did they have, sedated in the asylums? Is being made useful any worse than remaining lost to horrors nobody else can see? I don't feel qualified to judge.

"That's . . . enterprising," I say at last.

His arm drifts around me, his large hand lighting on my far shoulder. "But you don't wanna talk 'bout that right now."

I'd have to be an idiot not to know where this is heading, but I'm not sure how I should react. How long since Kai died? How soon is too soon? But Hon *is* gorgeous, and if I can procure safe passage with a few nights of sex, why wouldn't I?

"What then?" I let myself lean against him, surprised by his heat and solidity.

"Me, I think you don't wanna talk at all." He runs his hand beneath the weight of my hair, long fingers flexing into my neck, and it feels good.

I find myself tilting my head, though he's applying minimal pressure, and I think that's the point. Another exercise of power—I'm supposed to offer my mouth. *Wonder if he likes to play master/slave girl in the bedroom.* That's not my thing; I don't enjoy submission, but maybe I'll give it a try, this once.

Still, I can't bring myself to close the few centimeters between our lips. It's just not my style, and I enjoy being chased, like it when a man makes an effort. That says I'm worth the trouble to pursue, although it's been a long time. First, I was Simon's wife, then Kai's woman, although my toes curl, remembering the way Kai used to tantalize me.

Hon gives a low, husky laugh, as if he realizes I'm not going to prove an easy conquest. It'll take more than his proximity and the brush of his fingertips on the nape of my neck. And then he whispers, "Oh, I *am* gone enjoy you, pretty."

The flickering lights and the throbbing music only add

to the surreal quality of the moment, as he leans close. So close, I smell the wine on his breath. I can almost taste his kiss, and while I'm not advancing, I don't pull back, either.

I'm actually going to do it.

From a million miles away, I hear someone clearing his throat. "Jax. You're needed on the *Folly*. It's urgent."

Feeling giddy, I turn to see March behind us, and he doesn't look happy.

CHAPTER 29

So far, I don't see any urgency.

Doc has brought Canton Farr back to the ship to show him the formula he used in synthesizing the nutri-gel March has been smearing on his chest for almost a month. I guess Dina and Loras are still on station, enjoying the party. Farr is a thin man with nervous hands, the sort who spills things compulsively, then makes the mess exponentially worse with his apologetic daubing. It's almost impossible to imagine him living rough for years, as he reputedly did during his covert study on Mareq.

"I can't believe you did this," Farr's saying, not for the first time I imagine. "Stole one of the hatchlings. It's abominable."

"You'd prefer we left it to die?" March snaps.

Fortunately, Doc remembers we need this man's help, and adds in appeasement, "Yes, a regrettable necessity, to be sure, but think of the opportunities for study. You'll have a chance to verify all your observations at close range, won't you? I think it should be safe to take samples."

I still don't see why I'm needed here.

Farr brightens. "Well, that's certainly true. You seem to have gotten him—"

"It's a him?" Doc wants to know.

The scientist nods. ". . . past the initial hurdle, which means you're going to see an increase in activity. Typically the offspring stays close to its parent, participating in—"

March seizes my arm then, hauling me out of medical and down toward the hub, but he doesn't stop there, towing me toward the dormitory section like a derelict craft. I scowl up at him, yank out of his grasp, and stand there rubbing my biceps.

"What's the *matter* with you?"

"I need to talk to you privately," he bites out.

Around this point, I notice he's seething. Furious, in fact, although he's done a fair job of reining it back up until now. The door slides shut behind us; this is the first time I've seen his quarters, but they're standard, devoid of personal effects.

I fold my arms. "So talk."

"Are you nuts, Jax? Don't mess with someone like Hon."

Ha, I certainly never imagined he'd care about my virtue. I wave a hand dismissively. "Don't worry, I'm not stringing him along. It won't be a hardship to keep him warm while we're here."

He just gapes at me, like it's impossible for him to imagine someone sleeping with me. I know I don't look as good as I did before the crash, but I'm a rocket in bed. Maybe Hon knows that, so he's not put off the by the scars.

"You can't be serious."

"About what?" I ask, incredulous.

"Sleeping with Hon." His tone suggests I'd be whoring myself out.

"Why?" I start ticking off reasons to do so on my fingers. "He's gorgeous, he smells good, it's been a long time since I had sex, and he might kill us if we piss him off." Yeah, the last reason does sound like pandering, but still, if I want to, and it keeps Hon happy, what's the big deal? "Give me one good reason why I shouldn't."

I can actually see his jaw working, like he's struggling with something, then he growls, "How about this?"

And then he's in my space, body pressed up against mine. He's hard against me, and he cups my cheek in his palm as he lowers his head to claim my mouth with his. Oh Mary, I'd never have guessed March could kiss like this, deep and devouring. I kiss him back, arms up around his neck, biting gently at his lips. He tastes like sweet wine and promises, and his tongue strokes mine in possession, telling me wordlessly why he doesn't want me keeping Hon warm.

I feel his hands on my hips, tugging me closer. He breaks the kiss, leaning his forehead against mine, and I know he can feel how my heart gallops, hear my hitching breath. He probably senses more than that, come to it, my first soft pulses of arousal.

His voice sounds soft now, teasing. "How about it, Jax? Is that a good reason?"

"Maybe," I whisper.

"Maybe? Maybe, she says." But when I tip my head back, I see that he's smiling. "It's been a while for both of us. I don't see any reason for that to continue."

My words come out husky. Unsteady. "I'd just be using you for sex."

His eyes have the power to stop me in my tracks. I've been fighting this for weeks now, refusing to admit it even to myself. How much he draws me.

He gives me a slow smile. "I can live with that."

"Why would I pick you over Hon, though?" Oh, I'm a bitch for teasing him.

And it *is* a tease, because I've been noticing the breadth

of his shoulders and the round curve of his ass for weeks now. But I can tell he doesn't mind by the way he moves me against him, slow drugging circles, hip to hip.

"Remember who you're dealing with, Jax. I know all kinds of things about what you want."

"This is probably a bad idea." Last-ditch effort to turn things aside, even though I don't want to, and March knows it.

He had me as soon as he cupped my hips in his hands and moved me on him, just so. If I'm completely honest with myself, he had me weeks ago, when he promised he'd always come for me. I'm not sure I'm *ready* for this, but damn, do I want him.

"Mmhm." He finds my ear, licks a trail down to the lobe, then bites. "So tell me no, Jax."

Oh Mary, that's good.

"No," I breathe.

"You're saying no?" Now *he's* incredulous.

I give him a slow smile. "I'm refusing to say no."

Then we're a blur of questing hands. I want him naked, right now, although the desire to bare my scarred, skinny self is considerably less. He shakes his head in peeling my trousers down, and I don't need to ask to know that's meant as reassurance. I'd almost forgotten the perfection of sexing your pilot. He's beautiful: brown skin, broad chest, and a tight, etched stomach.

March pushes me back onto his bunk and I run my palms up his chest. I feel the residue from the nutri-gel, and that makes me smile, although it melts into a moan. He's not gentle; he wasn't kidding when he says he knows what I want. I feel his teeth next, almost enough to hurt, and the gush of response makes me draw my knees up, making room for him between them.

"Like that?" he whispers into my skin. "Like that, Jax?" As he trails his fingers down my belly, teasing me because he knows how much I want him to go lower.

"Like that. But more." I buck my hips, and he relents, dipping his fingers into me with a long, languid motion.

Oh Mary, the way he touches me—it's like he knows exactly how—but then he does, doesn't he? I whimper and arch, twisting beneath an intensity I've never known. He strokes me, his lips roving until I can't stand any more.

"Too much?" The bastard, he's taunting me.

"On your back," I manage to order.

It's his turn. Maybe I don't know his hot spots automatically, but I'll figure it out. With a smirk, March rolls over and I run my hands over his body, caressing here and there. Gauging his reaction. Grinning wickedly, I settle astride, my thighs framing his. He shudders beneath me when he feels my slick skin. My weight amplifies the sensation, and I seesaw on him, watching his face.

"Jax . . ." Now he's the one gasping, although it feels fragging amazing to me, too, as I run my hands up his chest. I see the scars I speculated about so long ago, long and livid. Yeah, he's seen combat. The one above his hip looks like they almost got him. That gives me a twinge that I don't like.

"I'm just using you for sex," I remind him, husky and low.

"So use me." His abdominal muscles ripple and go tight as he struggles to hold himself still. "Use me, Jax."

I need no further invitation. Taking him in my palm, I give him a squeeze, which elicits a groan, then I simply hold him steady and sink down. His hands come to my hips, guiding me.

Oh Mary, that's so good.

March doesn't need to be told how I want to ride him. We fill the room with liquid sounds and our labored breathing. Sometimes he moans; sometimes I do. I love the feel of his hands roving my body, demanding and possessive, pulling me down.

I feel the pressure building as I move on him, sweet, delicious heat, then he flicks his fingers down there again.

My whole body locks. He rolls with me then, pushing my legs up.

"My turn," he whispers.

And I don't have the energy to resist as he takes me his way, rotating his hips in slow, steady thrusts. I'm so relaxed that at first I don't register the tingles surging through me. *Again? Really?*

Then I hear March inside my head, just as he's inside my body. *Again, Jax. I'm using you for sex.*

Right now, I feel like that's about the best news I've ever heard.

CHAPTER 30

I sneak out like I'm leaving the scene of a crime.

As I dart into my quarters, part of me feels that I am, actually. I know it doesn't mean anything, and it doesn't touch what I felt for Kai. Because I'm alive, and I'm a biological organism, I know I need to be touched, but that awareness doesn't assuage my guilt. In some ways I think it would've been better if I'd picked Hon for some throwaway sex because I wouldn't have to see him on a daily basis hereafter.

In fact, I'm not entirely sure why March cared whether I slept with Hon. Maybe it's a man thing, which is stupid. It's not like I'm untouched. Between my marriage breaking down and falling in love with Kai, I did my share of fucking around.

But there was no premeditation with Kai; one night we were drinking and dancing, right after we tagged the beacon nearest the Belsev system—and he asked me how come we'd never slept together. He knew most jumpers and pilots do test the waters at least once, so he was wondering if I didn't find him attractive. That certainly wasn't the case; he was adorable, blond boyish good looks.

I didn't have an answer, so after some more drinking, we wound up naked. And it was fantastic. He was fun in bed, playful, but his best quality had to be how he listened. When he propped his chin on his hand and gazed at you with those liquid green eyes, you knew you were the only person in his world right then.

God, I miss him.

He certainly wasn't your typical man. Sometimes I'd try to make him jealous, point out someone I thought was delicious, and he'd give me a deceptively mild smile. "Go ahead," he'd say. "Try someone else if you want. But he won't be me."

No, baby. He'll never be you.

First time we talked about commitment, he said, "I don't believe in that, Siri. People stay true as long as they *want* to, regardless of spoken promises or legally imposed obligations. But we're good together, and I want to be with you as long as you want me back."

I meant to clean up, but instead I drop down on my bunk, startled by the yearning that overtakes me. Who knew sex would make me feel so fragging lonely? There's a dull throb inside me, the ache of long-unused muscles, and I press my knees together, trying to forget what I've just done.

If I let myself, I could cry, but I've done far too much of that in the last few weeks. Instead, I measure my breathing until the urge subsides; and then I do take that shower, washing away the evidence. Maybe this is no revelation, but it feels like one to me; good sex just isn't enough. I won't do that again for a while.

I dress in somber clothing that covers me neck to ankle, permitting no glimpse of skin. Now I'm not sure what to do; I don't want to sleep with Hon anymore, but I imagine he's not a man who handles rejection well, not that he receives much of it. Still, I'm not accomplishing anything cowering in my quarters, so I head out.

Although I know it's beyond idiotic, I can't help skulking, peeking around doorways, then making a dash for the engine room, where I find a spare remote. I pocket that. I'd like to avoid March for the next five to ten turns. Failing that, a day or two will suffice. I retrace my steps, and I'm surprised to find the door out of the docking bay opens for me automatically. I guess it's been coded to recognize me, a measure I didn't expect so quickly, and it makes me wonder what Hon's planning.

To my surprise, the party seems to be over. I would have guessed such things went on all night; shows what I know. There's just a few scruffy spacers left playing Charm, and they peer at me over their cards.

"Looking for the boss?" One of them smirks at me.

Might as well get it over with, right? So I nod. "Know where he is?"

"Yeah, he took the blond girl upstairs."

"The one who arrived with us?" I try to conceal my astonishment. There's a development I never saw coming, but then again, something about Hon . . . damn. Though I've made up my mind to stay off men, literally and figuratively, I'm still tempted, remember his smoky-spicy scent.

He nods. "You want us to deal you in?"

"That depends. You playing by Venice Minor rules?"

Dumb question, I know. Men rarely play Charm by Venice Minor rules unless they're competing against women. There's just no motivation to seeing each other naked, except in specialized circles. But I don't have any creds to wager. I bet my accounts have been frozen, and trying to access them would send up a red flag.

The men exchange a look and start laughing, then the spokesman answers, "Well, we *weren't* . . ."

I shake my head. "I'd rather look around. Will restricted areas be inaccessible or clearly marked?"

"Yeah, you won't be able to go anywhere you're not supposed to be. Be careful, though, we don't use the third deck, so no telling what's up there."

Nodding, I follow the corridor leading in the opposite direction. His mention of a third deck gives me a sense of the station's design, however, and I envision the slow revolution of each tier, creating gravity that keeps my feet on the floor. To my surprise, a large space past the throne room appears to be a library. Hon even possesses some ancient ink-and-paper books, though those are housed within a protective case.

"Find what you're looking for?" I spin to see Dina standing in the doorway. She doesn't *look* like she's been ravished, though.

I spare a moment to give thanks that she didn't see me slipping out of March's room. Mary knows, I'd never live that down. "I don't know what that'd be."

She offers a faint smile. "Nobody ever does until it's gone, then they realize they had it all along."

Depressing but insightful.

"The rovers told me you went upstairs with Hon." A nice, noncommittal statement, and yeah, okay, I'm dying to know but I won't *ask*. That would be rude. Wouldn't it?

At that she laughs. "Yeah, there's a bazaar on the second deck. I'll be heading back later with some trade goods so we can restock the kitchen-mate. The 'kingdom' runs primarily on barter." She lifts a brow. "You didn't think—"

"Of course not," I say quickly. "But . . . well, he *does* smell good . . ."

Dina rolls her eyes. "Male pheromones don't work on me. Now if he sprayed himself with bitch-in-heat, he might get somewhere."

Pheromones? Was that the smoky-spicy scent? Here I thought it was Hon himself who put me in the mood . . . and then I wound up on top of March—*ah, shit.* I want to cringe, but I refuse to give Dina any ammunition. Since I told her about Edaine, there's been a sense of amnesty between us, but I won't tempt her to break the cease-fire.

"Right. Guess I'll go check out the bazaar. Which way?"

"Follow the hall left, first right, down at the end is the lift. It's a bit temperamental, though." As I head out, she adds, "Be careful, Jax. Hon's being too cooperative, and men like him aren't prone to forgiveness. I feel like we're sitting in the eye of the storm."

I flash a half smile over my shoulder. "How's that different from any other day?" Then it occurs to me, she may be able to answer the question that's been bugging me since we docked, so I turn around. "What's the deal with March and Hon anyway?"

She shrugs. "I've been part of his crew maybe five turns now. He hired us out of Gehenna, right out from under another captain."

When she says "us," she must be talking about Edaine and the other pilot, which means March stopped flying quite some time ago. I wonder why that is, not that I'll inquire, seeing as I'll be avoiding him for the next month or so, at least. Now that I glimpse the big picture, Dina's been through a hell of a lot.

"Made a better offer?" I ask.

"We thought so, a cut of every job, not just flat wages. Anyway, maybe Loras knows; he's been with him the longest. Or you could try asking March."

I snort. "Yeah . . . 'Cause he's so forthcoming."

"Ask Hon. I bet he'd tell you." Dina smirks, sauntering down the hall toward me.

"I think you may be right. And that worries me."

"Me being right or Hon being willing to answer your questions?"

Pausing, I try to put my finger on what's bothering me. "Both?" I flinch when she slams her fist into my shoulder, playfully. This woman could kick my ass one-handed. "No . . . Hon, I think. His attitude strikes me as wrong somehow. You're right; he's too accommodating."

She sighs, plainly agreeing with me. And that's a first. "Well, you know what they say, sweetness. When you get a bad feeling, collect your creds and jump."

I nod. "Yeah, we need to get out of here as soon as possible."

But as Hon comes down the hall toward me, smiling like he's won a raffle, I think that may prove easier said than done.

CHAPTER 31

I am toured out.

Hon has shown me around, although I haven't seen his suite, and I thought that would be our first stop. Maybe I just overestimated his interest? Mary knows, it's not like I'm irresistible, but the juxtaposition bothers me. He's gone from amorous, aspiring lover to gracious guide in three hours, and that's just . . . not right.

Anyway, the back portions of the first two decks are allotted to housing, but I have no idea what an apartment here looks like. So I've duly admired the hydroponics garden, his extensive library, which he's had Canton Farr cataloging for the last two turns, and of course, the oddly intriguing bazaar, where permanent residents trade among themselves. Raiders have to do *something* when they're not raiding.

I particularly like the artists' section of the promenade. It's a touch of elegance I hadn't expected in such a place, but I suppose it's human nature to want to adorn one's living space, and when you're isolated, your best recourse is to tap your own creativity. So I commend the bold paintings and metal sculptures and various oddments.

There's even a dark-skinned woman, shaven completely bald, demonstrating the ancient art of the glass-dancer. Her movements flow smooth as the delicate treasures she creates from base chemicals, a sensual symbiosis of form and function. As I watch her, I think this ritual surely harks back to our Lady of Anabolic Grace, whose very name symbolizes the sanctity of change.

"Who is she?" I ask, admiring her.

"A priestess," Hon tells me, and leads me on.

Somehow I'm not surprised, and I cast a look over my shoulder. The artist dances, oblivious to onlookers, and I know I have never passed closer to Mary's grace than this moment. Of course there are more mundane vendors, selling refurbished droids, PAs, used clothing, footwear, hacking codes, weapons, oh, yeah, *lots* of those. There's a whole aisle of stalls devoted to them: shocksticks, blades, sappers, you name it, you can find it here, but the trick is finding something the seller wants in exchange because in Hon-Durren's Kingdom, they don't deal in creds. If this lay beneath an open sky, it would remind me of the starport market at Gehenna.

We stop last at the food stalls, just a couple really, people offering fresh fruit and vegetables, bread and wine. I don't know what they want in exchange, but when Hon stops by, they offer food and libation freely. Well, he *is* the king, after all.

I take a sip, more Parnassian red. Good stuff, but I don't let it go to my head this time. He still smells wonderful, but now that I know it's a chemical effect, I find him easier to resist. Plus, I've gotten laid recently, which doesn't hurt.

"So what happened between you and March anyway?" Dina said he'll answer me. Maybe he will.

He shrugs. "A woman, years ago, she chose him over me."

"Why in Mary's name would she do that?" I blurt the question before I stop to think about it, but fortunately he's flattered, giving me the wide, white smile that shines with gold. I mean, comparing the two, there's no contest, because Hon is gorgeous.

"Don't know, don't care. That was a long time ago." Now why doesn't that ring true? Dina's right, men like Hon don't forgive and forget. "Let me show you this, Sirantha Jax . . ."

I follow him, still thinking about why. And then I know. Makes me grin, imagining him using his gifts that way: *My great passions? Why, Somalan ale, antique beaded tapestries, and white-maned Old Terran ponies. Yours, too? How astonishing! It's like we're soul mates . . .*

March, you're such a bastard.

But I'm smiling as I continue Hon's infinite tour.

They've actually created a stable society, although they're short on women. If they got an influx from a failing colony somewhere, they'd soon start filling up all the empty places on station. I wonder what kind of future Hon sees for his people, and yes, although we mock him quietly for his ego, he's carved out a small place in the universe that's unquestionably his own, not an easy undertaking. And it doesn't lessen the achievement that his fief is rusted, badly in need of repair, and smells of hydraulic fluid.

"What you think?"

And I'm able to say truthfully, "It's a remarkable accomplishment." But to test my theory regarding his strange shift, I add, "Well, I appreciate your time, but I'd better get back to the ship."

He nods, his dark eyes inscrutable, and that's when I'm sure something's wrong. Because he hasn't asked me what emergency demanded my attention earlier. I feel the weight of his gaze as I make my way to the lift, trying not to break into a dead run while he watches me. I've never been very good at cat and mouse.

As soon as I'm out of sight, I sprint, and by the time I reach the docking bay, I have to press my hand against my side to try to soothe the stitch. I don't need to locate the remote, though. The boarding ramp descends as I approach the *Folly*.

Great, someone's been watching for me.

I'd lay odds as to whom, but I don't have the creds to back up my guess, so I simply dash up the loading ramp, make a hard right, and continue into the hub, where I startle the shit out of everyone but March. His dark eyes look like I've stolen something from him by creeping out as if he's my dirty little secret, but I can't worry about that now.

"Dina, did you get the supplies yet?"

She shakes her head. "Still assembling stuff to trade for the base organic to power the kitchen-mate. It's hard knowing what they're going to want. They don't seem to lack for anything, which is interesting, given their isolation."

"Hon said they make trade runs to other outposts in the Outskirts, in addition to hijacking Corp freighters." How that information helps us, I don't know.

"We have enough nutri-paste to make it to Gehenna," Loras offers. "We can restock there if we must."

Yeah, that's a bright side.

At least Loras isn't mad at me anymore. We're back to the lukewarm efficiency he offers me and everyone else. I wish I had a clue what makes him tick, but there's no time for that, either.

"Wherever we go, we need to get out of here. Like ten minutes ago."

March finally speaks. "What's wrong, Jax?"

I'm going to sound like I'm crazy.

"I . . . don't know," I mutter finally. "Something."

"What makes you think that?" There's no hint of the lover who held my hips and kissed me like he'd never tasted anything better in his life. I'm grateful for his discretion; I truly am. He must've written it off, as I have, as an interlude that should never be repeated. So I guess the awkwardness I feared will never emerge since we're pretending it didn't happen.

"Well. Hon's being too cooperative . . . it's like he's stalling us."

March raises a brow. "Anything else?"

"Well. He doesn't want to sleep with me anymore."

Dina can't be expected to pass up an opening like that, and of course, she doesn't. "I'd think you would be used to that by now, Jax."

They think I don't notice when March and Saul trade looks. I know what they're thinking—this is more manifestation of my paranoia. I'm flipping out here, just like I did when I thought March intended to kill me on Marakeq. And it's hard to believe they're entirely wrong. Maybe I have no intuition anymore; maybe I *am* just crazy.

Maybe I belong in that cell where they had me on Perlas.

Once, that would've drawn a look from March, maybe a whisper in my head, but there's only silence now, and that's exactly what I want. Right?

"That's pretty thin evidence," Doc says gently. "Perhaps you need some rest. Regardless, we can't leave right this minute. We need some supplies, and we still need to figure out what kind of gift we're going to offer Hon. He's shown remarkable forbearance in permitting us to consult freely with Canton."

That's just it, exactly. Why would he do that? He hates March; I deduced that much before I knew why. If he's being kind to us, then he's fattening us for the kill. But they don't seem to see it, except possibly Dina, who's lost so much that she probably feels a certain amount of fatal acceptance about such things.

I don't need rest. Mary forefend, it took us three weeks to get here. All I *did* was rest. But I realize there's no way

I'm going to convince them, maybe not until it's too late. Anyhow, I may have screwed us all—Farr emerges from medical, crooning to baby-Z in low croaks. Shit, I didn't know he was still on board.

It feels like every muscle in my body locks with tension, waiting for him to announce his intention to rush to Hon and confide my suspicions. Then again, he's not a stupid man, and if he says that, we won't let him leave. My own thoughts make me dizzy, the way they loop, and I almost decide Doc's right. I'm incapable of thinking in a straight-forward fashion anymore. There are too many monsters in my head.

Into the silence, Farr says, "You're right, and you've got to take me with you. I've been trapped for two turns, and I had all but resigned myself to the fact that I would die here. I didn't think anyone would come looking for me."

"You want to go with us?" March asks, sounding cautious.

"Please. Hon will extend docking privileges to anyone who isn't Corp, but leaving . . . that's the thing. I'm surprised he hasn't filled your ear with talk of eugenesis." Farr shakes his head and strokes baby-Z through the sling he's designed for carrying him. "Give him time. He's especially pleased that you brought a couple of new women."

Dina arches a brow. "Why does that matter, apart from the obvious?"

"New breeding stock," Farr says softly. "They're doing something dreadful up on third deck. I've only been there once, Hon doesn't know I know. I stole the access codes . . ." The scholar shudders. "You'd have to see it, and I'm sure it's worse now."

Our chances of getting off this station without a fight just decreased exponentially.

CHAPTER 32

"No. Absolutely not." I shake my head for emphasis.
We need to leave *now*, not go sneaking around the third
floor. "I'm not going."

March shrugs. "Then I'll go alone."

For this "reconnaissance" mission—although the chances
he'll do no more than fact-find are slim—the choices are an
alien who can't fight, a geneticist who won't fight, a scholar
who would piss his pants in a fight, and Dina, who's in
charge of acquiring supplies. I'm not sure whether she's
planning to trade or steal them now, and I figure that's up to
her. If she can swing it, though, I'd prefer she rips Hon off.

And me. The others have decided to pretend he never
came up with this mad notion, but I just can't. I follow him
to the ramp leading down to the docking bay.

"Why are you so determined to go? It doesn't even
make *sense*."

He pauses then, but doesn't meet my eyes, hands
clenching into fists. "Call it atonement, but I can't walk

away from people who need my help. I can't risk letting the monster loose again, so I have to be better, stronger, more . . . everything than anyone else. See, I don't get to be a callous son of bitch because I perfected it. I don't ask you to understand or to risk your life over this, so stay here. It's fine. If I'm not back in two hours, get the fuck off station. The AI can handle it."

Though it's a bad idea on a thousand levels, I want to touch him. Brush the dark hair out of his eyes and lean my forehead against his chin. We're both so fucking broken that I understand our strange attraction, a push-pull magnetism born of similar scars.

It's a foregone conclusion that I wind up heading back with March. I can't let him die alone, the unsung hero. I don't know what he thinks he can do up there, but I've got his back regardless.

I can't help wondering about the broken jumpers Hon admitted to kidnapping. Who else has he taken and why? I feel the pinch of an awakening conscience. Sometimes it's a pain in the ass traveling with a bona fide hero, not that I'd have thought to use that sobriquet on March a short time ago. But it applies.

I wonder if he's going to bring up the way I left and brace myself for awkwardness. He's quiet as we make our way back on station. Wish Canton Farr had been able to tell us more about security, but he spent most of his time in the library, trying to look harmless. So most likely, they're tracking our movements via that door. But there's nothing we can do; it's the only way into Hon's Kingdom.

"He told me enough about his operations that I don't think he intends to let me leave," I volunteer.

"Just figuring that out, Jax?" His tone sounds like nothing, though, no mockery, no teasing, and there's an astonishing coldness in his neutrality. "I told you not to mess with him. I've known the man a long time."

My mouth quirks in what can't rightly be called a smile. "I never claimed my brain is my strong point, apart from the J-gene."

I offer the opening, so I expect a standard March slam, but instead he falls silent. We pass through the throne room, eerily empty, even though I know it's the middle of the sleep cycle. I feel like a little kid sneaking to the kitchen after hours to pinch some cookies, but we'll get a lot worse than a warm bum if we're caught.

As we reach the library, he says, "Go on. Test the codes Farr gave us and see if you can use them to access complete schematics for the station."

When I do, the archives immediately unlock and the sys-term says, "Welcome back, Canton Farr."

It takes a moment, but I'm able to find the original layout and design. Without looking at March, I activate PA-245 and invite it to translate the data to its data banks via scan. The slim beam flickers over the screen as I pull each one up. I also snitch info about DuPont Station's initial weapon systems to give us an idea what might be shooting at us when we make a run for it.

"Compile the separate images into a single three-dimensional map, please."

"Certainly, Sirantha Jax."

That tears it. We *have* to take Farr with us, as it's inevitable this terminal will show what records he accessed recently. A man like Hon will place only one interpretation on such research—the correct one—and take steps accordingly.

PA-245 presents me a nice map of the facility, and I study it for a moment. March seems uncharacteristically passive, or maybe he's just distracted. Eventually, he comes over, peering at the clamshell terminal before saying, "The lift isn't the only way up there. We should access the maintenance shafts via the ventilation ducts."

I'd like to protest. Crawling about in dark, dusty ducts isn't something I want to do, but going straight to the third deck in plain sight seems too foolhardy, even for me. There's direct access to the maintenance tunnels, of course, but we don't have door codes. We're not authorized repair personnel. If we knew where they lived, March might be able to get the codes as he'd done on Perlas, but that just increases our risk of discovery for no guaranteed gain.

Sighing, I nod and indicate a spot on the display. "We can access it through a panel here."

"Let's go. With luck, Dina will have supplies on board by the time we finish up."

I follow him, and we retrace our steps, where I half expect to find Hon sprawled on his barbwire throne. But the room's still empty, and March leads the way over to the far wall, behind the table where the rovers were playing Charm, and drops to one knee. He tinkers with the catch, and it snaps open.

"Ladies first," he tells me, polite as a banker.

Yeah, sleeping with him was definitely a mistake. I miss him giving me shit, even the way we bickered. Now there's just this silence in which everything dies. But I know what's expected of me, so I crawl into the vent, where it is, not surprisingly, dark and dusty. My PA gives off a faint glow, enough for me to read the map and orient myself. Thank Mary, it's not dark enough to trigger a flashback.

"I guess we might as well get going. We have a lot of crawling to do before we reach the maintenance shafts."

That turns out to be an understatement. My knees are sore and my shoulders aching by the time we reach the hatch where we'll emerge in the tunnels. The station's riddled with them like honeycomb, permitting repairs to otherwise-impossible-to-reach pylons. I wonder how long it's been since anyone ran a safety check, though.

We're making for a ladder that will take us to the third deck maintenance tunnels. From there we'll backtrack to the vents and come out . . . who knows where? Or what we'll find. This time, March takes the lead, scanning side to side like he thinks there might be mines. Can he find or disarm them if there are?

"Yes," he answers without looking at me. "Stay behind me, at least three meters."

"You really think they'd do that? Don't repairmen come in here?"

He spares me a single glance. "I think we're somewhere we're not supposed to be, Jax. There may be security measures in place that we're supposed to know how to circumvent. And I prefer to be a bit careful. Now get *behind* me."

Bitching beneath my breath, I fall in, six paces back like a good, submissive Somalan wife. Part of me thinks he's enjoying this, and I feel cheated. I composed a speech mentally, dammit. I was going to tell him it was fantastic, but that it couldn't be repeated. March couldn't make it clearer that he doesn't want to talk about it, though. Shit, maybe if I brought it up, he'd read me my own speech. I scowl at his back, disgruntled.

March kneels then, running his fingertips over the welded metal seam between wall and floor, then higher. A red light higher up the wall flares in the gloom, then winks out. I tense, waiting for something worse, but March rises and wipes his hands on his thighs.

"A series of pressure plates all the way down," he says. "If they're triggered without someone inputting the disarming sequence . . ." Well, he doesn't really need to articulate it. "Interesting thing is, I don't think Hon installed them. This technology is older than that, more integral to the station."

I can't imagine how long it took to build this place; it's a relic, older than any other outpost in the Outskirts. But I'm not sure what this information means. "This was a Corp station, wasn't it? Before they decommed it and removed the last personnel when the star routes changed."

March nods, and I think I see the flicker of a smile, although it's pretty dim. "So what does that mean, Jax?"

"Oh no." I shake my head. "You're not going to get me to entertain you with another conspiracy rant. Don't think I didn't see how you and Doc looked at each other over my head on the *Folly*. Fragging patronizing, the lot of you, and I turned out to be right, even if I sounded crazy! You owe me an apology."

"Maybe," he says quietly. "But you're not getting it right at this moment. Let's go play hero."

"Can't we play master and slave girl instead?" It's a joke, but I flinch as the words come out. Mary, do I have a big mouth.

I can feel the heat of his eyes. "I don't think so. Come on."

As I start up the ladder behind him, I don't think I've ever felt like such an asshole.

CHAPTER 33

I know something's wrong the minute we crawl out of the vent.

The rest of the station looks like a pawnshop off Gehenna's pusher promenade, but the *third* deck, which everyone but Farr has been so careful to tell us isn't in use, well, it's like the disparity between the outside of the *Folly* and the gleaming well-kept interior. This level shines. Everything looks brand-new; it's a secure lab, and we've emerged in the middle of a hallway.

It's almost too bright after the gloom in the ducts. I've probably got something weird growing in my lungs now from breathing that air, some parasite that will eventually kill me, but what the hell, it was for a good cause, right? I wish I believed that.

Really, I'm testing March with these thoughts now and then. Waiting for his sarcasm, waiting for him to bitch at me and tell me I'm depressing. Something. *Anything.* But either he's not listening, or I just don't have the power to provoke him anymore. Why the hell does that *bother* me?

"Because you're fragging nuts, Jax." He gives me a ghost of a smile as he says it. "I thought you wanted me to stay out of your head."

"Since when does what I want matter? If the universe gave a shit about *that*, I'd be sitting in a café on Venice Minor, sucking on some choclaste nosh and admiring the working boys."

I take a minute to imagine that. *Mmm.* Given the choice, I prefer the slim, pretty ones, golden skinned, without a lot of body hair.

"You're truly an enlightened soul, aren't you?" March shakes his head, setting off toward a set of double doors at the end of the hall. The red lights that encircle it serve as an effective warning as far as I'm concerned, but March won't be deterred. "Come on."

Neither of us doubts Very Bad Things lie beyond this door, but there's a meter of solid titanium between us and . . . whatever. Mind, I'd be happy to turn around right now, but I know March. We're not leaving until he's seen this thing through.

"Whenever I follow you, we wind up in trouble," I point out.

"How is that different from what happens when you lead?"

I sigh. "All right, genius, how do we get in? There are no guards for you to—"

"Let me handle that." He withdraws a slim rectangle from his pocket, and I recognize it as a codebreaker, definitely black-market ware.

Slender silver filaments snake out from the device, gliding beneath the edges of the keypad to connect. I expect more animation, but it goes to work silently, and as it runs through numeric possibilities, the lights snap off around the door one by one. When all ten bulbs go dim, the door swishes open, leaving us looking into yet another hallway. I don't bother checking my PA; the map of the third deck is outdated, more than the other levels. According to those records, we're standing in an infirmary.

"This is really dumb," I mutter, as March sets off.

Presently we come to another security door, where he repeats the procedure. "I hope there aren't many more of these. This thing only has one charge left."

That much I knew. Like most black-market wares, codebreakers are crafted with a finite number of uses, then they break down to base chemicals, leaving no hint as to their purpose. Maybe a really good chemist, analyzing the residue, would be able to posit a guess, but there's still no *proof*, and for most criminals, that's the important thing. For obvious reasons, possession of them is outlawed on every Corp world, and as far as I know, they can only be purchased on Gehenna.

We hurry onward, trying to be quiet, although skulking in a bright corridor with no cover looks even sillier than it sounds. As we pause at the next—and hopefully last—set of doors, I say, "One of these days you're going to stop surprising me."

He gives me a saturnine smile. "And when that day comes, Jax, I'll miss you."

Bastard. But I don't mean it. Very few people can keep up with me verbally, and I wouldn't trade March for someone nice. Well, I don't mean that like it sounds. March is a good man, just not a nice one. Does that even make sense?

While I'm pondering, he gets to work, and the door whispers open. Even before I step around the corner to see, my skin prickles with wrongness. Yes, this is the place Farr warned us about, where they're doing dreadful things. I step into the room without waiting for March, scarcely able to take it in.

At first glance it looks like a med ward or possibly a morgue, so many rows of bodies, lying pale and quiet. The only sound besides our breathing comes from the low hum of the machines keeping them alive. And that's not even the worst part.

"Mother Mary," March breathes, coming to stand beside me. "They're—"

"Helping populate the station," a voice says from behind us. "We're growing only girl children right now. There are so many men waiting."

Shit. We've been had.

I turn to find Farr leveling a disruptor on us. Either one of us makes a sudden move, our molecules are going to find themselves painfully rearranged. And that's really not good for breathing and circulation.

"Canton," I drawl. "What an unexpected pleasure. Decided you don't want a ride off station anymore?"

As if he ever did. The last piece of the puzzle falls into place. Hon doesn't possess the scientific expertise to execute this plan by himself. My stomach roils, seeing how they're using these poor women as nothing but wombs. I'm afraid to speculate just how insemination takes place.

"Yes, I was rather proud of that performance. I had to think fast. But why would I? I can't study in the field anymore . . . my lungs were damaged on Marakeq, and I have a sweet setup here. Hon trusts me to take care of business, I'm his right-hand man."

"Where did you find all these women?" March asks. His hands furl into fists at his sides, and it doesn't take a specialist to read his body language.

"Med wards mostly, sometimes Psych. You'd be surprised how many throwaways there are, forgotten by friends and family." Farr shakes his head in what appears to be sincere regret, and I have to conclude he's just about the craziest bastard I ever met. He thinks it's too bad these poor women wound up like that but doesn't see anything wrong with *this*? "Don't worry," he adds, seeming to misread my look. "We test for genetic anomalies, and I'm keeping careful record so we don't wind up in-breeding."

"Thank Mary for that," I mumble, but Farr is immune to sarcasm. "You're behind the biomechanical work on Hon's jumpers, too, aren't you?"

He smiles, like we're having a friendly conversation, and if it weren't for the weapon in his hands, I might even believe it. "Yes, they're kept in a separate area, as it's a different project. Our goal is complete self-sufficiency, a settlement free of Corp influence, free from artificial cred-based commerce."

"What happens if one of these women wakes up?" March edges closer to the scientist by millimeters.

"Oh, they never do," Farr answers, and I can picture him smiling as he slides the spike behind their eyes, crooning, *This is for the best.* "And no one ever leaves Hon-Durren's Kingdom. Afraid there's no place for you here, March. Hon simply doesn't like you. We're keeping the women. Jax, after reviewing your Corp record, I don't trust you to be docile on your own, and you appear resistant to mental conditioning. The blonde's a mechanic, yes? We can use her expertise. The other two from your crew can join the rovers. I'm sure they'll all adapt . . . and if necessary, I can assist with that."

Shit, why didn't I see it sooner? He's just like the Unit Psych, Newel.

After a brief pause, as if thinking things over, March asks, low, "Will you take care of baby-Z for me, at least?"

No. Oh no. I find myself begging silently, *Don't you dare leave me, March. Don't you dare.* But there's nothing but my own thoughts, nothing to indicate he heard me.

"Of course," Farr says kindly. "I have him right here in fact." With his free hand he opens up his shirt and Z pokes his head out the top.

"Grrr-upp." For some reason, Z only chats if he can see someone to talk to. With his head covered up, he seems to assume nobody's around.

Fantastic. Now we're crippled because we need to be careful with the baby. Just when I don't think the situation can get any worse, March dives for the scientist's legs. Farr's faster than I'd have guessed, though, and he fires— blinding flash, so I hit the deck instinctively.

When my pupils adapt, I see March crumpled at Farr's feet.

CHAPTER 34

I've only got one shot at this.

As Farr levels the disruptor on me, a smug smile build-ing, he says, "You want to join your lover, Jax? Just how deep does that devotion go?"

"Frag you. Where's Hon? Does he know you're doing this?"

His look shifts from self-satisfied to irritated. "Like I told you, he trusts me to take care of business."

"I bet he's going to be pissed that you robbed him of the opportunity to take March one-on-one. How's he supposed to command respect from the rovers if he lets a weakling like you do his dirty work?"

I'm flat on the floor, gazing up at him. If looks could kill, he'd be a sizzling pile of meat, but sadly, he just stands there. I can't look at March again; his left arm's a mangled, bloody mass of displaced molecules. And he's so still. Mary help me, I truly am poison. Part of me wonders whether Simon's still alive, and if so, how he's

escaped the violent death that comes to all men who sleep
with me.

"I'm not a weakling," he responds tightly.

Good, I'm making him mad. That increases the proba-
bility he'll get careless. I'm neither brave nor heroic, but
I'm not dying here. If I can get that disruptor out of his
hands, I'll kick his ass, but I can't underestimate him. He
may be slight, but he's fast, or he wouldn't have been able to
drop March. And he's going to die for that, swear to Mary.

As I'm trying to decide on the best strategy, I see movement, a shadow thrown by someone coming down the hall.
Farr notices my shift of focus, but he thinks he's too smart
to fall for that. "Oh, there's someone behind me, is that it?"

"Actually there is," Loras says, stepping into view.

The scientist spins, and I launch myself at his ankles
and yank. He tumbles back, hits hard, and the disruptor
goes flying. I don't know what the hell Loras is doing here,
but both Farr and I scramble for the weapon. Since he's
about a meter behind me, he gets a kick across the chin as I
roll and come up with it in both hands.

"Let's not be hasty," Farr says, placating. He tries to
smile, and his teeth show smears of blood.

But all I can see is March lying behind him. I fire in reply, a chest shot, and then I stand for a moment just listening to him scream. His heart pulses sickly trying to pump
for a few beats before it bursts, spattering blood all over the
white lab floor. Loras looks like he's going to heave.

"You—"

"Damn right," I snap. "It's us or them. Remind me to
ask you later what you're doing here. For now, we've got to
get the frag out."

"What about them?" He nods toward the pale, gravid
row of women, bound to machines that do their living for
them. "What about their young? What will life be like,
born to serve the raiders?"

"I don't know, but I draw the line at killing unborn babies.

We can't save the world," I tell him wearily. "All we can do is save ourselves. Now let's go."

As we start toward the door, March groans.

"He isn't dead." Loras draws up short. "Help me, Jax. We can't leave him."

I pause, weighing our options. When I hesitate too long, Loras adds, "Jax!" like I've let him down somehow.

"Shit. Okay. *Okay.* I've got his left side."

My whole body cringes as the malformed meat that used to be March's left arm drops round my shoulder. He's so heavy. Between Loras and me, I don't know how the hell we can manage this. Not with all those raiders gunning for us.

But we have to try.

"I came up the lift," Loras says. "Best we go back that way. I don't think we can manage all the crawling."

That's quite an understatement. This way, we increase our risk of discovery, but it can't be helped. We limp along like that old joke, retarded man winning the three-legged race. Loras seems to know when the patrols pass, so we pause around corners and wait, clamping a hand over March's mouth when he moans. Give us away.

My heart sounds like a tribal drum in my ears as we finally hit the lift and—

"Wait, how the hell did you get the codes?"

"I told the guard that Farr wanted me for a special procedure," he answers quietly. "I knew something was wrong when he left. If he truly wanted to accompany us, he should've stayed aboard, fingers crossed for your quick return."

"Shit, that's clever," I say admiringly, as we step out onto the first deck. Now we just need to get to the docking bay. But here's the guard who let Loras go up, likely thinking he'd never come down again.

No hesitation—I fire, another chest shot, but I'm not fast enough to keep him from sounding the alarm before he starts screaming. More blood sprays out, a crimson fan over the guard station. I feel Loras looking at me with abject horror, but we need to keep moving. As the rovers respond to the alert, we're going to face more and more security. Time's the enemy now, along with about two hundred raiders who love nothing better than a fight.

Just need to clear the corridors, the throne room, and the last stretch to the hangar. *Come on, March, we need you awake.* As we take off at gimp speed, my shoulders burn beneath his weight, so I give him a little shake, hoping pain may do the trick.

"Shit," March growls, finally stumbling with some volition. He takes a little of his weight off us. "Where's baby-Z?"

Mary forgive me. I think I killed him. Inexplicably that hurts worse than anything that's happened so far. I feel the hot burn behind my eyes. *Forget Farr, I'm the monster.* But I wasn't thinking of anything but seeing him die.

"No time for that, stay with us. We're almost to the *Folly*. Just a little farther."

We're stumbling now, even with March half-conscious. Past the throne room, we can do this. We're almost there. But neither I nor Loras is particularly strong. Loras is smart, and I'm fast, but that's not helping us now. What I wouldn't give for Doc's burly back. He could probably heft March over his shoulder and go at a dead run. I hear booted feet behind us, and the Klaxons blaring remind me of Perlas Station.

Of course they do, this is a former Corp installation.

And they're going into lockdown.

No. Oh no.

I start to run, seeing the doors in the room that used to be the docking authority closing slowly. We need more speed, and it's all I can do not to shake free of them, sprint for all I'm worth. They're dragging me down, and right now I don't care whether they live or die. I'm not a fragging hero . . . I didn't ask for this, dammit, I shouldn't have to choose.

"Come on, you bastards." I'm sobbing as I try to pull March along, and we make it, bent double, beneath the first set of doors.

But I don't see how we can make the second set across the room. Still, I'm not giving up. I dig my fingers into his mangled forearm and rouse a scream of rage, of pain, but it doesn't have the desired result. Instead of goading him to speed, his knees buckle, and we all go down just before the second door.

I slither beneath on my belly; there's less than a meter of space now. In that moment I'm sure I'm the only one who's going to make it back to the *Folly*, but then I see Loras shoving March toward me. There's a terrible acceptance in his eyes as I reach for March and haul him forward.

"Thank you," Loras whispers, as March's boot clears the gap. "You gave me the power to choose."

The door clangs shut.

I feel tears streaming down my face, hot as blood. Part of me wants to stand here screaming, shoot the door with my disruptor, but I don't know what it does to metal, if anything, and I can't bring myself to waste the chance he's bought us. I refuse to listen to him die.

"Wake up!" I slap March as hard as I can, and he groans, trying to push upright. The bastard seems surprised when his left arm won't hold his weight. "Get your ass up. I am *not* leaving you, not after all this. Come on."

He doesn't even seem to know who the hell I am, but I get him on his feet. Just this last corridor now, and I don't know how the hell we're going to get through the docking bay doors. I doubt they'll open for us anymore, but—

There's a smoking hole where the door used to be, Dina standing there with a smile. "You two done sight—oh shit, is March . . ." She trails off, because obviously he's *not*, and the turrets in the docking bay are coming alive. "Where's Loras?"

I just shake my head, and she gets under his right side. "Head down now, it's going to be a shitty run."

CHAPTER 35

March is never going to be able to fly.

Doc's sedated him since the shock might kill him, and he's tending to the arm as best he can, but we need a real medical facility for proper treatment. He'll wrap it, get him started on a full series of preventives, and that's about all we can do. Saul will need to keep an eye on him, though, so that just leaves Dina and me.

"All right," she says grimly. "One of us needs to man the guns, the other needs to get us out of here. I'm usually in the pit, you ever pilot?"

"Hell no. But I've never been on guns before, either, so get back there. Cripple every ship in this docking bay, then blow the doors wide open. These aren't the only ships on station, but maybe it'll slow them down some."

"Yes, boss." She sprints for the gun pit, and the funny thing is, she didn't sound mocking when she said it.

I get my ass to the cockpit, and as I strap into the pilot's chair, I can't help thinking how wrong it feels. I've never sat over here on the left side, but I think I remember enough of that last time with March. Maybe I can figure this out.

I tap a series of panels from memory and feel vaguely surprised as the *Folly* powers up. It's not that I know what I'm doing, quite the contrary. I'm just seeing in my mind's eye how March does this. So far so good, the panels and switches seem oddly familiar. I remember how I thought, *I could almost fly this ship myself*, during our last jump. I need to stop doing that, because such mental boasts have an uncomfortable way of coming back to bite me in the ass.

This must be vertical movement . . . so this one is horizontal.

As I skate my fingers across the second bar, the vessel jerks hard and slings sideways, careening us into the far wall. *Shit, this thing is really sensitive.* I try to turn it, and it spins back, and soon we're just spinning wildly in the hangar, slamming into the ships Dina is supposed to be shooting. The *Folly* takes damage as we're whirling; I hear the steady barrage of hits along the hull.

"Hold this thing steady, dammit. I got no shot," she growls at me over the comm.

So I stop touching the controls for a minute, and I hear the roar of our turrets firing on the docked ships. Muted explosions tell me she's getting the job done. Now I just need to turn so we can get out of here.

We spin three times before I finally steady the *Folly* long enough for Dina to blow the bay doors, then we're out, although it's not in a graceful swoop like March executes. Instead, I bang around the exit, wincing at the painful sound of metal scraping along metal, but then we depart Hon-Durren's Kingdom. Finally.

With incalculable losses.

The comm crackles, and Dina's voice comes across with a mocking lilt: "Jax, as a pilot, you're a great jumper."

"Yeah, yeah." I flick the switch on her. "Computer, autopilot on, set course for Gehenna, maximum cruising speed."

"Acknowledged," the computer tells me cheerfully. "At our current speed, we will make port in approximately thirty-six standard hours."

"Alert me if there's any sign of pursuit or other problems," I say tiredly, unbuckling from the pilot's chair.

"Acknowledged."

I hope I never have to do this again. March usually stays up here awhile to monitor our course, but I need to check on how he's doing, talk to Doc, then get this blood off me. Rolling my shoulders, I head for medical. Not until this moment did I realize just how sore I am, but I feel like I've been beaten.

When I peek around the door frame, I see that Doc has sprayed March's arm in some liquid skin to keep out bacteria. I've never seen anyone shot by a disruptor before. They never perfected molecular transportation, but naturally, the Corp capitalized on the failed prototypes, turning them into a weapon that turns flesh inside out. Whoever invented that weapon was a sick son of a bitch.

Of course, I've killed with it twice, so what does that make me?

"How's he doing?"

Doc looks up from the life-sign readings with a creased brow. "He's strong, sound constitution, so that'll help. The fact that you got him back alive is pretty impressive."

"It was Loras, not me. He deserves all the credit." For a moment I think I might break down, tears simmering in my eyes. Sometimes you find your heroes in the unlikeliest places. *Wish I'd known him better. Wish—*

So many things.

Doc regards me as if he knows there's something I'm not saying. "March is in a lot of pain, though. Kindest thing we can do is keep him sedated until we reach Gehenna. I have some contacts at a clinic near the starport. They'll help us out without asking any inconvenient questions."

That hurts, too. If I'd done something differently . . . After a moment, I lock everything down, push it back into the compartment where wounded Jax lives. I'm the pragmatic Jax. "You can keep him nourished and hydrated?"

Saul sighs. "That's about all I can do with a wound like this, but yes, I can. What happened, Jax?"

I turn to see Dina standing in the doorway, waiting to hear the answer. Her eyes as she gazes down at March, so pale and still, almost like he's already dead, well, it's the look of someone who thought she'd lost everything, only to find more could still be taken from her. And I feel like I'm the harbinger of it all, although I didn't even want to go up to the lab. That was all March. But it doesn't seem to matter anymore. I was there, wasn't I? And everything I touch goes bad—just like that dead Gunnar said.

Taking a deep breath, I tell them. I don't spare a single detail, and I certainly don't paint myself in a better light. It doesn't matter if they hate me, couldn't be worse than how I hate myself.

But when Dina says softly, "It wasn't your fault, Jax," I almost fall down.

In fact, I have to sit down on one of the stools up against the wall, regarding her with incredulity. "You can't stand me. How can you say that?"

She shrugs. "Yes, you're a bitch for even *thinking* about leaving March behind, but you didn't, did you? It's not your fault he got shot. And it's not your fault that Farr was a crazy fuck. And it's not your fault that March wanted to go see if anyone up there needed help. That's just . . . March. And it *definitely* wasn't your fault that Loras didn't make it. He made a choice, Jax. And you gave him that power. I think when it came down to it, he wanted to die a free man, he wanted it to mean something."

"You spoke to him about my *shinai*-solution, didn't you?"

She nods. "It wouldn't have worked. He was touched you cared enough to put that much thought into it, though. And when he decided to go after you two, Doc and I respected his choice."

Even though we knew something could go wrong. Though I hear the unspoken words, they don't help much.

"She's right, you know." Saul turns from his examination of March's vital signs long enough to give me a solemn nod.

"And nobody who wasn't there can say for sure whether they'd have been thinking about what was under Farr's shirt," Dina continues, like she's determined to make me feel better. "If it was me, seeing my friend on the floor, I'd want the blood of the bastard who killed him, too."

"It is a tragedy that we lost Loras and baby-Z," Doc adds. "Fortunately, I have ten good DNA samples, so it's not a complete loss as far as the project is concerned. I took them when I was sure he was strong enough to bear it, shortly before we reached Hon-Durren's Kingdom."

The project.

Sometimes I think Doc's as crazy as Canton Farr. Maybe all scientists are. They don't care who has to die for them to test a theory. They lose sight of the important things; they spend so much time looking at cells that they forget those units are the building blocks of sentient beings who have thoughts and hopes, dreams and feelings.

Examining the cost objectively, I'm not sure I believe in this project anymore. With the bodies piling up in our wake—Jor, Mair, so many Gunnars, Loras, baby-Z—I don't think I can justify continuing this course. I can't imagine that it's worth it.

So what if the Corp continues to dominate jump-travel, so what if they own all interstellar commerce and travel? They always have—*status quo.*

But before I can tell them that I'm out, I don't want to do this anymore, the computer advises us, "I have detected two ships on intersect course, Sirantha Jax. Since they have powered up their weapon systems, I believe their intentions may be hostile."

And maybe I'm bad juju, dark luck.

CHAPTER 36

Dina scrambles for the gun pit.

I figure if March were awake, he'd be in the cockpit, so that's where I head, even though I know perfectly well we're better off on autopilot. At least the computer will continue to move us in the direction of Gehenna. Based on my performance getting us off station, the same cannot be said of me.

Regardless, as a good proxy, I take my place in the pilot's chair, even though I've got no clue what I'm supposed to do. I peer at various screens and panels until I get visual on the two ships. At this distance I can't tell where they hail from, but I'm willing to bet they've been sent from the kingdom formerly known as DuPont Station.

"Can you take evasive action?" I ask the computer.

"The autopilot is programmed with the standard S-68 dodge and 410 spiral. Please state your preference."

Shit, I have no damn idea.

I tap the comm, hoping she won't laugh at me. "Dina,

what's the difference between the S-68 dodge and a 410 spiral?"

"Huh?"

I get the feeling that encapsulates her knowledge on the subject. "Never mind. All weapons online?"

"Affirmative," she comes back. "We're going to be in range soon. Get the shields up if you haven't already."

Double shit.

"Computer, enable S-68 dodge with autocorrection based on trajectory of incoming enemy fire," I say, hoping that's possible.

Hoping it makes sense and the computer won't argue with me or call me an idiot. I certainly feel like one.

"Acknowledged. At current cruising speed, the pursuing vessels will overtake us in approximately five minutes."

"Shields online, extra power to aft section." That's where Doc and March are, and I don't want a hull breach back there.

The computer objects, "Insufficient energy, Sirantha Jax."

"Reroute power from secondary systems. I want stronger shields aft," I insist.

Maybe that's not the right thing to do, but I'm not trained for this. I'm not a pilot and certainly not one seasoned in space combat. Apart from the time I've been on the *Folly*, I've *never* had ship guns fired at me. I was Corp, for frag's sake—people rolled out the red carpet for Kai and me. How am I supposed to know this shit?

And the computer starts beeping and humming, hopefully doing as I ask. Don't know what I'll do if it doesn't because I'm not March. I can't program this by hand. I just hope my best is good enough up here.

After a moment, it announces, "All shields online, aft operating at one hundred thirty-five percent. Is that satisfactory?"

"We'll see."

That's really all I can do. So I cross my fingers and wait.

I feel the ship shudder as we take the first hit, but the shields seem to hold. And then the *Folly* begins what could only be standard dodge pattern S-68. Maybe the other pilots aren't academy trained so they won't recognize it. It's oddly silent, except for the odd jolt where they score a hit.

The comm crackles: "What the hell are you doing up there, Jax? We're slinging around like an old woman dancing drunk."

"It's called evasive action," I grumble. "Just shut up and shoot."

"I will if I can keep from puking."

But I see on-screen that she's got one of them. I hear nothing, but the ship crumbles into nothingness. It should be more dramatic, perhaps, but these are sleek, fast, one-man ships. Nothing else could've caught us, and they don't quite have the durability they need to take us on. Maybe they thought two-on-one odds would do it, but they didn't take a close look at the way the *Folly* is outfitted, heavy shields, hard-core guns.

And then I feel another hard lurch, just before something explodes somewhere starboard. "Imminent engine failure," the computer tells me helpfully. "Immediate maintenance required. Danger. Primary systems compromised. Immediate—"

I launch myself out of the pilot's chair. *Shit.* This pilot's smarter; he's not attempting to take us out by himself, just trying to cripple us. Leave us dead in space so that a larger vessel can catch up, then tow us wherever they want us.

There's no way I can repair those engines so let's hope I can figure out the guns. I don't know how to transfer controls to the cockpit, so I sprint for the gun pit, where Dina's already unbuckling. "Get your ass in there and take him out," she tells me, running for the engine room.

The ship shudders again, and now the whole area is lit with flashing red light, as if the blaring noise wasn't enough to alert us to the fact we're in trouble. I look at the panel in panic, trying to figure out—

Think I get it.

Inside the pit, I seem to spin as I tap the scope, and damn, Dina's right, this drunken lurch called dodge S-68 that we're running makes it hard as hell to target. But I mash the button, launching a volley toward the lighter ship. It swoops around us with a grace I can't help but envy with the autopilot driving and me on guns. If we make it out of this alive, it'll be a miracle.

I learn to spin the scope counter to our evasive maneuverings, and I can't help but shout when I hit the other ship. Just a glancing shot, didn't do any real damage, but it means I'm getting the hang of this. Maybe I can take him out before he destroys our engines completely.

Two hands on the controls, spin and target, then let it go. *Yes!* I can see he's crippled now, having trouble. There's a distinct dip when he turns portside, so I focus there, continuing to fire. I'm almost surprised when the other vessel seems to crumple, then there's a silent array of sparks. Now he's nothing but salvage.

I'm surprised to find I'm covered in a fine layer of sweat as I pull myself out of the gun pit. I already hurt from lugging March, and now every muscle throbs as if I've taken these guys on in actual physical combat. No wonder Dina's so strong; she fragging has to be.

I stagger out to the hub and don't see anyone. Eventually, I locate Doc in the cockpit, as he took over giving the computer orders when I hit the turrets. We find Dina in the engine room, using mechanic's tools and voodoo magic to keep us moving.

"How bad is it?" I ask, shoving the frizzy hair out of my eyes.

"Bad enough. This is just a workaround; we're not even running on main engines, and with what I had to do, the kitchen-mate isn't going to work, among other things. Enjoy your paste until we get to Gehenna."

If we get to Gehenna.

I'm so fragging tired, I feel like I could sleep for a week. One thing's for sure, though, I need to learn some shit. Because this boast of not knowing anything but grimspace isn't a good thing, and it just may get me killed, sooner rather than later. It's not enough to be a good navigator; I'm not a Corp celebrity anymore. I live in the real world now, like it or not, and that means expanding my repertoire.

I need to learn to pilot in case this happens again. I need to learn guns. I need to learn emergency maintenance. I need to learn—

Shit. I'm too tired to finish the list. But it's really long. Maybe it's to my credit that I've realized as much.

"Is March all right?" I roll my shoulders. *Think I pulled something.*

Doc nods. "I strapped him down before I went to the cockpit, but I should probably go check on him. I'll let you know if there's any change."

The old Jax would've taken his word for that, but instead I follow him to medical because I want to see with my own eyes. March has taken on greater significance than I can parse at the moment. He's like the last hope I have, the last chance to prove I'm not a living, breathing curse.

He's quiet and still, so fragging pale. It hurts me to see him like this, and for a moment my eyes sting because I can't make myself believe he'll ever wake up. I'm glad I don't have to see the mangled meat of his left arm. Doc's got that wrapped, and a steady burst of painkillers keeping March quiet. His vitals do look good, though, from what I know of such things.

I forget Saul's standing there, as I step closer to the table. It seems wrong to leave him strapped, so I start unbuckling him. When I'm done, I adjust the thin synth blanket, tucking it neatly around his waist. What I wouldn't give to have him wake up and tell me what a waste of space I am, chew me out over everything that's gone wrong.

But he's so fragging far away—I can't feel him anymore. Can't help but press my palm to his cheek, feel the too-cool skin, and trace the line of his cheekbone. I've lost so many people. Some I left on purpose and never looked back. Some were taken from me, and I never said good-bye.

March . . . he was supposed to be different, irascible but indestructible. As it turns out, he's flesh and blood like any other man. I drop my hand, nod at Doc, and leave Med Bay without speaking. I'm so tired, all the way down to the bone. The old Jax would've headed to quarters to shower and crash. She would've figured she'd done enough.

So I head for the engine room to begin my crash course in starship repair.

CHAPTER 37

We limp into port at Gehenna, not quite trailing smoke, but it's close.

Dina must've used every trick in the book to keep the *Folly* running. We all know we can't afford another battle or another delay. It may have already been too long for March. I won't speak that fear aloud, though. I put my faith in primitive gods right now, where you can keep the bad magic at bay by refusing to acknowledge it.

They say you never forget your first glimpse of Gehenna. Over the tall buildings the sky swirls with orange and red, true titian, a feature of the unique atmosphere. Of course that same air would kill human beings; hence they built the entire city inside a dome. Eternal sunset, that's why the place is so wild. You know the feeling you get, just before full dark? Sundown makes you feel like the world burgeons with possibility, and that's Gehenna for you.

Like any other romantic notion, it's based on bullshit, of course. Gehenna isn't the land of eternal sunset and infinite potential. The gas in the atmosphere just makes it impossible to see the sun.

The whole place is a rich man's experiment, really. If Venice Minor is famed for luxury and natural beauty, then Gehenna is pure man-made vice. At the open markets near the space port, you can buy anything from exotic weapons to designer drugs to trained slaves. Twinkling marquee advertisements beg for our money and our time. This club boasts "the most beautiful girls in the galaxy" and that one promises "the biggest jackpot ever, you'll break the bank," the one where a pair of enormous luminous dice seem to roll themselves, again and again. It's almost hypnotic.

I'm positive my landing skills aren't up to this challenge. Getting into the port authority requires traversing a complex series of locks; it's a measure that ensures the air inside the dome's not compromised. So when the docking agent contacts us, asking for our itinerary, I answer, "Our pilot is incapacitated, and we're coming in on auto. Can you transmit vectors?"

She sounds irritated that I've disrupted procedure. "*Svetlana's Folly*, is this trip business or pleasure?"

I don't know which this qualifies as, so I reply, "I repeat, our pilot is injured and in need of medical attention. This is an *unscheduled* stop."

That seems to appease her. "I'm sorry to hear that. We can bring you in safely if you accept the override."

Oh Mary, I get a cold chill, just thinking of turning control of the *Folly* over to strangers. For a moment I flash on Matins IV, but then I give myself a mental shake. This isn't a Corp outpost. It's a private playground, a smuggler's paradise. That's why it was built in the Outskirts, and as far as I know, nobody here is trying to kill us.

Give them time.

So I tap the panel to accept the override, and they bring us through the landing sequence, smooth as s-silk. There's no way I could have managed all these turns, the precise stops and starts while we proceed through the locks to the hangar. Maybe our computer could've handled it; I don't know. I'm glad we don't have to find out.

As we come down the boarding ramp, an official waits for us. "You said you have injured on board?" She's also outfitted in full hazard gear. "I'm afraid I need to check him to ensure you aren't carrying a contagious sickness."

"Go right ahead," Doc says, stepping back from the sled.

The dockmistress, or whatever the hell she is, runs a scan on March, head to toe, then nods, seeming satisfied. She pulls off her helmet, and I'm surprised to find she's quite young. "Note to log, merely an injury to an extremity, nothing infectious. Do you need transport?"

"That would be perfect if you can arrange it," I say.

I've only been here once before. Kai and I rented a sporty little two-seater, but that's not going to get the job done. And in fact, he handled the details, so I wouldn't even know where to start.

"I'll see to it," the official says. "I'll provide documentation for those traveling to the clinic with the patient. Here." She hands us an orange card. "But I do need someone to stay and fill out forms regarding your stay and, of course, pay the docking fee."

I'm about to volunteer when Dina says, "I'll do it." At my look, she shrugs. "I hate hospitals. No offense, Doc." But I can read the look she gives our helpful docking agent. "Afterward, I'll hit the market and see about parts for real repairs."

"Let's go then." Saul tows the emergency sled behind him easily, which is impressive, considering the thrusters that lift it don't do anything for propulsion.

As promised, we find a skywagon with an orange cross on the side waiting for us in front of the docking authority, and it's large enough to slide the sled in back. Doc gets in the front with the driver, giving directions, and I climb up with March. With a smooth swoop, we're off. Gehenna whirls around me, an impossibly bright collage of color.

I rest my hand on March's chest, feeling the slow, steady thump of his heart. The last two days I've found it impossible to sleep, and I'm somewhere past exhausted. Maybe I doze off sitting beside him, because it feels to me like we just got moving, then we stop. Someone opens up the rear doors.

I recognize Doc hauling on the sled, so I hop down. Guess he's already paid the driver, so we make our way into the clinic, a posh-looking place done in ultrachrome and diamante with a marquee that proclaims, "We build a better you" and a second sign that says "Where the stars come when they fall." I'm not sure what that means, but I follow Doc, hoping he knows where he's going.

"Saul Solaith!" calls an extremely affable voice. It turns out to be attached to a slim silver-haired man around Doc's age. "Why didn't you tell me you were coming? I'd have booked the twins and a suite at the Capital."

"Spontaneous stop," Doc answers. "I've got a friend here in desperate need of your expertise, Ordo. Do you have an op-room free?"

"Yes, yes, of course. And if I didn't, I'd put someone out for you."

The two men walk away, leaving me standing in the foyer with the potted plants and an impressive view through the skylight. I drop down into a padded orange chair. Overhead I can see an ad satellite orbiting the salmon sky, but I can't make out its slogan. Somehow it seems important, like it's a special message just for me, so I continue to gaze straight up, waiting for the moment when it turns so I can read it.

Working girls prefer Sapphire.

I don't know what that means, either, but over the next several hours, it works on me. The words must be a message written in code, and if I can just unravel their hidden significance, then March will be all right. But I can't work it out, and as I feel myself drifting off, I realize I've let him down.

Don't know how long I was out, but Doc wakes me with a gentle hand on my shoulder. "He's awake, Jax. You want to see him?"

"Yeah, please." I yawn as I push to my feet, scouring the sleep from my eyes with my knuckles. "Did you . . . that is—"

"We couldn't save the arm," he says gravely. "I had to choose between an organic and a prosthetic replacement."

"He wouldn't want a—"

"I know. It's going to take some time for him to build strength in the new arm, and it looks a bit different. But with physical therapy and exercise, he should eventually return to normal. Come then, this way."

He leads me through a warren of hallways and opens the door to a recovery room. With luxurious draperies, mosaic tile floor, and commodious bed with multiple settings, this space looks every bit as lush as the rest of the clinic; Doc wasn't kidding when he said he had connections here.

March sits propped up, his shoulder wrapped decorously in liquid skin. The new arm looks strange and pale, not to mention slim, almost delicate in comparison with his right. Every now and then he flexes the fingers of his left hand, probably testing to be sure they really work. I can't blame him.

"March," I say softly, and he looks up as if he hadn't heard us enter.

Lost in thought, I suppose. I would be, too. Doubtless he has a lot to think about. Neither one of us says a word in protest when Doc backs out of the room and closes the door behind him.

"I understand I have you to thank." He beckons me with his right hand, and I approach the bed, feeling oddly tentative.

Shaking my head, I sit down, careful not to jostle him. "What did Doc tell you?"

"Not much. And that worries me." His impossibly dark eyes search mine.

"It wasn't me," I say then. "It was Loras. And he didn't . . . he didn't make it."

I expect him to light into me, tear me a new one over everything that's gone wrong, but instead his long lashes sweep down. His mouth compresses into a white line, and I see his throat working. I don't understand what's happening any more than I understood the slogan *Working girls prefer Sapphire*. March reaches blindly for my hand, and I curl my fingers through his. Waiting.

"I'm sorry," he whispers. "You were right. There was nothing we could do up there, and Loras shouldn't have died just so I could find that out."

Tears burn behind my eyes, and he's hurting me with his grip on my fingers. But I don't pull back. "Maybe you can't save the world, but you'll never stop trying. It's the best thing about you."

He opens his eyes then, and they're so dark I can't see his pupils. I hope it's the drugs talking as he bites out, "Save the world? I can't even save the people I *care* about. It's just fucking hopeless."

I've never seen him like this, and I don't know what to say. Reassurance isn't my style in the first place, and to make it worse, I don't disagree with him. He's tapped into *my* worldview, but I don't like seeing it on him.

But in the end, the only answer he needs right now is the warmth of my hand wrapped around his as he fades out.

CHAPTER 38

I give them three weeks.

See, it never seems like the right time to say it, from the moment I made up my mind. First Hon's scout ships came tearing after us, then we had to get to Gehenna, March needed medical attention. Then I would've felt like a shit to walk into the recovery room, ask how he's doing, then tell him I'm leaving. Not that it's going to be any easier now, but at least I won't feel like I'm kicking the man while he's down.

So I bide my time, helping Dina with ship repairs when she's not seeing the docking agent, whose name is Clary. Doc seems to be taking advantage of the unscheduled R&R as well, raising hell with his old friend Ordo Carvati. But I'm glad when the clinic gives March a clean bill of health because it means I can finally get it out in the open. Stop pretending I'm in this for the long haul.

You'd think that wouldn't help me any, but I've learned March's partition trick. I know he's wondering why he can't read me anymore, but I've been careful not to give any sign of what I'm thinking. I didn't want to piss him off while he was recuperating.

Saying farewell aboard the *Folly* would prove impossible, so I've arranged to meet him for dinner at Molino's, got a nice little table in the atrium. I'm early. The ship's come to feel like home over the past months, but it's time to go.

I just want to step out into the throng and disappear. Live the rest of my life quietly. I'm tired of being pushed and pulled without my volition. I want to make my own choices from here on out, not do what someone else tells me. I don't give a shit about the greater good or changing the universe. A training academy isn't worth dying for. Shit, it's not even *my* dream. At this point, I don't know what that would be.

Yeah, I know it means I'll never see grimspace again, never feel the exhilaration that follows a good jump. But I guess I'm one of the rare ones after all. I can let it go.

Before he comes into sight, I know he's arrived. Don't ask me how; it's some March-sense I wish I didn't possess, perhaps a remnant of jumping with a Psi pilot. I wish I'd learned more about him, but it's too late now. I've already removed my things from the *Folly*; they're in the bag Dina gave me, stowed beneath the table. He strides between the tables, strong and vibrant, a little incongruous among the lattices and hanging vines. This part of the restaurant is meant to evoke a tropical garden, but thankfully they omitted the insects.

"Doc said you wanted me to meet you here," he says, but there's a question in his voice, echoed in his dark eyes. March rests his palm on the back of the chair but doesn't sit, as if he suspects this is just a stop on the way to somewhere else.

"They have great stuffed peppers," I say, and that seems to startle him.

"Okay, I'll bite." He drops down in the chair opposite me. "What's up, Jax?"

"Dinner?" Maybe he'll take the news better with a full stomach. Regardless, it can't hurt, and I really do like their stuffed peppers.

So we eat, but I sense the currents stirring beneath our casual conversation. When the waiters clear our plates and we're left with just our wine to finish, I wrap both my hands around the glass because I feel the need to hold on to something. This is harder than I thought it would be.

"You want to tell me what's going on now?" He sits back in his chair, propping his ankle on his knee.

I take a deep breath. "It's time for us to part ways. I've been doing a lot of thinking since we left the station, and I just don't feel this is worth it."

March starts to smile like he's waiting for the punch line. "No, seriously."

That's when I drop the mental walls he taught me how to build, and now I can feel his presence more than I ever could before. Perhaps it's a result of his absence; perhaps I'm simply developing a little of my own latent sensitivity.

"Seriously."

He shakes his head, seeming unable to believe what he's seen inside my head. "You can't go . . . we saved you."

"Yes, you did," I say gently. "And I saved you, too. I'll always be grateful to you for getting me off Perlas, but this isn't how I want to live. You don't own me."

I can tell he's getting angry. "What the hell do you think you're going to do, Jax? You have no creds and no training."

"Doc paid me the wages I should have earned during the time I've been with you. He said he didn't think I should be stuck on the *Folly*, unable to enjoy myself." I'm trying not to argue with him because it's not open for debate. My mind is made up.

"You think that's going to last forever? What the frag do you think you can do here? Wait tables?" He gestures at the handsome young man, who takes one look at March's face and heads the other way. "You'd kick someone in the head the first time he complained about the food."

I smile because he's right about that, but I've done some digging while we've been here. "I can probably get work at one of the fetish clubs. Gehenna caters to different tastes, you know." Scars, piercing, and body art are popular with a certain clientele.

"And *that's* what you want to devote your life to?" He sits forward then, elbows on the table, and his eyes sear me. "Letting freaks stare at you until you're so old they don't want to anymore?"

"No, but it'll put food on the table until I decide what I do want. Too many people have died, and I don't intend to be one of them."

"Nobody ever accomplished anything this big if people weren't willing to die for it. Maybe *I* won't see Mair's vision come to fruition, but we'll lay the groundwork so that others can come behind us and finish our work. One thing's for sure, though, I won't allow them to have died in vain because I'm afraid to see it through. You're a fucking coward, Jax, and you're running because you're scared you found something worth dying for, something more important than *you*."

I grit my teeth. "You know what I see? Someone afraid of finding something worth *living* for. Everyone you love dies, so you decided it's better to be a doomed hero, and you don't care who you drag down with you. Do you really believe in this cause, heart and soul, or is it just that there's nothing else for you? You're a pilot who doesn't want to fly because his ship's a monument to his dead sister, and you have the nerve to bitch at *me*? Get your own life in order before you come at me like you have all the answers."

As soon as the words leave my mouth, I'm sorry. I see him flinch although nobody else would have known they'd drawn blood. He shoves his chair back so hard that the scraping sound momentarily silences the low hum of conversation nearby.

"Part of that may be true," he growls. "But I don't use people, and I don't fuck my friends over. I get it, Jax, and I'll tell Doc and Dina you took the opportunity to jump ship as soon as we arrived somewhere you'd rather be."

"March . . ."

He doesn't turn, so I watch until his angry strides carry him out of sight. I don't have a chance to tell him it wasn't like that; I didn't lie to them, pretending to believe in what they were doing until I saw my chance to get away here. The cost just got too high, that's all. I didn't want it to end like this, but maybe I always knew we'd never wind up friends. Though I didn't always agree with him or even like him sometimes, March is a rock, and you don't run across those too often.

And losing him hurts more than I thought it would because I've come to count on him. If nothing else, though, I believed in March, and maybe deep down I hoped he'd see my point of view. If he hadn't reacted like that, I might have asked him to stay. I hadn't made up my mind, but his response decided matters for me. I finish my wine coolly, pretending the looks people keep sliding my way don't bother me.

Like none of you ever argued about anything. Or maybe you never cared enough.

It occurs to me then, he probably came down so hard on me because I hurt him. Maybe it felt personal, like a betrayal. And that pains me, but there's nothing I can do about it because it doesn't change my mind. I want a life, not sacrifice.

The waiter comes toward me like a child afraid of being slapped, so I muster up a smile and settle the bill. I collect my bag and leave with my head high. It's time to put all this behind me. I need to find work and a place to live. This is my new life, exactly what I wanted, and if I have a pain in my chest that won't go away, then I'll push it back.

That survival trick, you see? I've taken the old Jax and boxed her up. It's time to move on to the next Jax incarnation, but at this moment, even *I* can't see what kind of person she'll be, what she'll do for a living, or whom she'll love.

My future seems misty, shrouded just like Gehenna's sun, and maybe that's the way it's supposed to be.

CHAPTER 39

Have you ever watched a child learning to walk?

Before this week, I never had, but there's a certain grace to it. Well, if not grace, then tenacity. Fall down nine times—get up ten. And the tenth time you get where you're going, you don't stop, not for obstacles, not for other people *telling* you to stop. You don't listen to anything but that inner voice until you arrive where you want to be.

When do we lose that? Of course, maybe that inner voice needs some refinement because it apparently also tells us to eat what comes out of our noses, and that it's funny to hit people in the head, but I think maybe it carries a true message, too, something we shouldn't lose. I learned that working with children this week, not school-aged ones with the start of civilization impressed upon them. No, these are hardly more than babies, just learning to walk, little schooners of self.

It's strange how it worked out. I went to Hidden Rue, expecting to take my place on the stage. By all accounts it's a hard-core fetish club, where my scars might be an asset, but the old woman who owned the place took one look at me, and said, "You're too old, too scrawny, and your burns aren't interesting enough. What else can you do?"

For a moment, March's mocking words came back to me, and I almost said, "Not a damn thing."

Instead I did what I do best, spun a nice line of bullshit, the result of which is me, helping to watch the dancers' babies. Hidden Rue is a decent place to work. Domina, the owner, takes good care of her girls. Furthermore, she looks like she probably danced here in her day since she's tattooed, rit-scarred, and probably pierced in places I don't want to know about. They say an interesting life leaves its mark on your face, and if that's true, she's got one hell of a story. She's the one who told me that Sapphire is a line of cosmetics favored by strippers and joy girls.

The women have to stick together here because patrons tend to be rougher than what you get in a regular bar, guys who wish they'd inflicted those scars, those wounds. Or it's the other side of the spectrum, timid little submissives who imagine each dancer as their own personal princess of pain. Occasionally we get others, too, mainly aliens who don't seem to realize the club's skewed west of the human norm.

I don't work the floor, though, so my contact with the public is minimal. Instead, I spend my evenings trying to entertain fractious toddlers who want their mothers, wail for no reason, and upchuck whenever it's likely to do the most harm. I've been hired to assist a woman named Adele, who glows with serenity like nobody I've ever known. She's short and round, skin the color of choclaste, so of course I like her on sight. She wears her hair in loose graying curls and might be anywhere between fifty and a hundred, though her smooth skin makes the latter unlikely.

We see a steady stream of dancers in costume in the crèche during the course of a night. They want a quick cuddle between sets, but it usually leaves the little one crying. Still, I think it's nice of Domina to offer child care, although she does take a small cut from the dancers who use the service. That seems fair enough, no reason she should pay us entirely out of her own pocket. The babies I'm less sure about, although ironically my time with baby-Z has prepared me somewhat.

Adele even comments, "I can tell you've done this before. What happened to your little one, honey?"

"He died." I feel suffused with guilt all over again.

If they knew what happened, they wouldn't let me work here.

She accepts that with a shake of her head and says nothing more. Instead, there's a spill to clean up, and Mattin has hit Lleela in the head again. There's justice to dispense, and tears to dry; we're constantly moving until we get them to sleep one by one. This is my fifth evening on the job, and I go home bone-tired, but it's not a bad feeling. Instead, there's satisfaction in it, like I'm living a good life if not a large one.

It's penance. There's a reason I ended up here. I didn't do right by baby-Z, so I'll make it up as best I can. It's not what I'd choose to do, but I don't even know what that would be. The most important thing is that I'm accomplishing it by myself.

In the mornings, I like to shop. So first thing, I get up and head over to the market. Sometimes I look at the diaphanous veils and the belly jewels laid out, then at the next stall over I find totemic carvings and blessed kirpan waiting for those who believe in luck and talismans against evil. I linger over pottery and paintings. It seems as though I've never had a place of my own to decorate. In my parents' house, I had a room, of course, but I was never permitted to change it or make it mine.

As I turn to leave the market, an old woman catches me by the arm. "Your shadow troubles you."

I expect to find a fortune-teller soliciting me, reading cards or bones or peering into a cup to glimpse my future in sodden leaves. But this woman is simply garbed in black; she might be a cook or a housekeeper, certainly someone's grandmother, for her back is bent and her face withered.

"My shadow's fine," I reply with a frown.

"She is not," the stranger insists. "She has gone away and dreams another dream. You shift what lives inside your skin until she does not know you. And without her, I do not know how you will face this destiny hanging on you. So many ghosts walk behind you, so many ghosts . . ." She shakes her head and sighs. "I will light a candle for you at Mary's shrine."

At that she releases my arm, and I expect her to ask me to pay for her blessing or insight, but she merely wraps her black shawl around her head and hurries on, as if she's tarried too long. I leave the market and head for home, feeling distinctly unsettled. Adele rented me a room in her building; the word "garret" seems to apply. My flat used to be storage space before someone took the bright idea to replace half the walls with beveled glastique. Consequently, my ceilings slant beneath the line of the roof.

She told me it used to be an artist's studio; nobody's ever actually lived up here before. But I don't mind, the open vista and the altitude make me feel like I'm flying, which might make a mudsider uneasy, but I've spent so much of my life on ships, this place feels perfect. It feels like home.

When she brings a bowl of soup up for my lunch, I just have to ask, "Why are you being so nice to me?"

She gives me a Madonna's smile. "Mary teaches us that's how you change the world, one soul at a time, one kindness at a time. That's the only way it'll ever take root."

"Didn't they kill her for that doctrine?" I ask, taking the dish from her.

Adele shakes her head. "No, that was her son. They knew

better than to martyr her. It was meant as an object lesson from the authorities, but it didn't shut her mouth. She went on to live a good life."

I've never been religious, never thought much on the oaths I swear, but I pause in spooning up a bite of soup. "That's why she's revered? For living a good life?"

I don't mean to minimize its importance, but I can tell my tone struck a chord because she drops down on the battered old sofa that came with my apartment. "Isn't that more than it sounds like, Sirantha? It's easy to do right when everything *goes* right. But let everything go wrong, and see how difficult it becomes."

"That's certainly true."

When she calls me Sirantha, I think of my mother although I haven't seen her in fifteen years. I don't even know if she's still alive, but I don't harbor any illusions she'd be glad to see me. I made my bed when I ran away from boarding school and signed a contract with the Corp, when I decided not to be the pretty soulless accessory they were grooming me to be. And maybe I still don't know who I am, but it's not what they wanted. And that's enough, for now.

For some reason, I can't bring myself to tell Adele I don't have any faith. Mary is an idea, someone who lived long ago maybe, but she's nothing I believe in. I've never seen any sign of divinity or everlasting grace, except perhaps a whisper in the movements of that glass-dancer.

Hard as it may be to swallow, I think this shot's all we get. Science has proved there's nothing to the talk of ghosts and spirits, no proof anything like the soul exists. And to my mind that's an argument against the existence of an omniscient force. I think people believe whatever makes living easiest, and who am I to deny someone comfort?

So I just shut up and eat my soup.

CHAPTER 40

I haven't been sleeping well.

It's been six weeks, and I can't get the old woman's words out of my head. Sometimes I catch myself looking over my shoulder for my shadow, and I never find one. I tell myself it's part of living on Gehenna, where there's no direct sunlight. Most citizens take regular UV treatments to make up for the deficiency.

But that's not the reason I wake up dripping sweat, hands fisted in my bedcovers. Where I sleep would give anyone else vertigo, mattress flush against the glastique wall. That's not my problem, either. First thing I do is roll over and look out over the city, see how the 'scrapers strive toward the unassailable sky. The skycabs and private hovercars swoop with silent grace, and I lie there listening to my heartbeat.

On another world, it would be dawn now, and I wake from the same dream, night after night, exactly this way. I run my palm over my biceps and feel the skin marred by scars, further roughed by goose bumps. I don't know what to do.

He's the last person I want to see when I close my eyes, and yet he's there, always the same. Since I'm a new Jax, building a new life, I try not to let myself think about March, but he comes to me in dreams. I see him sitting on the edge of his bunk, elbows on his knees, head sunk into his hands. That's all, really, but it doesn't begin to encapsulate his solitude and despair. It's like he's one of the ghosts the old woman claimed she saw following me.

I hate how much I miss him. There's a hollow where he used to be, and it echoes with self-imposed loss. This is the life I *chose*, first decision I've made since I was seventeen and ran away from finishing school, so I need to make the best of it.

I want to be happy, but my heart won't let me. In crowds I see his face. When I close my eyes, I see his face. And in dreams—

With a muffled groan, I crawl off my mat and collect my bath basket. I don't have a san-shower in my garret, so I go down and borrow from Adele. She lives just below me, and most mornings we breakfast together as well. Usually it's darjing tea and toast with good marmalade.

She's coded the door to recognize me, so I don't wake her slipping in to take my shower. This morning I manage to get cleaned up and make the tea before she stirs. Scratching at her sleep-rumpled hair, she sits down at the small metal table that looks as if she salvaged it from a rubbish pile. Perhaps she did. But it's meticulously clean, if dinged and dented.

Adele takes one look at me, and says, "You dreamed of him again, hm?"

I give a curt nod in reply, wrapping my fingers around my mug for warmth I can't seem to generate on my own. It's like I sweat away my heat in fitful sleep, then for the rest of the day I walk around with a chill I can't dispel.

Doubtless the old woman from the bazaar would say it's something to do with my missing shadow.

She can tell I don't want to talk about it, though, so she falls quiet, and we eat listening to the bittersweet melody of the music she calls folkazz. Before work, we go to the piazza and listen to them play, old-fashioned instruments with reeds and strings. I like it, but there's a certain melancholy in their faces that says they know they belong to a lost era. Their music makes me think again of the ghosts that follow me.

Tonight, the children are especially querulous. If Gehenna experienced weather, I would say there's a storm coming. Perhaps there is, a dry lightning tempest somewhere beyond the safety of the dome. Mattin will not climb off my lap, even to hit Lleela in the head, and that little girl has attached herself to Adele's leg; she will not dislodge herself for toys or treats. The others seem less affected, but they do quarrel more over small infractions of rights or personal dignity. And none of them will sleep.

So we get no peace until the last of the dancers collects her offspring, then we walk home together through the titian-tinged streets. Though the hour is late, Gehenna looks exactly the same, like a whore who paints her face night after night and holds secret the ravages of time. I decline Adele's offer to come in and trudge up another flight to my flat. There's a lift in this building, but she tells me it hasn't worked in years.

Even before I let myself in, I smell the scent of a man's passage, but I don't expect to find him standing in my flat. I know how it must look to him: poor, eccentric, squalid. But it's mine. His back is turned to me, and he seems to be admiring the view. It's strange to see him amid my eclectic furnishings, my sleep-mat, the battered sofa, a softly glowing lamp with a fringed shade. But he spins as he senses my presence, even though I don't speak.

"It's been a while," Doc says, folding his hands behind him. "Hello, Sirantha."

"I thought you would have gone by now."

Long before now, actually.

"Oh, we tried." And there's certain heaviness to his tone that unnerves me. "We were so lucky to find Edaine. She failed basic academy training, but not through incompetence. One of her instructors took a fancy to her and gave her low marks when she refused to sleep with him."

"Yes, I imagine that's pretty rare. Would you like something to drink?" I keep my words neutral.

"No thank you. I won't stay long." He studies me for a moment, as if seeking something in my eyes or expression.

"How did you find me?" I thought I had well and truly disappeared.

That bothers me. If he found me, then the Corp could as well, not to mention bounty hunters. Gray men don't always work as a unit. Sometimes they dispatch a solo quietly to neutralize targets on worlds they don't control. It's not unreasonable to posit one such might be searching for me here, even now, and I can't be on my guard all the time. To make it worse, my presence might pose a danger to the children and to Adele. That I cannot permit.

"My old friend Ordo has excellent connections," he answers.

I suspect that's an understatement. Ordo Carvati can accomplish anything he wants in Gehenna. He's from one of the First families, and he's old money. It's to Doc's credit that he doesn't flaunt his friendship with such a man.

"But he can't find you another jumper?"

He hasn't moved from the center of the room, and none of his body language tells me this is a friendly visit. In fact, I would say he doesn't want to be here at all. That tells me a great deal about his state of mind.

At that he smiles, although there's a sad slant to it. "He cannot make miracles. I know what March has said about you. And I've listened to Dina's thoughts as well." By his careful phrasing I can well imagine the way the other two cursed me. He takes a step forward, and the glow from my fringed lamp finally touches his face. "Two days ago Dina had a shunt installed. Ordo wouldn't do it, so she went to a black-market surgeon."

"A shunt?" I repeat blankly. "Why?" But even as I ask, I find myself fingering the jack hidden in my wrist.

"She says there's no one else," he answers.

Now I understand the heaviness in his voice. "That's crazy. She isn't trained."

I can't even imagine what grimspace would do to someone untrained, someone who doesn't possess the J-gene. Don't know whether it will kill her, drive her mad, or if all of them will be lost. I could find out, research the early days when they first discovered the Star Road, but something tells me knowing won't make it easier to bear.

Doc shrugs. "She seems to think determination and mental strength should make up for that. They don't know I'm here. March was supposed to ask you back, perhaps two weeks ago. He said you refused."

That hurts. As long as I had known him, March never lied. And yet he's learned how in order to avoid seeing me.

"He never came," I say quietly.

"I didn't want to believe what the others said, Sirantha. Now that you know, I can't imagine you'll let her do it."

"I won't." My heart sinks as I say it. But like Gehenna itself, these past weeks have been nothing but an illusion. I can't hide here. I can't live a quiet, simple life. "Of course I won't. Just let me get my things."

Dina has lost so much. She imagines there's no reason not to take the risk. She might even see it as a way to get back to Edaine. The people we love and lose never return to us, though, no matter how many shades we chase. And March . . . March would do anything to keep his word to Mair, no matter what the cost.

As I brush by him, Doc touches my shoulder. "You may

not want to admit it, but you are a vital piece of the puzzle. No one has been the same since you went away."

I know there are probably other difficulties, mounting docking fee costs. Obstacles I haven't even considered. As in my dream, March sits on the edge of his bunk, night after night, trying to find a way to succeed, trying to find a way out.

"It's not that I don't want to admit it," I tell him, weary beyond belief. "But I've spent my whole life doing as I'm told. This was the first time I ever did what *I* wanted. But it turns out I'm not allowed, so I'll live and die on someone else's agenda. Burn out jumping, no matter what I want."

"Oh . . ." His expression tells me he hates putting me in this position but not enough to leave. And it's probably best that I go. It would kill me if anything happened to Adele because of me. "If it makes any difference, I don't think you *can* burn out."

I pause in stuffing my belongings into my bag. "What are you talking about?"

"I didn't want to say anything until I was sure. But I've compared your before and after images to other case studies, quite extensively over the past weeks." He shakes his head. "Sorry, I am getting ahead of myself. In your first scan, I detected brain lesions consistent with AGSS. That test indicated burnout was inevitable and quite soon. Your next jump should have been your last. Instead, you came out, slept for three days, and when I took the next reading, all lesions had disappeared. Your brain looks as if you never jumped in your life, a student straight out of the academy."

The duffel slips from my hand. "How is that even possible?"

"I don't know." Doc shakes his head. "It's something to do with the L-gene I isolated, but that's . . . not a human trait."

"You're saying I'm—"

"I'm saying you apparently don't need to worry about burnout."

I feel numb as we head out of my glastique flat, like I don't know what's true anymore. Doc takes my bag from my nerveless fingers, and I tuck my favorite lamp beneath my arm. Although it's late, I tap on Adele's door, declining its offer to let me in.

She answers soon after, groggy but not alarmed, and her eyes go immediately to the man behind me. I glance at him, and it's like he's been hit by lightning. They simply stare at one another until I feel superfluous and clear my throat.

"I'm leaving," I say without explanation or apology. "I'm sorry I can't stay until you find a replacement for me at Hidden Rue."

Her eyes are so gentle. "It's all right, child. I knew your fate didn't rest with me. Call it a fuel stop for the soul, hm?"

Yes, that's exactly what it was. I hug her, then murmur, "This is my friend, Saul Solaith. Most people just call him Doc, though." To him, I add, "This is Adele."

She smiles with unearthly sweetness. "I'll be seeing you again, I think."

I don't know whether she's talking to him or me. It doesn't matter, really. We go then, down many flights of stairs and into Gehenna night, which looks the same as Gehenna dawn or Gehenna dusk. I think maybe I'm ready to go. Doc doesn't speak during our return to the space-port.

As I walk up the ramp to the *Folly*, I glance back once and see my shadow.

CHAPTER 41

I'm unpacking when the door to my quarters slides open.

They've erased all trace of my presence here; the room-bot doesn't even recognize me any longer. So I have no personal control over my environment at the moment although I have propped my fringed lamp up at the end of my bunk. Without turning, I know that it's March standing behind me.

"You were going to let Dina die before asking me for help?" Attack is the best alternative here. "And then you lied about it? Asshole."

I face him then, but it's a casual movement, born of stowing my now-empty bag into the bottom of the storage closet where I've hung my clothes. Though I manage not to react, I'm shaken by how haggard he looks. He's visibly thinner, lean jaw unshaven, and there's a terrible darkness in his eyes that has nothing to do with their hue.

"Yeah," he says with a flicker of his old bite. "And that's

so much worse than abandoning people who depend on you."

You know, I've never been in this position before. Never had to remember who I used to be and try to become that woman again. Who was I before I walked away? I remember it hurt me to say farewell to this man. I bled when he left me sitting in Molino's, his accusations etched in acid, eating at me from the inside out. And now those feelings return as I wriggle back into her soul.

My soul. A thing I didn't believe in until I spent time with Adele. *Oh Mary, I'm so broken.* Never realized how fragmented I've become until this moment. I'm a mirror where someone sunk his fist, a thousand tiny images refracted from that fissure, and none of them complete.

"I couldn't make you understand then," I say softly. "And I can't now. I hoped you could find someone else. I don't see myself as irreplaceable."

He steps fully into my room, and the door swishes shut behind him. "You think jumpers grow on trees? Why do you think we settled for you in the first place?"

That sends a stab of fresh pain through me, but I don't let it show. Maybe he can feel it. I don't know anymore. "I thought it was tied to Doc's research."

"Trust you to be literal." March glances around my quarters, which seem smaller with him standing there. He flexes the fingers of his left hand; that's a new nervous habit. "Yeah, it had to be you. But if you're just going to run away again—"

"No, I'll see it through." *Like I have a choice.* I'm bound here, and I don't know why I didn't see it sooner. "March, I'm sorry for what I said about your sister."

His intake of breath sounds so loud. "She wasn't why I stopped piloting."

"I know. I was mad, so I put two and two together to make twelve." Hesitate for a moment, then add, "And I wanted to hurt you."

"You did."

The words lie between us like a gauntlet. I don't know what he means, so I choose the coward's course. Apropos, I think. "I'm sorry."

He shrugs. "It's nothing new."

"What—"

"You think it didn't cut me every time you thought of him?" His jaw clenches. "You think I didn't bleed when you left my bed to scrub away my touch and deify his memory? You think it didn't hurt when you *left* me? Jax, you've been slicing me to bits for months, and there's damn near nothing left."

"March . . ." But he's not interested in whatever I might say.

He shakes his head. "I'm not letting you do that to me anymore. It's going to be different this time."

I know what's coming, and I'm not going to let him say it, not when I'm just starting to figure things out. "I didn't think about him when I went away." I step closer and his whole body tenses, although whether in anticipation of pain or pleasure, I couldn't say. "I dreamed of *you.*"

I can't believe I told him that. But the moment thrums with such stark honesty that I can't offer him less. I never knew I had the power to hurt him, only that he possessed the power to hurt *me.*

His ridiculously long-lashed eyes search mine, as if for some sign I'm going to turn this into a cruel joke, but I hold his look, letting him see the truth. Funny how I can tell when he's reading me now; it's a little prickle on the back of my neck.

"You mean it," he says, after a moment.

"Yeah." That same candor compels me to add, "I wouldn't have done anything about it, though. I wouldn't have come back."

"I know." He smiles then. "We're great ones for burning

bridges, you and I. Slamming doors hard enough that we're not tempted to knock on them again."

"That sounds about right."

March touches my hair, tentative, as if he thinks one wrong move will frighten me away. I close my eyes and draw a deep breath at the feel of his fingers on the nape of my neck. When I don't recoil, he pulls me close, and I wrap my arms around his waist, running my hands up his back. He's so thin I can count his ribs with my fingertips.

Oh Mary, I missed this. He feels . . . right, just as he did on Lachion. I remember how he drove away the bad dreams, even then. I remember how his arms always felt like they could protect me from anything, but maybe I was afraid because I never accept that from anyone. I never admit I might need it.

"Tell me this isn't what you were running from." Lacing our fingers together, he flattens my palm over his heart. "I can't compete with a ghost, though. I won't even try. So if you want me to let go, just say so and—"

I shake my head. "I don't know, it may have been part of it, but I . . . laid him to rest somewhere on Gehenna."

March tips my face up, studying my features intently for a moment, then he swings me up in his arms, and I realize I haven't even asked about his recovery. He must be all right, though, because he carries me over to the bunk and settles with me in his lap. I feel him running his hands up and down my back, stroking my thick, coarse hair. I expect . . . *more* I suppose, but he doesn't even kiss me.

"No," he says, shaking his head. "That was too soon, and I paid for it. Probably should've just let you sleep with Hon. I just—"

"Couldn't stand to see someone else touching your woman?"

He exhales into my hair, and I shift enough to glimpse his sheepish expression. "I know. Big cliché, right?"

I find myself reassuring him. "A certain amount of

territoriality between mates is natural. I know we're supposed to be enlightened, but some things just don't breed out."

His smile widens into a grin, and it's only then that I grasp what I've said. But I don't try to take it back. When March tilts his head against mine, my mind swims for a moment, then I'm full of him. He shows me everything, a barrage of impressions, and I understand why I can't resist him. He's exactly like me: compartmentalized, broken, a jumbled mass of jagged edges he conceals beneath biting wit and confidence.

"You can't imagine what it's like. Hearing secret thoughts, then listening to lies spoken with a smile. It kills the soul, Jax. I was a monster when I met Mair. She turned me into a decent human being and taught me to control it." He hesitates, shuddering, and I reach up to stroke his cheek. I know he's not going to be in a confessional mood forever. "But after our first jump, I'd find myself in your head without any clue how I got there. It scared the shit out of me. I'd stopped piloting because Mair said there were risks associated with a Psi-sensitive using wetware."

"I guess it would. I thought you just were doing it to piss me off." I smile up at him to take the sting out of my words, but I have to wonder what risks Mair was talking about. Wonder if she left anything in my PA. "Do the others know?"

"No! They wouldn't understand. They'd be afraid of me, afraid of what I know. Jax . . ." His tone turns wondering. "Do you have any idea what a miracle you are? What you say is exactly what I see in your head. No disparity, no dirty secrets. Even when you detested me, you made no bones about it."

I grin at him. "You like a little honest hatred, huh?"

"I guess I do. Spices things up." He pulls me closer, resting his chin on my head, and I listen to his heart.

Hard to say who's most surprised when the door slides

back. Shit, I forgot it will open for anyone right now. Guess it's a good thing we're just curled on my bunk together. Doc still looks astonished, though.

"I wanted to say that we're clear for departure." He clears his throat. "Anytime."

"We didn't kill each other," I say with a grin. "We'll head to the cockpit shortly."

Right now, March looks more at peace than I've ever seen him, and it's a little hard to reconcile that serenity as being related to me. I shake things up, create chaos and agitate for change, but I've never been accused of being restful.

He cups my cheek in his palm, and murmurs to Doc, "Five minutes. Now get out."

I truly hope we're going to make good use of that time.

CHAPTER 42

We're not going where I thought we were.

As March and I emerge from quarters, we find Doc and Dina waiting for us in the hub. To my surprise, neither looks like they want to kill me, although Saul's expression gives me pause. He sighs and powers up the comm station. I avoid touching it whenever possible because Loras is supposed to be sitting there.

"I think you'd better take a look at this."

When I lean forward, I see an old holo-newsfeed, dated almost two months back. A dark-haired woman with a small mouth and a perfect coif smiles without showing teeth. This is notable only because she manages to speak without showing them, either. I think she mistakes this facial immobility for a proper "grave business" expression.

"Citizens of the Conglomerate, we urge you to be on your guard. Although we've tried to contain this matter internally, we of Farwan Corporation cannot in good conscience"—I snort at that—"continue our search without revealing the in-herent danger we all face. This woman, Sirantha Jax . . ."

Here, an unflattering picture of me flashes in the upper right-hand corner of the screen. "A former employee has escaped from our secure facility on Perlas Station, where she was awaiting trial for her involvement in the death of eighty-two souls aboard the *Sargasso*. We do not know the names or identities of her accomplices, but we speculate they may be the terrorists responsible for the strike against the conference on Matins IV. Their reign of terror contin-ues unabated. Our operatives tracked them to DuPont Sta-tion, where for reasons known only to themselves, they—"

My breath hisses out of me in a rush. "We didn't blow the station!"

"No, we most certainly did not," Doc agrees with a sigh. "But so far as the rest of the Conglomerate is concerned, we *did*."

"Why would they do that?" My knees feel shaky as I keep seeing the explosion, time and again. "And how did they even know we were there?"

Dina finally speaks but she sounds matter-of-fact. "My guess is, Hon contacted them, intending to cut a deal. Maybe he was tired of playing mad scientist with Farr and wanted recognition from the Conglomerate. Maybe he was tired of worrying about them showing up to evict him if he ever became a threat instead of an annoyance. But he wouldn't have been able to negotiate without you, Jax."

"He didn't want to kill us, just stall us until they ar-rived," March agrees.

I feel his hand light in the small of my back, a propri-etary gesture. The other two make note of it, but they don't comment, which had to cost Dina. She even smiles at me. Just what the hell is going on?

"We don't know exactly what transpired," Doc says, "but they've clearly pinned the blame on us. And that's not the worst of it."

"There's more?"

"Indirectly." He picks up the device he was showing Dina when we emerged from quarters and starts indicating readings that don't mean anything to me. "The problem is, they've closed the doors to us that we need most."

"You don't need me for this," March interjects. "I'm getting us off this rock while you bring her up to speed."

I guess he already knows this stuff. And yeah, maybe I'm a *little* disappointed when he walks off without looking back, but I redirect my attention without being obvious. I already knew March is practical. He's never going to sit at my feet and write me poems, which is good because I hate poetry, except dirty ones that rhyme.

"Anyway," Doc says pointedly, and I roll my eyes. Sometimes he reminds me of my professors. "I've been studying your scans, comparing them with the sample I took from the Mareq." I flinch, but he seems not to notice. "Your DNA isn't entirely . . . human. I alluded to it back at your flat, but the truth is, in all my case studies, I've never seen the L-gene append to the J-gene, as it has in you. I was hoping to *achieve* that through years of engineering, but it appears that our work has been done for us, either by nature or design."

"You're saying—"

"I don't know. I don't even know how this is possible." He bites the words off. "What we need to do is retrace your steps, dig into your early life and try to discover how this happened, so we can duplicate it. That may be the best shortcut available; otherwise, we'll spend months gathering samples before I can even begin work."

The *Folly* trembles, powering up, and Dina pushes away from the console. I think she doesn't want to look at it anymore, and I can't blame her.

"By making us infamous, they've shut the door on us," she mutters. "We can't use official ports, and you grew up on New Terra, right? *That's* where we need to be."

"The three of you can go. They said they don't know who my accomplices are. I can wait on the *Folly*. Maybe you can find something out."

She shakes her head. "That's bullshit, Jax. We registered on Perlas. They know the name of the ship, and they have our sequence codes. How else did they send this?"

Saul fires up the terminal again, saying only, "What I showed you before, that was just the attachment. This is the message."

A man with sea-blue eyes and elegant, chiseled features comes on-screen. I drop down hard in Loras's chair because I recognize him. For several moments I see his lips moving but no sound registers, and Dina touches my shoulder.

"You all right?" At my mute nod, she says to Doc, "I think you better replay it."

"Sirantha, this message has been bounced off all public relays. I implore you, surrender now. Turn yourself in at the nearest Corp outpost, and we will tend to your treatment. You're confused, unwell, and perhaps do not realize that your actions are wrong."

Shit.

Simon always was a persuasive bastard. On-screen, he's the image of a concerned husband. I haven't seen him in years, but now they've got him acting as the face of Farwan, hoping to entice me back? They must really think I *am* crazy. I don't understand why they've painted me as an interstellar terrorist, though. Is it spin, covering up their negligence on Matins IV, or are they using me to hide something else entirely? Whichever the case, I suspect they're widening the net.

"The only place we're safe is in here in the Outskirts." Both Dina and Doc nod, waiting to see where I'm going by stating the obvious, I guess. "But you think something in my past could provide answers?"

"It's our best hope," Saul replies, stroking his goatee

with two fingers. "Also the most dangerous course for obvious reasons."

I glance at Dina, but she picks today to begin keeping her mouth shut. "Then that's where we need to go."

Can't imagine what my parents are going to say after all this time. Assuming we can find a place to dock. After all, New Terra is a Conglomerate world, firmly in the clutches of Farwan Corporation. It's going to take all our combined ingenuity to keep from winding up in a cell.

The ship lifts, a subtle jolt. We steady ourselves on the console as March guides us through the locks that will liberate us from Gehenna. Now that I've tried flying this damn thing, I can't help but feel impressed. Consider how rusty he must've been on Perlas, and yet he's taking us out of the atmosphere so smoothly we can scarcely register the shifts in altitude. He's really, really good.

"I'm sorry," I say to Dina.

"For what?"

I don't see a scar on her wrist or even a bandage. The surgeon must have been first-rate. *Rare in a black-market doctor.*

"Leaving."

She cocks a brow at me. "I don't blame you for wanting some leave, Jax. It's been a pretty fragged-up run, hasn't it? And we could scarcely have found a safer port."

I narrow my eyes at Saul. "You lied to me."

He turns, offering me a layered smile. "Dina never doubted you were coming back. So I had to make that happen, didn't I?"

They never told her I left for good?

Doc's ice blue eyes tell me things I never knew about him: He'll lie, cheat, or steal to unearth this truth. On the surface, he's the model of chivalry, courtesy, and kindness, a gentleman scholar. But he analyzed the situation and told me exactly what would get me back on board. And here I am.

"What's going on?" Dina glances between us, interested but wary. And so I fill her in. By the time I've finished, she can't get her breath for laughing. "Just how stupid do you think I am? If you took off, we'd stay till we found someone. Like hell do I see myself as a jumper; I had fun with Clary. Wouldn't have minded hanging around another couple of weeks, but Saul said you were ready to get back to it."

Beneath his intellectual exterior lies a ruthless bastard. And this is the first time I've seen it. I experience a frisson of unease, as if I've been sailing along a smooth sea, unaware of dangers that lurk unseen.

Between March and Doc, I have been *handled*.

CHAPTER 43

We bitch at each other throughout the entire jump.

I've never done that before, didn't even know it was possible. We're lucky we didn't wind up past the Polaris system, halfway to Old Terra. I unplug and bounce out of the nav chair, glaring at March, hands on hips.

"I can't believe I bought into this again. You and Doc, you two would say anything to keep me here. What about the stuff you said in my quarters? Was that bullshit, too?"

"No," he answers, setting our cruise course for New Terra. "He said he'd figure something out, but I have never lied to you."

"No, you have lackeys do that for you."

"Are you *looking* for a reason to fight with me?" He unstraps and pushes to his feet. "I can't fake anything with you. I had no fragging clue how he meant to get you back here. And when you said that about Dina dying, I almost said, 'Huh?' "

"So why didn't you?"

"I wanted to find out what he told you." March cups my shoulders gently. "Look at me and swear you honestly don't believe I thought you were never coming back."

It's true, he looks like shit, but I don't want to be persuaded. I want to argue. "I don't know." Both my hands curl into fists at my sides. "I'm tired of having nobody I can trust. Tired of people keeping secrets from me, tired of not being sure whether I'm even working for the *good* guys."

"Jax, I can't promise we're squeaky clean, but look at the opposition. They killed eighty-two people on the *Sargasso* for unknown reasons. They blew up DuPont Station with two hundred souls living there, not counting the unborn." He breathes like merely thinking of it hurts him. "But I'm solid, right?"

"I guess so," I mutter.

When he pulls me toward him, I lean my head against his chest, wondering if I can truly trust him. Wondering whether I can trust my own judgment. I've known from the beginning they intend to use me, and March is bound by so many debts and promises, none of them to me.

His hands play over my back. "I know you're mad. Did you yell at Doc?" Feeling sheepish, I shake my head. "Why not?"

"I'm afraid to provoke him," I confess, low. "I don't know him like I thought I did."

"You're afraid to provoke Saul," he repeats, looking incredulous. "Who's a *pacifist*. So you take it out on me." March shakes his head. "You're one of a kind, Jax. We've got eight hours before New Terra. Come on."

Put that way, I know it doesn't make a lot of sense. I think about it, trying to quantify the feeling, but I can't. Maybe I'm mixing Doc up with the Unit Psychs or even Canton Farr. Do I really think he's capable of greater malice? I don't fucking know. At best he believes the end justifies the means, and I can't sort it out. So when March reaches for me, I take his hand and let him lead me to his quarters.

As he guides me to the bed, I whisper, "I thought you said it was too soon."

He kisses my forehead. "Not for this. I'm tired, but I want you with me." In an economy of movement he drops onto the mattress, then rolls to his side, back to the wall. "Unless you have somewhere else you'd rather be." There's a certain vulnerability in his voice, and maybe I play on that while I gaze around his cabin, pretending to take in the bunk built out from the wall, the closet adjacent to the san facilities, and the personal sys-term on the opposite wall. "Jax?"

"I think I can clear my schedule for you."

The bunk feels firm beneath my knees; it doesn't give as I slide down onto my side, facing him. One thing's sure; whoever designed the *Folly* didn't anticipate the crew sharing their sleep space, which seems a little shortsighted. Only centimeters separate us, then he drapes an arm over my waist, pulling me closer.

"Lights off."

I'd know him in the dark. He always smells of citrus and a darker woodsy scent, like standing in a cedar forest at midnight. His heat washes over me, chin to shins, and my toes curl.

"Do you ever think about him?"

"Him who?" March sounds drowsy. He runs a hand over my head, knotting his fingers in the coarse curls. But gently, like I have silken princess hair.

"Baby-Z."

We've never really talked about that night. It's about time we did if we intend to move on from it.

He stirs then, pushing up on one elbow. "You feel guilty."

"Yeah." That seems inadequate, but I don't have words to translate that moment where we knelt, mutually awed by the small miracle unfolding at our feet to how I felt when I realized I had splattered a helpless, living creature along with Canton Farr.

I don't know anything about what his life might've been like, or how his parents may have felt when they awoke to find one of their young missing with no explanation. I don't even have the framework to grieve properly.

I squirm, sick with remembrance of my casual brutality. Beneath the guilt, I suffer the certainty I wouldn't have shot so fast if it had been a human child in Farr's arms. Deep down I'm another thoughtless bigot who believes in human skin privilege. My life is worth more because I have a particular biochemistry? The realization repulses me.

And it devalues the heroism of someone who gave his life for me.

"I can't absolve you," he says quietly. "All I know is, if it had been you on the ground, I'd have done the same thing."

"You feel this way a lot? Like nothing you do could be enough to make up for it."

In the half-light, his eyes go strange and distant, fringed in those impossible lashes. "You get used to it. And occasionally you run across something you can do to try to brighten up the dark places."

March doesn't say it, but I know that's why he feels like he needs to try twice as hard as anyone else. If he lets down his guard, he might go skidding down that slippery slope again. And maybe I won't recognize what comes out the other side.

"Thus you play the hero."

With a nod, he brushes his lips against my ear. Sparks just shimmer down my spine. This man's pure narcotic, delicious and addictive. Don't know how I thought I could walk away from him for good.

"Jax, I can't think about what I'd do if something happened to you, if it *had* been you on that floor." His mouth compresses into a thin white line, and a shudder runs through him. "You just don't know . . . the things I've done. What I'm capable of. I hope you never do."

When he gets like this, he scares me a little. I run my fingers along his jaw, feeling the tension thrumming through him. That would be why he still keeps certain things partitioned when we're jacked in. I hope he trusts me enough to let me in, someday.

"Let it go," I say quietly.

And realize the suggestion applies to me as well, but it's easier said than done. I can't just write off the guilt or stop wishing things were different. Neither can he. March acknowledges the rightness of my thought with a half smile.

Mary, I've never had this kind of connection with anyone. How does he bear being part of me? Sometimes I can't stand *myself*.

"I'm sorry about baby-Z . . . he's just one more weight on me. If we hadn't gone to Marekeq, he'd have hatched by now. Be living out his normal span. Instead, he's just a bunch of samples in Doc's database."

"I did that."

"Yeah. But a hundred turns from now, baby-Z will be remembered. He's making a contribution. Maybe that will help, someday, when the academy is more than a dream."

I exhale against his throat in a long sigh and close my eyes. "I don't imagine that would console his parents much. I wish we could tell them. Somehow."

"Maybe we can. Somehow. Get some sleep, Jax. We can't fix anything right now."

March makes a good point. And I'm flat busted, so I take his good advice.

Don't know how much later it is when I stir, finding my-self wrapped tight in someone's arms. *March.* I'm on the *Folly* again. It all comes back to me although I'm not mad anymore. How can I be when I wanted this, deep down? I couldn't sleep for dreaming of him. To reassure myself that I'm awake, I run my hand across his waist, finding the gap between shirt and slacks. I delight in dragging my nails lightly over his lower back and feeling him shiver. Goose bumps spring up wherever I touch.

His eyes open to slits, dark choclaste, golden caramel flecks. "What're you doing?"

"Stroking you." I pillow my cheek on my forearm and continue inscribing patterns on his spine.

"I'm not a pet," he murmurs. "And you're making it hard to sleep."

"Am I?" I smile and hook my thigh over his. The way I figure, it's time. Life-affirming ritual, seal unspoken promises to each other, and a lot of other psychobabble that boils down to wanting sex.

And I do. But it's more than that, this time. I needed the time away to reflect and heal, but I needed to come back, too, even if I would never have done it on my own.

"You know you are."

He skates his palm from its innocuous resting place between my shoulder blades to curl around my hip. The heat feels good, but it pales in comparison to the tingles that sparkle through me when March slides his hand lower, cupping my thigh. Deftly, he searches out nerves on my inner thigh, caressing through the thin fabric of my trousers. I squirm against him a little, not an intentional tease; I just can't help it.

Then he looks into my eyes. I register the silent question and nod, but as he tilts his head against mine, I realize I haven't said yes to what I intended. Thought he was going to strip me naked, but instead he comes inside me another way. My head's full of him, awash in sensual images I only half process as they amplify my arousal. My breasts ache, as if he's sucking them, and I feel hot, damp, between my thighs, so ready. He hasn't even touched me.

"March . . ." At that he shifts his head away, leaving me lonely and shuddering. "Wh-what did you do to me?"

"I could bring you off that way," he whispers. "Just me, inside your head."

Instinctively I know that's not an idle boast. He left me so close, panting on the precipice, and if he moves, I might lose it, grinding myself against him like I'm in heat. The very idea wrenches a moan out of me.

"Have you done that often?" I'm surprised at my tone. Oh Mary, I hate the thought of him making anyone else feel this way.

But he shakes his head, a faint smile pulling at his mouth. "Two things make this possible. Our theta waves are compatible, and you're wide-open to me. Even untutored minds have basic shields that prevent such intrusion, Jax; it's a fundamental human trait. With other people, I skim the surface and only see their superficial thoughts. I've never been . . . part of anyone before." He cups my cheek in his palm, long fingers stroking my temple. "That's what I want without you running away afterward. I want to fall asleep and know there's no place you'd rather be."

I tremble, afraid to envision it. Though I know some pilots and jumpers do it jacked in, I always dismissed it as a kink. March doesn't need wetware, though. I find myself unable to resist the mental images, our bodies straining as he saturates my senses completely, no sense of self, drowning in mutual pleasure.

"Yes."

I seek his mouth in the artificial darkness, finding it first with my fingertips. His lips part, a flicker of heat as he licks my skin. And I replace my hand with my lips, starving for him. This time I'm the aggressor, nuzzling the tenderness of his mouth to taste him, explore the texture of a rough velvet tongue, the smooth bone of his teeth. His whiskers scrape my skin, contrasting to the softness of our mouths. I want to crawl inside him, devour him.

Can't remember feeling this way before.

With a muffled groan, he rolls me beneath him, and I know a moment of pure euphoria. He can't resist, no matter what he said about it being too soon. I want everything he described, everything—

Shakes.

So hard we tumble from the bunk and hit the floor, hard. March is good, but we're not even having sex yet, so I don't think I can claim the earth moved. *Of all the Mary-sucking luck.* I can't get my breath for a variety of reasons. He landed on top of me, and . . . I think he broke my rib.

"Shit, you okay?" he asks, crawling off me.

The ship's alarm sounds on cue.

CHAPTER 44

Lucky we aren't scrambling to get dressed as we stum-
ble into the corridor.

The *Folly* listing like this can mean only one thing, and
we take another hit as the four of us intersect in the hub.
The bombardment continues. I smell something burning,
and Dina looks . . . panicked. Never seen that expression
before, so whatever's gone wrong, she can't fix it.

Shit.

"We've got a breach," she says, breathless. "Cruised too
close to New Terra, and now their Satellite Defense Installation is all over us. No surprise, we're on the shit list. Only
thing we can do now is try to sneak into the atmosphere
with the shuttle."

"Why didn't someone wake me before we got in range?"
March growls. "I didn't plan on coming up to the front door
and knocking!"

"You didn't tell us to, you brainless hump." Dina glares

at us both. "Besides, you're the one who left it on autopilot to go roll around with Jax."

"The only rolling came when we fell off the bed." That's probably an unnecessary correction, but trivia keeps me calm.

"There is no time for this," Doc says. "I suggest we get to the shuttle immediately."

To think I could still be on Gehenna, wiping baby spit off my shoulder. I spare a thought for Adele and Domina, Mattin and Lleela, and for my lovely glastique flat. I want to go back; it's home. I want to make love with March there, so it feels like we're flying.

First we have to live through this, however.

Doc's logic can't be argued, so March answers, "Get anything you need from quarters, only necessities, and meet back in two minutes. The shuttle's leaving in three. *Move*, people."

We spring into motion. In my case I'm heading to quarters to grab a change of clothes and my PA. *I just unpacked, dammit.* It's hard to tell what I've got, but I cram it all in the bag and move down the hall at a dead run. When I reach the hold, I see Dina waiting. She's got the doors open, and I regard the boxy little vessel dubiously.

"How the hell is this thing going to get us to the surface under fire?"

"It won't be fired on," she assures me. "I can trick out the energy readings so our signal will be lost amid the big boom the *Folly*'s going to make. Just got to time it right."

"If you say so." I climb aboard and buckle myself into the second row of seats.

She follows, but she gets in front, choosing the copilot's chair. Better to make the techno-mojo, I suppose. My hands feel like I've been squeezing squid, and my stomach keeps trying to push out my throat. If I hate terrestrial driving, then I hate shoe boxes like this ten times more. A kid on a scooter could take us out, let alone the kind of damage those SDIs are dealing.

March and Doc arrive simultaneously, although the geneticist frets as he clambers in beside me. "I hope I retrieved all my data. Got the Mareq samples . . . but I've discovered some unexpected links since I've been studying your most recent scans—"

"Shut up and strap in." Nice to know March doesn't reserve his charm for me alone.

"Yes, of course." Doc piles his things at his feet and complies as the larger ship feels like it's shaking to pieces around us.

"Life support's online. We've got maybe two hours before the air starts to go bad," Dina tells us, as if we didn't have enough to worry about.

"Get the loading doors open, Dina. We're going for a ride." I'm disgusted to detect a note of pure exhilaration in March's voice.

Swear to Mary, he thrives on adversity, and if that's the case, no wonder he wants me around. Where I used to be charmed, everything I touched turned to gold; since Matins IV, it's like I stepped through a witching mirror to the other side. But hey, at least March enjoys my jinx, right?

"Sure thing, boss."

As the doors swing open, I decide there's nothing scarier than seeing space with just a few centimeters of poly-metal alloy between you and horrible asphyxiation. However, there's a bright side. If we wind up out there, we'll only have about ten seconds to feel sorry for ourselves.

"I give the poor girl thirty seconds," Dina says, hushed, like someone's dying.

At first I think she's talking about me, but then we almost seem to drift off the *Folly*. March uses power sparingly, and I glimpse the first hint of what Dina meant. With hull splintered, huge hunks of metal adrift, she looks like she's about to break in two. Yet the SDI fires with the relentless precision of a machine-driven attack.

I can't watch, so I squeeze my eyes shut. It feels like we're moving too slow; any minute the SDI could figure out that we're not wreckage. But maybe that's the key here, just as it is in nature. In my survival training, we learned never to run from a predator; it just makes it think you're something that should be chased.

At least my ribs stopped hurting—nothing like adrenaline to cure what ails you.

"Now," Dina orders. "She's going to pieces. Head for the surface!"

In such a small craft I feel the speed especially in my stomach, and I become aware of Doc, gray-faced and sweating beside me. He lied to me, so why I should I care if he looks worse than I feel? *But we're a team, whether I like it or not.* Wordlessly I offer my hand, and he squeezes it as if he wants to make blood shoot out my fingertips.

We come screaming into the atmosphere like an angry comet. Did we leave a trail? Is anyone coming behind us going to be able to tell what happened? Any minute I expect the shuttle to shake apart, but March manages amid cursing that does Mair proud.

Dina monitors panels and sensors, muttering suggestions. "Ease up, dammit. You're going to burn out the stabilizers, and I don't think we want to test impact resistance in this thing."

He spares her a look. Not just a look, *the* look. "You want to fly this?"

Huh, I'm not the only one who gets that.

"No, but just remember—"

Oh, that noise can't be good.

"Told you to ease up." She sounds so smug, considering that the shuttle wobbles like it wants to start spinning and not stop until we collide, hard, with the ground.

Although I'm not an expert, I tend to prefer that doesn't happen. They bicker back and forth while Doc crushes the shit out of my hand. Maybe I believe too much in March, but I don't think we're going to crash. Sure enough, even with the unsteady shimmy, side-to-side stir-fry action, he manages to slow the shuttle, skimming over the ground as he looks for a place to land.

March puts us down just before the stabilizers crackle for the last time. Doc staggers out as soon as the doors open, falls onto his hands and knees. I turn away so I don't have to see him getting sick. My stomach still feels shaky, and that's not helping. I step away, and then scrape a palm over my face. *Time to take stock.*

We're in the middle of a field.

If Old Terra is a ghetto world, an urban sprawl stripped of natural resources, then New Terra is its farm colony. Cities here are few and far between. I lived in New Boston, where my parents styled themselves "society," but this infinite expanse of golden grain boasts no landmarks. Overhead, the sky looms heavy and gray, indifferent, but the wind smells of damp earth and growing things, an echo of my childhood clear as a phantom with twin plaits and a handful of sweets.

"So where are we?" Dina asks. To my vast exasperation, they all regard me with expectant expressions, even March, like I should be able to pinpoint our location via some native global positioning system.

"New Terra."

Doc straightens, wiping his mouth with the back of his hand. "I believe she meant more specifically, Sirantha."

No shit? The man really has a penchant for stating the obvious. That's the trouble with geniuses; most of them seem to lack anything like a sense of humor, so they're forever "clarifying" for other people when they were, in fact, being smart-asses.

"You know it's been like sixteen years since I've been

here, right? And I wasn't a world traveler before I signed with the Corp, not that there's too much to see." I wave a hand at the vegetation, which, thanks to the wind, seems to wave back. "But it's definitely a Conglomerate world. The Corp has their home office here."

"Well," March says, "since we can't fly the shuttle, we need to get some distance from it. I don't think we want to be found here if someone comes looking."

That's the first sensible thing I've heard. We have gray men and bounty hunters looking for us. Neither will stop until they bring us in, the former for order and honor, the latter for the payday. Now that we're stranded in enemy territory, shit's only going to get harder. March glances at me, smiling. He really does love this.

Dina shrugs. "If we're going, let's go. We're burning daylight."

I sling my bag over my shoulder while Doc fidgets with various bits of gear. What he took to be essential seems like a lot more than what the rest of us grabbed.

My stomach growls. Can't remember when I ate last. Jump-travel has a way of lagging the shit out of your biosystems. "Did anyone think to snag some rations?"

"I've got a week's worth of paste." March doesn't look delighted by the prospect, though, and he's the survival specialist.

"Perfect," Saul says, all loaded up. Good thing he's strong; he'll need to be. "It could always be worse, hm?" he adds, sounding determinedly cheerful.

Nobody responds to that, but before we walk ten meters, it starts to rain.

CHAPTER 45

March is the only one who brought bivouac.

Like I said, he's the survival expert. Doc packed all his lab gear, various scanners and samplers, other stuff I don't know the names for, while Dina brought her tools. As for me, I grabbed my favorite shoes and clean underwear. What can I say, some of my mother's lessons stuck, although I refuse to put my hair up, and I haven't worn a dress in almost twenty years.

If she had her way, I'd have a vanilla husband and a dignified career as an art dealer, selling to the cultured at an exorbitant price. Instead, I'm plodding through a field, lost, while my belly chews through my backbone. For a fleeting moment I wonder what the life I left behind would've been like. Just as quickly I dismiss the curiosity; I'd have choked to death in their world.

We walk until true sunset. I pause, gazing up at the streaked sky, tear trails of scarlet blurred over cobalt. Damn, haven't seen one of those since we left Lachion, though I'm not sure how long ago that was. I wonder how Keri is faring among the clans, whether she's married the Gunnar yet. Nobody says much as we set camp near a scrubby copse of trees that exist only to demarcate one field from another.

The rain subsides into a miserable mist, drizzling down through our clothes until we're all irascible. Dinner takes all of thirty seconds, but my mood improves marginally when I see Doc and Dina wrap up in rain slickers and bed down on the wet ground. Seems like I may end up the same way since all I have is clean underwear, but then I see March beckoning me from the mouth of his sleep cylinder. This thing only holds one person, but I manage to wriggle in beside him. He fastens the end up, and we elbow each other more than once in getting settled.

As he pulls me close, I hear Dina grumble, "Shit, *I'd* sleep with him to get out of this weather."

Into the silence, Doc stage-whispers, "So would I."

I break down as March calls back, "No thanks, I'm good."

Guess I am crazy because even though I have no earthly reason to believe things are going to work out, right now I'm happy. Maybe I'm like March, and I thrive under less-than-ideal circumstances. What a fragging understatement.

"Please don't make me listen to you shagging," Dina cracks. I hear Doc laughing, like this is an adult sleepover. "The rain's bad enough."

"You're just jealous you didn't get me while you had the chance," I shoot back, before March shushes me with a kiss.

But there's no room for anything else, even if we were so inclined, and I'm *not*. Though I'm fine with the other two knowing about March and me in the abstract, I don't get into V&E. My kinks are pretty tame, come to that. His body heat warms me, and I fall asleep listening to him breathe.

In the morning, it's more paste and some bitching for breakfast. No surprise that I bear the brunt of it because I just thought to check my PA. As it turns out, 245 *does*, in fact, possess a navigation system, even if I don't.

"Greetings, Sirantha Jax. It has been six days since your last entry." Do I detect a trace of censure in 245's synthesized tone? I'm telling you, this little gadget is not like other AIs.

"Sorry about that."

"Are you still having the dreams? Would you like to—"

"Er, no. Let's not talk about that." My cheeks burn as I try to shut the machine up. Yeah, I talked to 245 when I was on Gehenna. I cringe, remembering the way I rambled about March. "Can you figure out where we are? I saw that you have—"

"What world is this, Sirantha Jax? I possess the ability to calculate geographic location based on latitude and longitude, but I need to assimilate certain local parameters to ensure accurate computation."

"New Terra." I give the same answer as yesterday, but it offers significantly different results this time.

"According to my best estimate," 245 says modestly, "the nearest settlement lies eighteen kilometers north-northwest. Unless I have erred, this would be Maha City."

Shit.

I can see in their faces, they have no idea what that means. But we're halfway across the continent from New Boston. "Thanks, 245. See you later." With that, I snap the sphere shut, only to notice the way the others are staring at me. "What?"

"It's your best friend, huh?" Dina smirks at me.

"No, that's you, sweetness."

I make like I'm going to hug her, and she shuts up real quick. She even backs away like I'm dangerous, deranged, or diseased. Doc glances up from organizing his gear to offer a half smile. He's been too quiet.

"Not a bad hike." March tips his head back, assessing the clouds.

I could tell him it's not going to rain. Today, the sun beats down on us from a pure blue sky, drying up the muddy patches. Even the grain glitters in the distance, throwing golden sparks row to row with each ripple of the wind. But it *is* going to get hot.

Sighing, I say, "Let's see how far we get then."

Nightfall finds me exhausted and bitchy, although the other three hold up better. March wants to press on. Doc and Dina don't seem to care, irritatingly solid, both of them, so I drag my feet and mumble. I feel sweaty and wilted; my scalp itches, and every exposed inch of skin has been stung or bitten by something. We've passed several farms and outbuildings, but we agree that it's a bad idea to linger where strangers must be scarce. So I suck it up and keep going, but I draw the line when I overhear the whispered conversation taking place as the first city lights come into view.

"She's got to," Dina murmurs, low. "You know she's the one they're looking for, and with all that hair—"

"What about my hair?" I stop in alarm, gathering the wild mass in both hands.

"I don't know that it matters," Doc says with a strange, tight smile.

My eyes go to March, who produces a wicked-looking knife. "I'm sorry, Jax."

"No! Come on, I can . . ." But I come up with nothing, so I bend my head dumbly, the sacrificial goat.

I'm not brave. As March starts hacking, my vision blurs, and I can't help but sniffle. I don't *remember* the last time I had my hair cut; it's my trademark. Maybe it's frizzy, unruly, wild as an Anduvian ice otter, but it's me—

And that is exactly why it has to be shorn.

But he's not content just to slice it short. I start when I feel the blade scraping across my skull. "What the frag—"

"It'll help you pass for a boy," Dina explains. She takes a closer look then and gives me a roguish grin. "Or a really cute butch. Rawr. Er, anyway, try to keep your head down until we can do something about those eyes."

"What's wrong with my eyes?!"

"They're memorable," March says, wiping the blade on his thigh.

Sweet, but it doesn't make me feel one bit better about being bald. The wind feels too cold against my naked scalp, and I run my fingers over the rough shave with a pained little whimper. I think I might cry.

"For Mary's sake," Dina grumbles, "it's just hair. It'll grow back."

"Want me to shave yours?" I growl at her.

She shrugs. "If it'll shut you up."

"Let us give them a moment." Doc guides her away, probably whispering that she needs sensitivity training.

March bends his head to mine, kissing me in a delicate brush of warmth. "You're gorgeous. All that hair hiding such beautiful bones, I can't believe it."

Though I know he's bullshitting me, trying to smooth me past the desire to throw a fit, it helps. "You're so full of it."

March shakes his head, solemn as a barrister. "No, really. You might even look better this way." I narrow my eyes on him, knotting my fist in his shirt. "Too much?"

"Uh, yeah."

After lacing our fingers together, he leads me toward the others. Maha City twinkles against the dark, glints of scarlet and silver snaking together as if to form a cogent image. We're just not high enough to appreciate the art.

"So who are you, Jax?" I see him smiling, teeth gleaming in the moonlight. Oh, he's teasing me, but his comeuppance is nigh. "My little brother?"

I shrug, studiedly casual. "That's not what you need to worry about."

His thumb slides over my index finger in a soft, proprietary caress. "And what would that be?"

"Being the guy who wants to shag your own little brother."

That's the first time I've gotten the last word with March.

CHAPTER 46

Our credits are running low.

I made enough to get by on Gehenna, but Outskirts currency possesses no exchange value on Conglomerate worlds. Keri could wire us funds, as Lachion is nominally a Corp world, but it would link her to us, and that's something we need to avoid, considering our infamy. If anyone suspected them of bankrolling our activities, that would be the end. So I'm not sure how we're going to pay for somewhere to stay, or how we're supposed to make our way all the way to New Boston.

Worry nags me like a frigid wife. We can't take public transport because I can't use official stations. It would be disastrous if I tried to travel using my own identity, and it would take both creds and connections to acquire a good forgery. And we don't know anyone except my parents, and it's not like I can ask them for help. If they're alive, they're mortified at how low I've sunk and are telling everyone they aren't related to me. I don't realize I'm scowling until March smooths the lines from between my brows.

"We'll figure something out," he assures me softly.

Maha City spins out in concentric rings. At the center lies the posh upscale area, including the business district, the metropolitan museum, and the municipal center. I gleaned that much from looking at the map 245 showed me, but what I didn't realize is that the farther you go from the city center, the worse it gets.

We pass through shantytown first, hovels scraped together from spare parts and scrap metal. A dog sits in the road, gazing at us with uncanny eyes. Its lips curl back from its muzzle, and it growls deep in its throat as we pass by. The only vehicles seem derelict, rusted, and we find a family asleep when we peer inside.

"I'd rather camp than look for a room here." Dina speaks for all of us, for once.

"I thought the Corp promised prosperity for everyone." The skin on the back of my neck prickles, as if we're being watched. As we continue deeper into the city, I feel glad that from my silhouette and shaven head, I look like a boy although that wouldn't discourage the determined.

"Only in advertisements," March murmurs.

A yawn that crackles my jaw overtakes me, the sort that leaves your eyes watering, but we can't rest until we find a safe place. Dying in our sleep won't solve anything in the long run, even if a nihilist would argue it's coming down the pike at some point anyway, so we might as well embrace it.

The moon hangs over us, bloated, gibbous, and yellow— its beams look tainted as they slide over the corrugated shelters in rivers of oily light. We trudge along until the streets start getting brighter, and we're greeted with a collage of low-slung buildings, flophouses and speakeasies. Distant, mellifluous notes slink toward us in the dark like melancholy whores.

No structure stands over two stories tall, as if they squat here in fear of giants that tear such hubris down, but an acrid smell hangs heavy in the air, declaring the machinery functional. We're unlikely to do better at this time of night. So we turn at random into a white building with a sign that proclaims with laconic largesse: rooms.

We transact business with a greasy man wearing a shirt stained with a week's worth of dinners and armpit sweat. Hair bristles from his face in a porcine fashion, and his grunts as we pay for our rooms reinforce that impression. He handles our rental through a metal grill, densely woven, only a slot large enough to slide a credit stick through at the bottom.

"Twelve, fourteen, and sixteen, down toward the end. There's a communal san-shower, last door." He manages to speak without moving his mouth, without making eye contact. Just as well because I'm not supposed look at people until I get some tinted lenses.

This isn't the sort of place where they ask for names or identification, and I'm glad to go. The office smells of rancid meat and human sweat, loneliness and despair. Back outside, we follow the broken walk, counting the prefab housing units until we find ours. These rooms don't have palm locks because that would require configuration technology. He's given us three digits that open the metal tumbler latching the door, and there's no telling how many others know it.

"Be careful," I tell Dina and Doc, as they go on to their rooms.

She laughs. "Anything that comes in on me tonight better be prepared to die."

March pauses at the door, spinning the numerals until I hear a snick. The room revealed barely qualifies for the name, squeaking in by virtue of its four walls and ceiling. No windows, no san facilities, no furniture, there's just the ragged sleep-mat that appears to be affixed to the floor.

I flash him a wry smile. "No wonder I like you. Since you take me to such nice places, and you do hair, too."

He has the grace to show chagrin as he runs a hand over my bare scalp. "I really am sorry, Jax. But it was for the best."

"I know. You want the shower?"

Shaking his head, he drops his bag, then kisses the tip of my nose. "You take the first one. It's only fair, considering what I've put you through. I might sack out, though, if you take more than five minutes." He gives me a sleepy smile.

There's the fist again, squeezing at my heart. Shit, I don't *want* to feel like this, but sometimes, sometimes the man can be so sweet. It's getting harder to remember what an asshole he can be. "Thanks."

I can't wait to be clean, so I head for the san-shower. It's black in here, stale, sour air that smells as if it blows upward from sinister, sulfuric places in the earth. I bump the door shut behind me with my hip, and I'm immediately sorry.

"Lights on."

Standing here in the dark convinces me the facilities must be manual, so I fumble around, hearing my own breathing. My heart resounds in my ears as I find the switch. Sudden illumination. I swallow a shriek as a swarm of chittering insects scuttle across the floor and out of sight. Being dirty seems *much* less objectionable, but I refuse to concede defeat. So I close my eyes and scrub up, amazed at how fast it goes without hair to wash.

I dress quickly, watching my feet for the return of those creepy things. Crunchy bugs make the inside of my stomach shudder. Shouldering my bag, I step out onto the walk, flick the switch, then shut the door behind me.

My heart gives a wild thump as Doc steps out of the shadows. *Right, he's in room 16, the last before the shower.*

But I thought I heard the murmur of him talking to someone, although I don't see anyone else around.

"You scared me."

Mary, he looks so strange in this light, something about the way the moon shines his eyes, almost blind but feral. I feel the same unease as I did aboard the *Folly*, after I discovered his deception.

"Did I?"

"Yes." I back up a step, wrestling with an irrational instinct telling me to run.

"Intuition is an interesting thing," he says. "Sometimes it gives us cues that cannot be explained by logic. Don't you find that to be the case, Sirantha?"

"Doc wouldn't have lied to me." I take another step back, finding myself flush against the building. "He wouldn't. Who *are* you?"

In a movement so fast I can't track it, the creature whips an arm around my throat. "Excellent. I'm tired of this skin." His flesh seems to liquefy, then it sloughs away to reveal a bony carapace with black holes where the eyes should be. The creature's body elongates, no longer short and stocky. "So cramped and limiting."

"You're a Slider," I breathe.

I've heard of them, so dubbed because they can slide into someone else's life seamlessly. They're the best bounty hunters in the known universe, native to Ithiss-Tor, but who expects ever to *meet* one? They're rare like chi-masters and glass-dancers. I should feel flattered that the Corp set one on me. Instead, my stomach knots, and my palms start to sweat.

"An unflattering designation." Its mandible flexes, a sign of displeasure, undoubtedly. "You were so cooperative, coming to New Terra with me like this."

Shit.

"M-maybe we could cut a deal—" I try to stall, find out

what it wants most. Maybe someone will come out and surprise it. If I scream, will it kill me? Am I worth more dead or alive? I fragging wish I knew.

"How much do you care for them?" it whispers. "If you refuse to accompany me to the rendezvous point, my associates will descend on this place and kill everyone for the inconvenience. But if you cooperate, I will let them go. There is no bounty on them, and I care nothing for this 'project,' although the doctor's research is . . . interesting. However, I have not been hired to safeguard Farwan's interests, only to retrieve you."

I feel its claw tracing a caress across my throat.

CHAPTER 47

My bag slips from my fingers.

When they discover it, they'll know something is wrong. Whether that will help me in any fashion, I don't know. It's clear that I have to go with him, however. I have a better chance of survival if I cooperate. Maybe I can escape from the Corp facility. Maybe I can escape en route, but if I struggle or scream, this Slider will slit my throat. I could rouse the others, but I'd be dead before they could help me. Backed by a long, proud history of not-dying, I *know* when someone's serious.

Beyond all that, I won't let him miss the rendezvous. I won't permit these bastards to descend on Dina and March. I think this is the only semiselfless thing I've ever done in my life.

"Time is money, Sirantha." The talon on my jugular depresses, and I swallow, feeling my pulse pound like I'm prey.

"Let's go."

Can't wonder what happened to Doc.

"A wise choice." It snaps something around my wrist. "If you move more than two hundred meters from the control device on my belt, the slave bracelet will detonate. I have never taken a target foolish enough to test it, but I understand it does significant structural damage to the human form. Let us depart. I am sure you are no more eager to linger in my company than I am to have you."

The broken walk leads us away from rented rooms and silent sleepers. I follow him, docile as a pet. That scrapes against the grain. Now that his claw's off my throat, I picture myself killing him, removing the belt and taking it with me until I can get the bracelet off, but . . . that doesn't solve my immediate problem, even if I could get the best of him, which I doubt, unless I strike while he's asleep. Regardless, I still have to protect Dina and March, and I can't see any way to do that except by going to the Slider ship.

March. What if he thinks I ran again? I know I don't have a rep for being reliable, not like him. Former acquaintances would say, "Sirantha Jax values her own ass above all others." *But I didn't leave you because I wanted to, baby. Not this time.*

"I don't know," I mutter. "I don't imagine you're any worse than the Corp."

The thing makes a curious sound in its throat. "You are a strange woman." I can identify the tone as amusement, so that noise must have been laughter.

"Not the first time I've heard that." Maybe I should be terrified, but so far as I understand, Sliders are pragmatic. If I don't give it any trouble, it's going to turn me over to the Corp in one piece. Of course what comes afterward will probably make me *wish* I was dead. "So what should I call you?"

Beside me, its movements strike me as distinctively mantislike. "Why must you call me anything?"

"You're a person," I say, trying to sound reasonable as

every moment moves us farther away. "So am I. There's no reason we shouldn't keep this civil."

"You are not a person, you are my captured quarry. But you may call me Velith if it pleases you."

"Nice to meet you." I'm determined to be polite. Maybe if I'm nice enough, I can make it feel guilty about turning me over to the Corp. *And maybe Mother Mary will descend from heaven to deliver me.* If I'm going to hang my fate on an impossible hook, then I may as well dream big. "So what's it like on Ithiss-Tor? I've never been. Your people don't encourage tourism."

"No, I suppose they do not," he agrees, but his pitch disturbs me. I hear dual harmonics that make me feel as though I am listening to more than one entity. "As for the homeworld, I have not returned in many years."

"Why not?"

"If you believe our relationship is such that I shall confide in you, Sirantha Jax, you are much mistaken. Now keep silent."

Velith picks a careful path back toward the shantytown. Appears we're not going deeper into Maha City, which make sense. Nobody notes the comings and goings out here. If nothing else, there's a certain freedom in abject poverty, I suppose. When we reach a truly impressive junkyard, he pauses and activates one of the devices I didn't recognize. It glows gold, and then there's an answering hum from a ship well concealed among the derelicts.

"Seems your associates are punctual," I observe unnecessarily.

"It is one of their few redeeming qualities."

"That good, huh? I can't wait to meet them. Bet you're a bundle of charm in comparison, the 'face' man of the organization."

He—she?—makes the odd choking noise again. "You are not what I expected, based on the holo-footage and the dossier Farwan provided."

"No, I'm not really the blow-up-a-space-station type. More likely to kill a carafe of Parnassian red and flash my tits. Or . . . I used to be. Not much of that, lately."

"I recommend you keep your chest covered on board. My associates are more likely to take it as an invitation to dine than as a mating overture."

Shit.

"You mean they aren't more—" I break off before I can piss Velith off by calling his race Sliders again. Trouble is, I can't recall the respectful term. Theirs is an obscure world, seldom studied in our exoanthropology courses, not that I ever took such a thing.

"No," he says dryly, as if I'm an idiot for envisioning a crew comprised of Sliders. "But you will see for yourself, soon enough."

As if on cue, the doors flip up with a soft hiss of decompression. Slim and sleek, shining with ultrachrome, the ship appears to be a Silverfish, good for them, bad for me, as it's the fastest transplanetary vessel available today. Once I climb aboard I'll be delivered to Corp headquarters in Ankaraj in less than two hours.

Velith curls his hand around my unshackled wrist, and I'm surprised to find that his palm feels leathery but not unpleasant. The chitin of his face gives me the crawlies since I can't stand insects with a hard carapace, the way they crunch when you step on them . . . *Oh Mary.* A shudder runs through me.

He glances back, seeming to misinterpret my reaction. "You have nothing to fear from me, Sirantha. You have comported yourself as a model captive, and I will deliver you to your destination unharmed."

"It's not you I'm worried about," I answer truthfully, as we board via three small steps that flip down from the low-slung craft.

"That is . . . most unusual."

I think I've managed to surprise him. Looking like that,

no doubt he's used to people pissing themselves once he sheds his human skin. I wonder if he can smell the acrid tang of terror, whether our emotions manifest to him in the olfactory spectrum. If so, it probably tells him something about his prisoner's intended course of action, and I would do well to remember that. A jump in my adrenaline levels might communicate itself to him in some fashion, warning him I'm about to try something.

Sighing, because I truly needed something else to worry about, I take stock of my surroundings. The interior of a Silverfish is cramped, not intended for extended use. I count ten seats and five of them are filled.

"Mother Mary," I breathe. "Your crew is made up of—" Velith claps a claw across my mouth as a growl goes up from the fanged collective. It occurs to me that they would find the term derogatory.

Glad he didn't let me say it.

"Yes. As you noted earlier, I am the charming one. So I suggest we get under way before you precipitate a problem."

One of them squeezes my arm as I walk by; it's not a warning or a cruelty so much as . . . well, testing my flesh for texture, I suppose. To them, I must look like dinner on the heel. No wonder Velith told me to keep myself covered, although breasts wouldn't be as tasty as they look, all glands and fat.

Velith hisses and chitters, gesturing with both claws and mandible. What I take to be an argument ensues; maybe his crew wants to eat my extremities before delivering me? If I arrive alive but truncated, that would still fulfill the terms of their contract. Finally, one of the Morgut straightens its lower limbs and skitters upright. I find the movement both horrifying and hypnotic. This is a creature, who by all evolutionary standards, should not exist, and it's heading for the cockpit.

How the hell am I going to get out of this?

"Just a misunderstanding," Velith assures me, as he

sinks into a seat with the mantis motion that seems comforting compared to the appalling otherness I discern among the Morgut. That's human slang: We named them so for their insatiable appetite . . . more gut than anything else. They are the stuff of terror vids and bedtime stories told each other by children in hushed, gleeful whispers.

He pats the space next to him, surreal but cordial. "Make yourself comfortable, Sirantha. This will all be over shortly."

Yeah, that's exactly what I'm afraid of.

CHAPTER 48

*I manage to sit beside Velith quietly for all of ten min-*utes.

The inside of the vessel carries a strange sweet-and-sour tang. I'm not sure if it's an odor given off by the Morgut or a food source concealed somewhere. It's all I can do to keep from staring over my shoulder at them, but I don't want to show interest, either.

As a species, they're intelligent but savage, seldom seen on human worlds, primarily because they view us as a delicacy. Gehenna is the most liberal of ports, but after constant incident reports, they became the last non-Conglomerate world to restrict Morgut travel. Here on New Terra, they used to require a permit and a trainer sworn to control them and assume liability for their damages. That sums Farwan Corporation up right there. They don't care about loss of life, just property damage.

"How come they don't eat you?"

"I beg your pardon?"

He doesn't need to turn his head to glance at me. The disconcerting placement of his eyes permits him to study me at his leisure. I'm almost accustomed to the insectile quality of his mannerisms, but I can't figure out how he manages to speak universal. Maybe he has a vocalizer implanted; that would seem to make sense.

"The Morgut'll eat anything. How can you work with them safely?"

His mandible twitches. "My body chemistry renders me poisonous to them."

"Oh. That's convenient. I guess they make incredible enforcers. Strike terror into the hearts of hardened criminals."

"Yes." He inclines his head. "Though it is occasionally difficult to persuade them that our bounties would not be better served with a sweet glaze and mixed fruit."

I grin a bit. "Was that a joke?"

"Perhaps."

"I have to know, were you the ones who chased us into grimspace?"

"Your pilot is good," Velith says. "The ghosts were clever and made tracking you exceedingly difficult."

"I don't suppose—"

"No. Go to sleep, Sirantha."

"I should have known you weren't Doc," I mutter. "He never calls me Sirantha. And he doesn't need me to hold his hand during a landing, and he *doesn't* suffer from motion sickness."

"I did not interpret him well? I adjudged him a scholarly individual, a beta male, who would behave with some timidity in certain situations." He reacts like a vid-actor being advised his performance was over the top.

"You did all right faking the science stuff, although it helps that none of us have a clue what he's talking about half the time, but for personality, no. Not even close." I sigh, tallying up all the inconsistencies. "Where is he, by the way?"

I don't want to believe he's dead. Nutty as it might

sound, I sort of like this Slider. I don't doubt he'd kill if it were necessary, but I'm beginning to get a sense of his intellect. He prefers to think his way around problems.

Velith lifts one jointed shoulder in a fair approximation of a shrug. "I left him in a storage locker. I would surmise he has gotten out by now in some fashion."

No wonder he pushed to get us off Gehenna as soon as possible. Some of the tension eases out of my shoulders, but then I realize I have something else to worry about. "That stuff you said about the lesions . . . did you make that up?"

He hesitates. "I . . . examined all the data and Dr. Solaith's notes, but I am not a scientist, and I needed you to jump to New Terra. The Morgut could not pass on Gehenna for obvious reasons, and I feared I would require their assistance to subdue you."

"Why in the hell would you think that?" I put my hand to my head, meaning to mess with my hair as I tend to do when I'm nervous, but I find nothing but rough skin. Fragging bastard, no wonder he said it didn't matter if I shaved my head, and now I'm bald for nothing.

"You are a cunning and dangerous woman, Sirantha, wanted on every Conglomerate world for mass murder and wanton acts of terrorism."

Shit. From his point of view, he's the good guy, and it's astonishing he has been this polite to me. How ironic; it speaks well of him. I wish I had 245 with me; she could probably figure something out. But she's in the bag I dropped outside the san-shower.

Has March found it yet? Do they know I'm missing?

Desperation laces my voice. I've got less than an hour to think my way out of this. "Did it ever occur to you to that the Corp is guilty of disseminating false information? I'm the only survivor from the *Sargasso* but I didn't do that. The landing authority used override codes on our vessel and supplied incorrect coordinates, the wrong trajectory. They fragging *engineered* that crash."

"Every convict claims he is innocent."

I nod. Every scum-sucking lowlife he's captured has probably begged and pleaded, professing his innocence. I'm just one more in a long line; tough shit for me that in my case it's actually true. For the first time in my life, I can't see a way out.

He'll deliver me to the Corp, where they'll turn me over to Unit Psych Newel, who will work on me until I'm broken, until I confess to anything they want: Matins IV and DuPont Station, who knows what else. After all this, forget Whitefish, they're going to execute me. And the Corp comes off squeaky clean.

I can't fucking stand it. And then I realize there's another way. It goes against all my instincts, but my back's to the wall, and I will *not* let them win. There's one last act of defiance I can offer.

"At the hostel, would you have killed me if I screamed?" My voice sounds hoarse, urgent, and he turns his head then.

His mandibles flex as if he finds the question impolite. "Yes. Then your associates would have rushed to your aid too late; mine would have descended on the place like locusts. A messy situation, best avoided."

Then I accomplished what I intended, saved Dina and March. *Huh, so this is what altruism feels like. It chafes a bit.* But I can't let myself think about March, or I won't have the strength to continue. I force the words out before I think better of them.

"Please . . . if you'd have done it then, do me this kindness. Do it now. Feed me to the Morgut afterward, I don't care. Just don't turn me over to the Corp alive."

Velith clicks his claws together, a sound I interpret as exasperation. "I am not a murderer, Sirantha. I kill when I am presented with no viable alternative."

Wouldn't you know it? A bounty hunter with a conscience. That's it then. I'm out of ideas. Then my eyes light on the bracelet he slapped on my wrist. When we get off the ship, I can try to run, hope to reach two hundred meters out before I'm caught. Don't know whether I'm fast enough to manage it. I don't know if I'm brave enough to do that to myself on purpose.

But if I run, I might incite their predatory instincts. The Morgut might eviscerate me. And as far as I'm concerned, that's preferable to returning to a cell, going back to Psych Officer Newel. There comes a time when speculation ceases to matter and all planning comes down to instinct. Thinking has never been my strong suit anyhow. I just need to—

Grab Velith's arm and slash his claws across my forearm. He scrambles out of his seat like he thinks he's under attack; I'm finally showing my true colors, the crazed killer the Corp has painted me. But by the time he figures it out, it's too late. I work my thumb feverishly over the vein just beneath my elbow, and the blood really starts to flow.

It drips down my forearm and over my fingertips, crimson drops spattering the ki-pants I put on after my shower, intending to curl up next to March. The blood looks dark and obscene against the pale fabric, living art.

"What is the *matter* with you?" I can tell by his tone that he doesn't understand. Not surprising, this isn't something a sane person would do.

His long, thin body blocks the path to the cockpit, as if I would try to take over the ship. That's fine; it even works in my favor, as I'm heading the other way. Bracing my palms on the back of the seat, I bounce over, then it's clear to where the four Morgut sit, conversing in a low chitter.

Deliberately I draw my arm back and fan it across their faces. All four of them draw back as if struck; and then, as one, forked tongues flick out to sample my flavor. Watching their faces, seeing how the slit-pupil eyes dilate with a different sort of lust, I feel like I could puke, but instead, I murmur, "Good? Want more?"

And all hell breaks loose.

CHAPTER 49

I expect to die.

When the first Morgut launches itself at me, I don't even flinch. The others follow in a fury, but I simply squeeze my eyes shut and stand my ground. But instead of going down beneath a wave of rending limbs, Velith shoves me behind him. I have no idea what's going on in his head, but he pushes me back so hard that I overbalance, slamming my head against the seat.

My vision fills with little flecks of light as I hit the floor. I hear grunts, sounds of scuffling, and weapon fire as if through a tunnel. Feel something hot and viscous spattering my face. I could crawl under the seats. Wait. Instead I push to my hands and knees, dizzy and nauseous. I don't know how much blood I've lost.

When I force my eyes open, the ridge along my brow throbs; maybe I hit my face on something on the way down. The carnage astonishes me. Of the five, only Velith's left standing, but he looks really fragged up. Two of the

Morgut bodies are still convulsing, pestilent ooze boiling out of their wounds.

"Why? Why did you do that?" We voice the question in unison, although we're asking vastly different things.

"All I wanted was to die," I whisper. "Why didn't you let me? You still get paid."

He's bleeding in four places that I can see, a thin, delicate stream. Thought his blood would look different, but Vel is more like me than the Morgut. He's not a monster.

His claws click together, and it makes me feel his agitation. "I captured you alive, Sirantha. Never has a target been slain while in my charge, and *no one* is going to sully my impeccable record, not you, not them. Now sit down and shut up before I am tempted to see how much damage you can survive."

The Silverfish slows. Even though it's a graceful descent, I feel the lessening altitude in my belly and in the way my knees bend slightly as if gravity asserts more influence closer to the ground. Don't know whether we've reached Corp headquarters or if the pilot heard the commotion, but I'm betting on the latter.

A low, unpleasant noise comes over the comm system, and Velith cocks his head, listening. "No. *Nicht*. Do *not* come back here. Everything is fine. Keep going." Then he lapses into the chittering I find unintelligible.

But whatever he's saying doesn't appear persuasive, and the Morgut pilot puts us down so deftly I barely feel the touchdown. Whatever else may be said of them, they know their way around a ship. I hear the door to the cockpit unseal with a soft whoosh, but Velith greets him with a shot to the head, and his brains spray out bile green against the bulwark, more modern art.

He seems to read my reaction and lifts a shoulder in that endearing almost shrug. "I never liked him."

That strikes me as absurdly amusing, but I manage to

contain my laughter, knowing it will come out sounding like hysteria. "Why did you kill him?"

"They were clutchmates. He would have attacked us if I had not reacted thus, and I am in no condition to engage in unnecessary violent confrontation."

I shake my head. "You're crazier than they say I am. You should've let them kill me. What's waiting for me at Corp headquarters is so much worse."

With that I turn and head for the door. I'm not afraid of him anymore. My peaceable surrender has accomplished something that I don't quite comprehend, but it seems he feels honor bound to protect me until we reach our destination. I can use that to my advantage. As he pointed out, he isn't in top shape right now. Neither am I, so we'd be two cripples mixing it up with our crutches, so to speak.

Hope neither one of us is that dumb.

I hit the button that unseals the outer doors, and the stairs lower with the smooth sound of well-maintained machinery. A gust of frosty air sends a chill straight through me, and when I peer out, I see that we're in the middle of nowhere. *Big surprise.* But instead of a field full of golden grain, we've landed in smooth, white tundra, mountains in the distance, also white-capped. I'm fragging hungry, so they remind me of choclaste cakes with cream sauce on top. The sky looks as if it may snow, and the light diffused through the clouds appears touched with gold.

We can't be more than a half hour from headquarters by Silverfish flight, but as previously noted, these ships are insanely fast. I have no way of calculating the distance from here to Ankaraj, although the Corp is probably tracking our flight in some fashion.

Sure enough, the comm crackles to life in the cockpit. "*Spiral*, this is control. Do you need assistance? We show you stalled in the Teresengi Basin."

Velith bounds for the cockpit, leaping with unsettling grace over the corpses that litter the aisle. Being battle-sore hasn't decreased his agility. Tapping the panel, he replies, "Yes, but I would also appreciate some information. Why does my target claim that Farwan Corporation is responsible for the crash on Matins IV? Why does the target prefer to provoke a pack of Morgut to being extradited into your custody?"

His questions meet with an uncomfortable silence.

Shit.

Now I'm the one running for the cockpit. I struggle to turn off the feed, but he holds me away, waiting for the answer. My heart starts to pound because I know . . . I *know* we're in danger. They're not going to send aid now; they're going to send aerial assault. I know how they think. I know about their damage control. When he started asking the wrong questions, he ceased to factor for them.

"She's insane," the controller finally responds. "She would say anything. Just sit tight, and help will arrive shortly. We have a unit en route."

"Come on." I tug at his arm. "We have to get out of here. Right now. We *cannot* be on this ship when they get here."

"They claim you are mentally unbalanced, Sirantha." I wish I could read his expression, but I'm incapable of distinguishing anything but the twitch of his mandible and the clicking of his claws, and maybe I interpret those incorrectly as well. "Your behavior suggests paranoia, at best."

"You half believe me." I grab him by the collar. Mary, he looks strange, still wearing Doc's clothes that are too big and too short, so badly shredded by Morgut fangs. "Or you wouldn't have mentioned it. I've raised some doubt in you. Give me this much. Come off the ship with me. Over there . . ." I'm pulling him now, and I'm surprised to feel him follow. With my free hand, I point to a dark jumble of rock in the distance. "To wait. If they really intend to rescue us, there will be a search party and we'll go to meet them peacefully. I won't give you any more trouble, and you can forget you ever saw me. But if I'm right . . . then we don't die when they blow the *Spiral* all to hell and claim it crashed. Velith, please."

"Very well," he says finally. "A test. But we will need some supplies if we are to wait with any degree of comfort."

He packs with an economy of motion that March would envy and hands me the bag to carry. That's when I notice his shoulder, half-torn from the socket, and I wonder how he can bear it. Before we step out onto the crisp snow, covered with an icy crust that professes we're the first to have stepped foot here in a long time, we wrap up in blankets. The outcropping sits a little farther out than it seems, but we make the trek just as I glimpse the white trail in the sky that means something's headed our way.

I know he wants the ship to land, but it won't. So I crouch down, flattening myself against the dark stone. Make sure the gray blanket wraps around my head, which feels like it's covered in hoarfrost. Velith hesitates, then mimics me.

"You have succeeded in making me uneasy," he whispers.

I don't reply to that. There's no need. As soon as he asked those questions, he turned himself into a security risk and a liability. Why would they pay him when they can just kill us both? But then I know how they think, and I got him to listen, praise Mary.

The Corp vessel overhead spots the Silverfish, and instead of lessening altitude to land and offer assistance, I see the blue-white flare of guns overhead. Beside me, the bounty hunter watches, barely breathing, as the *Spiral* goes up in flame. We hold very still as the ship seems to skim the area overhead, then wheels off, returning to headquarters to report us as loose ends tied up.

Without a word, he reaches over and inputs a code on my bracelet. It drops off my wrist and onto the snow. For a moment longer we watch the *Spiral* smolder.

"So how does it feel to be dead?" I offer him a bittersweet smile, hating what I've done to him, what I've taught him.

Sometimes there's nothing worse than the truth.

CHAPTER 50

"Cold," he says, after a moment's reflection.

Taking in the vast expanse of snowy landscape, I can't
help but agree. In slippers and pajamas, even wrapped in a
blanket, I'm not going to last long out here. There are no
settlements within visual range, but maybe Vel brought
something useful from the ship.

I dig into the bag and glance over at him. "You already
knew, didn't you?"

Not waiting for his answer, I don the thin, insulated suit,
right over the top of my clothing. My teeth chatter as I
stuff the blanket into the bag, but oh Mary, it feels good
once I get the gear fastened up. I'm covered from head to
toe, just an eye slit providing perfunctory visibility. He
dresses more slowly, seeming to consider my question.

"You were ... persuasive in your paranoia," he answers finally. "And I preferred not to perish of exposure,
if you were right. A good bounty hunter always has a
plan B."

I continue prowling through the bag. "What else did you bring?"

"Nothing that will keep us alive indefinitely."

"You're one of the good guys now," I tell him, stepping away from the shelter of the rocks. "Although I don't suppose that helps much."

"Not especially, no." His wry tone amuses me because it contains a thread of self-deprecation, as if he knows he brought this upon himself.

Yeah, well, anyone could tell him, trouble starts with listening to Sirantha Jax.

"So what now?"

Velith gazes up without speaking. I tip my head back and discover that the sky has gained the heavy opacity of impending snow. *Just what we need.*

"Shelter. Beyond that, I need some time to process events."

I can understand that, but if ever I've been told politely to shut the frag up, it's right now. So we start walking—far as I can tell, we seem to be making for the mountains. Out here I feel impossibly small and inconsequential because everything else is so huge. From the towering mountains to the wide-open sky, the elements seem actively hostile, like even the wind wants its pound of flesh.

It rushes against us, making progress difficult, until all I can hear is my own breathing and the crunch of our dogged tread on virgin snow. My lashes ice up, making me conscious of the exposed flesh around my eyes. They feel frozen, as if I can't move them side to side. I don't notice when it starts to snow, not until it becomes heavier, stinging my skin.

"Where are we going?"

I don't want to whine, even inside my own head, but I'm so fragging hungry that Velith is starting to look good. Not to mention the fact that I'm cold, exhausted, and my raw forearm throbs in a painful counterrhythm. Most of all, I'm worried about March. The way he looked when I came back . . . and now I'm gone again.

"Almost there."

There turns out to be a shallow cave, reached only after fifty meters of slippery, heart-stopping ascent. But, Mary, it feels good to get out of the wind. Crouching, he leads me all the way to the back where the stone slopes to meet the floor. It smells stale and a little funky, as if some animal might occasionally den in here. Not bad enough to drive me back out into the storm, though.

The sky has turned to slate, and the wind howls, white with blowing snow. I let myself slide down and watch him pull out various items. As he does, I realize he packed this stuff when we were evacuating the *Folly*. And these aren't Doc's devices at all.

"Do you really have the Mareq samples?" Suddenly that seems of paramount importance; otherwise, we've wasted all this fragging time and accomplished *nothing*.

"I do actually," he answers absently, his attention on what he is assembling from a battery, a coil of wires, and four metal plates. "I could tell they were valuable from reading Dr. Solaith's notes."

I'm astonished to see a sweet red glow rise from the cube he put together. "A chemical heater?"

"Among other things. Do not touch it, it warms all sides equally." He tosses me a metal cup. "Fill this with snow, and we can make soup."

"No paste?" I'm so glad to hear that, I could hug him, but instead I make my way back to the mouth of the cave, pack the mug full, and return to the copper-tinged shadows.

"Cannot abide it. I keep powdered rations in my emergency kit. If there is no water nearby for hydration, then I am in a world of trouble, regardless."

A world of trouble, that sounds about right.

"So how bad off are we?"

He doesn't answer for a moment. As I watch him slitting

envelopes and tipping the contents into a metal cylinder, it occurs to me that he no longer sends a shock through me. The bounty hunter responsible for my capture, a Slider no less, is now making me dinner. When he seems content, he sets the tube on the heater, then turns his head toward me, his faceted eyes glittering in the ginger glow. I can only see a little through the protective weather gear.

"I have been in worse spots, Sirantha. The storm will work to our advantage, covering our tracks if they should send anyone to double-check our demise. When the foul weather passes, I will beam a distress signal to the Guild. Someone should arrive within a standard day or two, depending on whether there are other operatives on world. Our supplies are adequate to that end."

"Guild? You're calling in more bounty hunters?" For a moment, I feel nothing but pure strangling panic.

Velith touches my shoulder. "Relax. You are now deceased. As such, your bounty will be removed from the active rosters. And so far as my colleagues are concerned, you are my apprentice. The pretense will suffice for our purposes."

"Bounty hunters take apprentices?" That's a new one on me.

"Athnid encourages it. When a bounty hunter begins to think of retirement, the Guild asks that he find an apt pupil to carry on his art. Other collectives possess much less in the way of tradition, nicety, and honor."

"Were the Morgut your apprentices?"

"They were meat. Muscle. Hired because I believed I might require assistance with you. I did not anticipate you would surrender to protect your comrades." His tone sounds odd somehow.

I have to grin. "Don't believe everything you see on the vids. Most of it is bullshit or Corp propaganda or both. How's your shoulder?"

"It hurts."

That has to be an understatement, and I'm suddenly glad I haven't bitched about my arm or my sore eye. Warm enough now, I push my hood back but can't restrain a wince when the cool air rushes over my scalp. That's going to take a lot of getting used to. About a meter away, Velith judges the soup done and pours some into the same mug I filled with snow.

"Careful, it is hot."

So I just hold it for a while, feeling the heat through the insulated fabric. When I take a sip, I find it bland but not bad, a legume and broth staple that will sustain us well enough. If I believed in Mary, I would send up a prayer right about now, but maybe Adele is doing that for me.

"Thank you. I guess I was pretty lucky to wind up with you."

"One could not make the same argument in reverse," he returns wryly, pushing back his hood to eat.

And I almost drop my empty cup. "Vel, what . . . why . . ."

He turns guileless green eyes on me. "I thought you would find it comforting to see a familiar face." *Not just any face. Kai's face.* "I found his image in your dossier. On a more mundane note, the generation of such tissue provides greater insulation in inclement weather."

Does he know what Kai was to me? What kind of reaction is he trying to provoke? I feel my fingers trembling so I clench them together. Kai's slender, lanky build suits Velith's natural form better than Doc's stocky musculature. Probably feels less cramped, too, but that's like a distant intellectual thought running down a different pipeline. I can't shut off my visceral response to seeing him again.

Though I know it's not him, even though I *know* that, I want to brush his hair back off his forehead. I want to touch the line of his cheek as I have so often. It's almost more than I can manage not to burst into tears or throw myself into his arms.

Kai, baby . . .

If he wasn't gazing at me with Kai's eyes, his sweet half smile as he sips his soup, I'd be asking about the functioning physiology, how the transformation takes place. I didn't see it happen beneath his weather gear, but I can't think of anything but—

Oh Mary, I could have him back.

CHAPTER 51

I back off that thought so fast my head spins.

That's the insidious whisper of a psychotic break. This isn't Kai, and I'll never see him again—cold, hard fact. Velith is a mimic, albeit one I like well enough, but if I accept him as my dead lover, then I'm lost, and I'll never find my way back.

Reality is March out there grieving. Reality is how he watches me when he doesn't think I'm paying attention. Reality is the way he always keeps his promises. Reality is . . . him loving me although he's seen every scar, every fault, inside and out, magnified a thousand times. Reality is him saying to himself: *I want her, no matter what. She's mine.*

I've got to get back to him.

"Can you change it up a bit?" My voice sounds hoarse. "Eye color, nose, mouth, something? I can't look at you like that."

He looks perplexed. I can interpret his expressions when

he's wearing human skin, no problem. Perhaps in time I'll learn all the Slider variations. I guess he thought he was giving me a present. Maybe one day I'll be ready for that, but not now. It's too soon.

"As you wish." His eyes darken to hazel and his nose seems to flesh out further. Now he's nobody I know, and I feel the tension ease out of my shoulders. "Will you tell me about the project, Sirantha?"

Making myself as comfortable as possible on the stone floor, I start from the beginning. He interjects with occasional questions, incisive, intelligent ones, and sometimes I don't even know the answers. I think he'd work really well with Doc; they possess similar mind-sets.

"And that's where we are," I conclude.

A little depressing to realize we've made no more progress than that toward realizing Mair's dream of a rival academy. But it makes me smile to see him tapping his fingertips against the rock wall as he processes the information. I'd be hearing thoughtful clicking right about now if he were wearing his native form.

"Once you remembered what occurred on Matins IV, you should have begun investigating *why*," he advises me eventually. "What did Farwan Corporation stand to gain by crashing the *Sargasso*? They would scarcely have chosen such a course if it had not presented the greatest value."

Why? It never occurred to me that there must be a reason. To my mind, they're just bastards, that's all, but now that Velith's got me thinking, which I've stated isn't my strong suit, I decide he's right.

"I don't know," I say aloud. "There were delegates, dignitaries, representatives from all Conglomerate worlds heading to Matins IV for a conference. No one ever told me what would be discussed there, at least not that I recall."

"Then I will find out, as it is highly probable that the purpose of that conference impacts Farwan's decision to terminate those on board."

Nodding, I shift my weight onto my hip and thigh, curling sideways against the slant. "I should've done that, but I guess I just wanted to start over. Strike back at the Corp by founding a new academy."

"A worthy goal, but you cannot escape your past, Sirantha, particularly when they engage me to hunt you." He sounds amused.

"That's right, rub it in."

I'm surprised when he slides over and offers me his good shoulder instead of the wall, but even though I know what lurks beneath the skin, I'm too tired to care. In fact, at this point I consider his true nature an advantage because I don't imagine he has any interest in me.

"You sure this is all right? You're pretty beat up."

He doesn't answer—I guess it ranks as a stupid question. So I put my head down and close my eyes.

The emergency rations ran out yesterday, and we've been reduced to drinking melted snow. And san facilities, well, you try pissing outside when it's snowing. The only thing to do is talk. Velith wants to know all about me. Wish I knew why. But he's a good listener. I tell him all about Kai and March, more than I should have, probably. Maybe it seems like I've said too much, but there isn't much else to do, and it keeps my mind off the others. Stops me wondering whether they're all right.

I know how I'd feel if March disappeared on me. I'd want to kill someone. Shit, when Farr shot him on DuPont Station, I couldn't control myself, couldn't even think. I never felt that kind of rage before in my life. When I lost Kai there was too much physical pain, confusion, and disorientation, further exacerbated by the Unit Psychs and dream therapy.

Please make March stronger than me. Adele, light a candle for us on Mary's shrine. We need all the help we can get.

At first, I wonder if it's safe to beam out a message, but Vel assures me he is using a frequency unique to the Guild. So I try to simmer down, but the time passes so slowly. I get him to talk on the second day, learn why he became a bounty hunter. "It is not an entertaining a story," he says, as if that's going to blunt my curiosity.

"Tell me."

"Females on Ithiss-Tor"—I remember that's his homeworld—"are dominant. They take lead roles in government and in family hierarchy. Additionally, they are not always . . . gentle with their mates, a regrettable trait remaindered from more primitive times. Rather than remain on planet, I confined a visiting human and took his place on an outbound ship. I met my mentor, Trapper Harley—"

"Wait, you *knew* him? How old are you?" There's no twitching mandible this time but I can tell by his drawn brows that I've been rude. "Er, sorry. Go on."

He doesn't, though. I've pissed him off, so that's pretty much all the conversation until I doze off propped up against the rock wall. By the third day, I start wondering whether anyone is listening. *Cheerful thought.* Not only are we in danger of starving, the risk of freezing rears its head again.

As the ginger glow from the depleted chemical heater fades on the fourth day, leaving us in darkness, his comm unit finally crackles to life. It's a live feed, too, means our savior is on planet, not bouncing a delayed message on a relay.

"This is Sheppard. In a spot of trouble, are you?" A crisply accented voice comes across, but I can't get a look at its owner, the way Vel tilts the vid screen.

"To say the least," Velith returns. "We need a pickup in the Teresengi Basin. I will pay standard rates, plus hazard bonus."

There's a long pause, then: "Shit, that's a proper mess. Double hazard pay for even thinking of having a go at it."

"What mess?" he asks, as I consider trying to yank the comm unit away from him.

The other bounty hunter sounds incredulous. "Where've you fragging been the last three days? Living in a cave?"

Can't help but snicker as Vel answers, "Yes."

"Oh. Well then. Farwan shot down some poxy terrorist. In retaliation, her people set bombs all over Ankaraj headquarters, demanding the head of the bloke that gave the order. They're holed up with hostages, and the Corp's shut down all air traffic within two hundred kilometers of the city, so I'm going to have a bitch of a time getting to you."

March. I feel as though someone punched me in the chest. He believes I'm dead, or he wouldn't be doing this. It's vengeance now—he doesn't see a way for us to win. In his own eyes, he failed me, failed Mair, so this is the only thing left.

Even though he told me his gift kills the soul, though I glimpsed the darkness in him, because he always tried so hard to do the right thing, I didn't realize the truth, the scope. I rise to my knees, gazing into darkness. He would kill the world for me.

I have to save him.

Mair gave him back his soul. I can't be the reason he loses it entirely. I won't be.

"Triple hazard pay," Vel offers. "Perhaps you can arrange land transport just before you reach the no-fly zone."

Our potential rescuer sighs. "Greed's going to be the end of me, but done deal. I'll make the arrangements."

"You would never abandon a Guilder in trouble." Velith sounds a great deal more confident than I am of that, but credits always make a good case.

"Right. Send coordinates then. I'm on the way."

I make sure the feed's dead before I say, "You sure you can cover that? Won't your accounts have been frozen when the Corp reported you flatline?"

He pauses in packing up the remaining gear, what's still usable anyway. "Perhaps. But I do not keep my assets wholly within Conglomerate banks. I will have access to funds from investments on Venice Minor and Gehenna. Guild barristers will straighten out legal issues arising from any dispute of my existence."

Now that would be handy. "I'm starting to wish I'd become a bounty hunter."

With a neat tug, Velith ties up the bag. "If you had, think of all the fun I would be missing right now."

I take my figurative hat off to the master of deadpan, just hope it's not symbolic.

CHAPTER 52

Longest wait of my life.

But eventually, Sheppard comes through. He's a lean man with deep-set eyes and a weathered face. We find him waiting for us at the base of the mountain in a trawler, big-ass hunk of all-terrain machinery. I have no idea how he got ahold of it, but I don't care. Vel and I slip-slide our way down to meet him and pile inside. *Mary, it's so warm in here.* Settling in back, I pull down my hood and start peeling out of the insulated gear.

Almost forgot I'm still in pajamas. Haven't bathed in days, not since the hostel in Maha City. It highlights how bad off I am when I feel nostalgic about that shitty san-shower with all the scurrying bugs. Miracle my arm isn't infected . . . Vel won't let me look at his shoulder, largely because that would mean shedding the human skin keeping him warm. We take off in a rumble of treads rolling over the snow.

"Right," Sheppard says by way of greeting. "We'll have to make for—"

"Ankaraj. Please. Drop me as close as you can."

"Your boy's a bit mad, eh?" he says to Velith, ignoring me.

Boy. Shit, I forgot about my head. "I *mean* it."

Vel glances up from whatever he's doing. As soon as we got in, he jacked into the portal sys-term, sending spiders out to retrieve data at a speed I can't even track. Watching his eyes scan back and forth as he reads makes me feel a little queasy. And then he compiles the info, his fingers deftly copying to a spike.

"Ankaraj," he affirms. "Take us straight to headquarters."

"You're both barking mad. The city's in lockdown, they'll never let us in." But a look from Vel seems to change his mind. I wonder how he'd react if he discerned what lurks beneath the unremarkable exterior, Guilder or not. "Right, Ankaraj it is then. We're not too far off, though you wouldn't have made it on foot."

Glancing out at the stark black and white of the landscape, capped by a hopeless gray sky, I can only agree. We plow onward, and I find myself bouncing one leg until Vel reaches over to still me without looking up from the screen. "We've got them," he tells me, powering the sys-term down.

Before I can ask what he means, the sun breaks from behind the clouds, reflecting too bright off the ultrachrome-and-glastique horror that is Ankaraj. Active defense towers, uniformed guards monitoring the expressway into the city. I see two squads of gray men trying to subdue the panic of a populace unused to open warfare. I can almost hear them crying out, "But we're too civilized for such things, aren't we?"

March, what have you done?

"I hope you two have got some idea as to how . . ." Sheppard starts to say, as the trawler reaches the checkpoint. "Oh, hello, Officer. It's imperative that we—"

At that I sit forward enough that the guard can get a good look at my face. "I'm Sirantha Jax. And it is imperative that I reach my people. I can stop this."

Poor bastard. He thinks I'm crazy at first, but then he glances between my bruised face and the ugly picture they have splashed all over the holo-feed. "But . . . you're dead."

If it weren't so fucking urgent, I'd laugh. "Not so much. Let us in."

That galvanizes him into action, and I hear his voice reverberate over the city comm. "Armed escort immediately. Clear the roads. First priority."

Sheppard keeps stealing glances at me when he thinks I'm not looking. "You . . . you're . . ."

"That poxy terrorist. Don't worry, my reputation's somewhat exaggerated."

He sighs. "Right. And you're his take, yeah?"

Velith shakes his head, looking thoughtful. "Quite the contrary. You will soon see, along with everyone else."

I hope that means he's got a plan. Surreal. I feel as though we're leading a parade, so many armored vehicles behind us, and people following on foot, since the checkpoint seems to have been abandoned. As I wanted, Sheppard takes us straight there.

"One favor," I say to our driver. "Bounce a message to this private sequence for me. Say, 'I'm sorry.' It doesn't need to be encrypted."

It's all I can do, an acknowledgment of my failure—my only consolation is that Keri hasn't been drawn into this mess with us. At least, they've got distance from it. Maybe they can start over, someday. Then I climb down without waiting for them to finish transacting Guild business.

A hush falls over the crowd assembled outside the squat, sprawling building that serves as the Corp home office. This is where I came to sign my contract, so long ago. I realize they're looking at me, and I can only imagine the picture I present: bald, barefoot, coming into the cold wearing only bloodstained pajamas. I know I'm gaunt, my nipples making sharp points through my thin cami, but I don't let myself shiver.

No weakness. Hold your head high.

People part when I pass as if I am the Holy Mother come to bless them or the Dark Lady come to reap their souls. To their minds, I've risen from the dead, which is as close to miraculous as most people ever get. Or perhaps it has something to do with the gray men closing on me. Velith holds up a hand, stepping between them and me.

"You shall not touch her." His voice carries that terrible dual euphonic tone, and they fall back, cowed.

There's something uncanny about Velith, but since he's on my side, I don't delve into it. "That's best. I'll stop this if you let me go."

The squad leader glances at his men, then he says, "Stand down."

I've never seen that happen before. He knows there's no way I'm getting out of here alive. Already knew that, though. They're letting me in because that's exactly where they want me, and I can help inside, but getting out again, that's another story. Once March releases the hostages and reveals the location of the explosives, we're done. I know that; I just don't care.

"Where are they?" I ask.

"Third floor, communications center."

We pass into the neutral light of the building, although the floor feels no warmer against the soles of my feet. The foyer is deserted. I presume they've long since evacuated all inessential personnel, other than the hostages.

I pause and glance at Velith; he has so much more to lose. He could've walked away, played it safe. I don't understand him at all. "Why are you doing this?"

"Perhaps I have always wanted to play the hero, Sirantha." That's not an answer, but I let it be, as wc proceed through silent halls.

So ironic. I ran so long and fought so hard to escape the Corp. And now here I am, returning all but naked and unarmed. It doesn't matter anymore. All I know is that I can't let it end like this, where March becomes a conscienceless butcher because of me, even if they are Corp automatons and wage slaves. He's better than this. Better than *me*. And I'd die for him. That's why I'm here. Nothing else makes a bit of difference; I'm here to share his fate.

Finally found something more important than me, baby.

My throat burns. There's nobody anywhere in the building, but on the third floor, we run into two MPs dragging a struggling man in a suit toward what I presume to be the comm center. I guess they finally decided to give up the button man. The Corp certainly doesn't hold human life sacred, after all.

"You're dead," he shouts. "You're supposed to be dead. Mother Mary of Anabolic Grace, what will it take to *kill* you?"

"People keep saying that." But then I take a closer look at him, straining against his captors. "Simon?"

Vel frowns, glancing between us. "You know this man, Sirantha?"

"Not well enough to have foreseen this, but technically he's my husband."

I disregard whatever Simon's screaming as they tow him toward the doors. Had no idea he'd climbed so high on the Corp ladder that he'd be placed for involvement in something like this. Then again, he always was ambitious. I think he chased me because he thought it would help his career, being married to a nav-star. Too bad I came equipped with a mind of my own and no compunctions about telling him that he couldn't get me off with a handbook.

"Save the reunion," the guard says, clapping a hand over Simon's mouth. "Let's take this inside before that crazy bastard in there starts making people explode."

"I told you, nobody gets in but the one responsible for her death." Every muscle tenses at hearing March on the speakers. Mary, I've never heard him sound like that. Cold. Determined. Hopeless. He's likely monitoring the building from inside. "Keep fucking with me, and this whole place goes up. We planted enough charges to take out this whole quadrant, and I'm tired of waiting."

"Just, please, let us in," the guard begs, sounding like he wishes he was in another line of work. "We brought him for you, didn't we?"

There's a long, tense silence, and I'm almost afraid he's going to snap before we get inside. But then the lock clicks, and the doors swing open. I don't wait; I can't. My feet pound the floor as I break into a run. But I draw up as I realize sudden movement is a really bad idea.

The room smells of stale sweat and terror, faint acrid reek of urine. People lie facedown on the floor. I recognize Dina and March, note a couple strangers with disruptors, hired guns most likely. *Oh Mary, look at what I've done to him.* He carries hell in his eyes, the set of his mouth. He regards me with a blank, dead stare.

"You fragging twats," he says, a low, hoarse voice. "You'd try anything. Trying to fool me with a dupe? Get that bitch out of here."

"March, it's me, baby. I'm here. I will *always* come for you."

I move toward him, knowing he might shoot me in the chest. I can feel that he's gone away somewhere inside his head, a fire-washed wasteland where nothing matters, and the burning never stops. I know the place all too well.

I'll wind up there myself if anything happens to this man.

CHAPTER 53

I keep walking.

"Dina, you dumb bitch. Why'd you let him talk you into this?" That earns me a sharp glance. I sense it more than see it. Less than two meters to him now. I see his fingers trembling on the weapon. "Remember when I sat on your lap in the rover? I expected you to grab my ass, but you never did. Guess I'm really *not* your type."

"Shit," she breathes. "March, it's Jax. It's really her."

He comes roaring into me then, although he doesn't move, not gentle exploration, more of an invasion. I feel everything inside him—the despair of my own death washes over me, and I stop. My chest feels tight; it's almost impossible to breathe.

Then I don't see anything at all because he crushes me in his arms. My ribs contract as he squeezes me, trying to make me part of him. The hired gunmen are screaming at the guards, and Simon adds to the clamor, but I can't make out what they're saying over the roaring in my head. Distantly,

I'm aware of a woman sobbing, hoarse and desperate in the cadence of her weeping.

"I wanted him to die," March whispers. "I wanted the whole world to die. Jax, Jax . . ." His fingers tremble as they brush across my scalp, down over my temples to my jaw. He touches my bruised eye with such reverence that I might be a holy artifact.

I don't know what might have happened then, but everyone in the room freezes as the forty vid screens around the room light up, and Velith steps away from a sys-terminal, looking pleased. The first thing that pops up is a document. It's a meeting agenda with the heading: *Matins IV—a Conglomerate summit to vote upon deregulation.*

Deregulation . . .

A chill washes over me. But that's not all. Up on-screen, we see footage from the crash, smoldering wreckage, and I suddenly know what Vel's doing. *Mary, he's fragging brilliant.* This is what he was splicing in the trawler, but I'm still surprised when the display patches to the grainy record taken from his cranial cam. Didn't even know he had one, but I guess it eliminates any question of how a capture went down. I see myself pinned, his claw on my throat, hear myself surrender to save the others.

Then we bounce to the Silverfish, where I say, fuzzy but audible, "Did it ever occur to you to that the Corp is guilty of disseminating false information? I'm the only survivor from the *Sargasso,* but I didn't do that. The landing authority used override codes on our vessel and supplied incorrect coordinates, the wrong trajectory. They fragging *engineered* that crash."

And now everyone watching this feed, not sure how many that is, knows it, too. But he's still not done. Vel shows the world the way I provoked the Morgut, feeding them my blood like a moron, and we hear his voice on the comm. "Why does my target claim that Farwan Corporation is responsible for the crash on Matins IV? Why does the target prefer to provoke a pack of Morgut to being extradited into your custody?"

"She's insane," comes the soon-to-be-infamous response. "She would say anything. Just sit tight, and help will arrive shortly. We have a unit en route."

The last scene shows us crouched behind the rocks, as the Corp ship blows the *Spiral* all to hell; and then it starts to play all over again. Outside, I hear the crowd roaring, the impact of something exploding against glastique. Farwan Corporation murdered the last hero the whole galaxy recognizes, Miriam Jocasta, because they were afraid of the vote. Afraid the Conglomerate would vote to deregulate jump-travel and permit freely established academies.

Security's going to have a hell of a time containing the riots—if they even bother. The public never likes being duped. Hostages clamber unsteadily to their feet because even the hired gunmen look stunned and numb. Nobody stops them.

"It is finished," Vel tells the guards. "I bounced that feed to every Conglomerate world, and it is only a matter of time before they arrive demanding justice for their murdered representatives. Once exposed, a secret loses all its power."

He's right. Although it may flail around like an enormous decapitated beast, doing collateral damage, Farwan's days are numbered. They failed to break me before March got me off station, and now it's too late. They should've killed me instead of trying to turn me into their sacrificial goat. I've said that all along.

I can't even begin to imagine the economic ripples this is going to have. I foresee world after world seceding from the Conglomerate until it ultimately dissolves. And who can prosecute a company so large, it essentially became a galactic government? But perhaps a strong leader can hold it together. They'll have to create a tribunal, so much ground-breaking here. It's a new universe, or will be, once the shock waves cease.

The security officers exchange a long look, then pull the patches from their uniforms. Silently, they drop their weapons and nobody stops them when they leave the room. I guess they're unemployed now. A lot of folks will be before this thing is done. Hard times are coming, but I think perhaps it's a good thing. Change is good, chaos can be beneficial, and this will open a lot of doors. Maybe ours won't be the only start-up academy; maybe we'll have competition. And that's exactly as it should be.

"I was only following orders," Simon whimpers. "They told me to select someone expendable, and you've been jumping a long time. Statistically speaking, you should have burned out long since. Sirantha, please . . ."

Deliberately I turn my back on him, content to let the incipient tribunal deal with him and all the rest of his ilk. I hear the sound of one of his former employees shutting him up. It's distinctive, the repetitive thud of a fist hitting a face. The room empties, some hostages looking broken, others disbelieving. I can relate; rather suddenly, the face of the universe has changed.

March pulls me back into his arms then. He let me turn when the screens came to life, but now he's compulsive, running his hands over my back, my shoulders, my hips. He holds me as if it hurts him to breathe, and he can't seem to find his voice.

Dina comes up behind us, and I'm surprised to feel her arms encircle both of us. "You stupid bitch," she mutters. "I don't need you dying for me. I need you to stick around because . . . you're my best friend." She squeezes us with her corded arms, then steps back, clearing her throat. "We got a message from Doc, by the way. He's all right, just stuck on Gehenna. Said he had some news for you, but he didn't say what."

"I'll bounce a message to him later," I answer.

But I think I already know, something about the L-gene appending to the J-gene. Maybe he knows why since he's had nothing but time since we left and access to the excellent Carvati research facilities.

"Come on," she adds to the hired guns. I hear explosions in the distance, shattering glastique. "Let's loot this place before the angry mob gets inside."

Then it's just the two of us. I meant to thank Vel, but he's gone, and I didn't see him leave. Maybe for him it was as simple as getting to the truth. Maybe we didn't bond like I thought we did, but I can't think about that right now. I'll locate him later if he wants to be found.

It's time to say the words. Wherever he is, Kai knows my feelings now don't lessen anything we shared. March is such an odd dichotomy of buried cruelty and brutality, overlaid by the kindness and compassion that Mair taught him. He'd kill the world for me, so it's my place to make sure he never has to.

Yeah, they proved there's nothing spiritual, no such thing as a soul, but I'm not sure I can wholly put my faith in science anymore. Miracles are possible. I believe.

"I love you," I whisper, lifting a hand to his cheek.

He catches my fingers and carries my palm to his lips, not a kiss so much as homage. I feel his tongue against my skin, tasting what I've been through as he comes into me, gentler this time, sharing instead of raiding.

"Once in a while," he murmurs, low, "a man would like to rescue the woman he loves. You can't keep saving me."

I shake my head, wrapping my arms about him. "You had your turn, remember?"

"Jax, when you never came back . . ." I feel him trembling. "I found your bag, and 245 showed us what happened to you. She captured it, so we knew you meant to die for us. Started falling then, but I never hit bottom, just—" His voice breaks, and he squeezes me with all his strength. "And then we saw the newsfeed . . ." He gives me everything he felt, rage and anguish, washing over me in waves that never ebb.

It hurts, but then, what doesn't? Pain proves that we're alive, gives us the ability to appreciate pleasure—everything in balance, everything in its time.

"You don't need to be afraid of falling," I murmur, raising my lips to his, whispering into his skin, "when there's someone around to catch you."

I'm Sirantha Jax, former Farwan navigator, and that's my job.